Donation

Hideaway
at
Silver
Lake

A Snowflake Sisters Novel

Jennifer Greene

AVON
An Imprint of HarperCollins*Publishers*

P.S.™ is a trademark of HarperCollins Publishers.

HarperCollins books may be purchased for educational, business, or sales promotional use. For information, please email the Special Markets Department at SPsales@harpercollins.com.

FIRST EDITION

Designed by Diahann Sturge

Snow Globe illustration © Giraphics / Shutterstock

Library of Congress Cataloging-in-Publication Data has been applied for.

ISBN 978-0-06-324113-8

22 23 24 25 26 LBC 5 4 3 2 1

To Stell

I was blessed with extra grandmas, but no one as special as my next-door neighbor when I was growing up. She taught me the art of sharing special secrets—like the recipe for "Spaghetti Ice Cream." I still miss you. Always will.

Prologue

CAMILLE HEARD HER cell phone chime, but since it was four in the morning and she was violently trying to stay sleeping, she ignored it. A full day of rowdy sixth graders was going to descend on her life, and sanity, in less than four hours. She needed every hour of sleep she could beg, borrow, or steal. It was a matter of survival.

She pushed a pillow over her head, barely closed her eyes again when the landline rang and the answering machine kicked in. Naturally, the message was from Marigold, her younger sister. *"Call me, Cam. It's important."*

Marigold. Awake at four A.M.?

It had to be appendicitis. A guy crisis.

For darn sure, something on the level of Armageddon—to her sister, anyway.

She hurled off the covers, yanked on the light, and reached for the phone. "Just tell me. What's wrong?"

"It's Poppy. She's gone."

"What do you mean, she's *gone*?"

Marigold normally had a voice softer than sunshine. Now it was sick-shrill. "I couldn't sleep. So I gave up, curled up with a blanket and a hot cup of chai and my iPad. And my phone. That's when I started seeing all the messages."

Cam tried to concentrate on keeping her eyes open, but her eyelids kept slipping down. She just wanted sleep. The need to sleep lured her like a lover she couldn't have. "What messages, Marigold? Speed this up."

"Poppy said she sent you texts and emails, too. She's gone. Disappeared. We're not going to see her until after Christmas."

"Come on. That's impossible. In fact, it's downright ridiculous."

"Camille. Wake up! Go read your email and your texts. Then call me back."

Her younger sister hung up. Cam stared at the phone in disbelief . . . and felt the sprouting roots of panic. Marigold was as happy-go-lucky as a basset hound. She had no nerves. She couldn't spell the word *stress*. She woke up high on life and went to sleep the same way—even when life kicked her in the teeth. Even when the rare nightmare kicked in. Even when some creep hurt her.

Cam wasn't good with disorder. She liked rules. She liked organization. And corny or not, she still believed in loyalty. And honor. And doing the right thing. And protecting family. But if someone had hurt her little sister, all bets were off. She'd annihilate the son of a sea dog without a qualm.

She jammed her feet into slippers. Grabbed a robe. Caught a glimpse of herself in the antique mirror over the dresser—her hair was the same rich, thick auburn as her sisters'. But both Marigold and Poppy had cut theirs. She'd left hers long—which was an absolutely silly thing to notice, when it was predusk dark, the wind whipping leaves into a frenzy outside. Right now her hair looking witchy-wild was relevant to nothing. Cam was calm, cool, and collected in a crisis. Any crisis.

She sprinted into the kitchen, picked a hazelnut pod, started the Keurig, pulled out the mug that read "Be Wary of a Well-Read Woman"—her lucky mug. She opened her laptop while she waited for the brew.

And read the emails from Poppy. Then the texts from her phone. Then punched in Marigold's cell number again.

It was so easy to imagine the rage, the protectiveness, the fire if someone hurt Marigold.

But Poppy . . .

Poppy was their world.

They'd been little girls when their mom died. Poppy, the oldest, had only been eleven. But she'd somehow managed to do everything. Keep them together. Put food on the table. (Sometimes a little iffy, that food.) Everybody did the wash and put-aways, even when Marigold was barely old enough to reach the table. Poppy got them to school. She patched up their skinned knees. They slept with her when they were scared of the alligators under the bed.

Their dad was alive. He was just never what anyone would

call "present." Either Poppy took care of them or no one did. And she *had* taken care of them.

Cam couldn't imagine—refused to imagine—that anything could have happened to her.

When Marigold answered her cell, Cam could hear the tears in her sister's voice.

"No," Cam said, but gently. "We're not crying. We're going to figure this out. Do you know what's going on?"

"No. I told you. I thought everything was like normal until I got all those texts."

"Well, she hasn't disappeared. And she'd never willingly leave us at Christmas. So something's obviously wrong."

"I know."

"Is she sick? Mention anything odd in the last few weeks? Do you know if she had a doctor appointment, or lab tests, or anything like that?"

"No, no, and no. She never mentioned anything being wrong."

"Okay, okay. Let's calm down."

"I can't."

"I can't either," Cam admitted, but not willingly. "Could she have lost her job?"

"Are you kidding? They love her and she loves the job."

"I know, I know, but I'm trying to think. It hasn't been an accident or something like that, or she'd have called. Or we'd have heard. Ditto if there'd been a fire or a robbery."

"I've been thinking the same way, Cam. But if it isn't any of those *normal* catastrophes, then it could be something worse than that. What if she has, like, a tumor? Something so awful she couldn't face telling anyone, even us? She'd *need* us."

"Poppy does not have a tumor."

"How do you know that?"

Because Cam just knew. She couldn't imagine life without her older sister in her world, in their world. It was unthinkable.

It was unbearable.

"Look, all she says is she needs time to herself. So let's get our minds off terrible possibilities and concentrate on the constructive things we can do."

"Like what?"

"Like finding her. Like tracking her down. Like figuring out what we can do to help her."

Marigold was silent—and Marigold was almost never silent. "All right," she said slowly. "We both have keys to her house. How about if I go over there, look around, see if I can find addresses or phone numbers or suitcases—all the kinds of details that would give us clues to where she's gone."

"Her lab rats might know. Her whole staff loves her. I could try contacting some of them."

"I could talk to her neighbors. Not *saying* we're worried. Just seeing if she told anyone where she'd be."

"I like it." Cam pushed back her hair. "The more we brainstorm, the more ideas we'll get. And I guess I could talk to Dad, but . . ."

". . . but we both know that's likely useless. He'd probably forget Christmas if we didn't remind him."

They both knew their father, all too well, but Cam still volunteered, "I could still pop over. He might remember something she said. No harm in trying."

"Better you than me."

Cam almost chuckled. But already relief was starting to calm down her panicking heart rate. It might take a bit of time, but they could do this. They'd find Poppy. Someone, somewhere, had to know where she'd gone, even if they didn't know why she'd left. The mailman might have a forwarding address. Poppy would have let someone know what to do if the furnace failed or there was a blizzard. Poppy was on contact lists if anything happened to her or Marigold or her father.

So. It might take a little time, but they'd eventually track her down. Then they could see her. Find out what had happened, what was wrong.

After that, the rest was easy.

They'd help her. They'd be there for her.

If anyone had taught them to be a family—to be there for one another—it was Poppy.

Chapter One

WHEN POPPY MCGUIRE finally spotted the fish-shaped mailbox, she let out an exuberant "YES!"

Not that she'd been afraid, but over the last hour, she'd had a few teensy doubts that she was ever going to survive this drive. That was definitely the silliest mailbox she'd ever seen, but it was unquestionable proof that she'd found the cottage. She'd *found* it. She'd made it here. She wasn't lost—at least not anymore.

The wild, screaming wind and slashing snow hadn't let up in forever, but the blizzard no longer mattered. Ahead, she could see the hazy outline of the cottage, and it looked like a picture in a book of fairy tales, as if a giant had draped the roof and windows with huge, pillowy marshmallows.

Her ten-year-old Subaru lumbered over a couple heavy snowdrifts until Poppy braked and turned the key. She was bone-tired—heart- and soul-tired—and the whole back of the car needed to be unpacked before she could crash. Yet she sat back for just a few seconds, savoring the look of her pretty haven for the next couple of weeks, her mind replaying the long day behind her.

At five that morning, she'd been so raring to go that she couldn't sleep any longer. Whistling the whole time, she had packed the car, cleaned out the fridge, turned down the heat. She checked with her lab one last time—her team had just finished a terrorizingly important study for a big-money grant—but there was no point in submitting the materials before the holidays. Nothing would happen with the results anyway. Until then, she and her team all had a break from the long work hours.

Poppy's last task was the most important. She checked to make sure the texts and emails she'd sent to her sisters had gone through. They were going to hate her being gone for Christmas—and she felt a bit guilty that she was leaving them around the holiday. But it couldn't be helped. This was the first time in forever that everything came together—the grant finished, the university Christmas break, her projects all under control. She could carve out a block of two whole weeks for herself if she just grabbed the chance.

So she had.

By noon, finally, she had climbed in the car, ready to boogie. The GPS claimed the drive from Madison, Wisconsin, to Silver Lake would take around two hours. At this time of year, darkness started coming on around four. Her goal was to arrive at the rented cottage by midafternoon, be unpacked and set up before the sun went down.

A perfect plan.

Almost.

The first fat crystal snowflake popped on her windshield before she turned on the highway. She smiled rather than worried—and, yes, of course she'd listened to the weather forecast. But it was December. A forecaster promising snow was like saying the sky was blue. A yawner. And anyway, the storm predicted was more like typical weather for that part of the country.

Only, within a half hour, the sweet splash of snowflakes turned into a downpour of heavy, wet snow. It was pretty clear that the forecasters had misjudged . . . again. The wipers couldn't keep up and fog smoked the windows. The defroster started whining. Then the wind started, first with a grumble and then with a primal howl.

She considered howling herself.

Another hour passed. Another and another. She couldn't stop, simply because she couldn't see the edge of the road, couldn't see buildings. The GPS couldn't help because she couldn't follow the directions. Curbs and crossroads were indecipherable because of the blinding snow. Snow and sleet had crusted on street signs, making them impossible to read. Traffic lights danced and pranced in music only the wind could hear.

But now the nightmare was over.

Poppy pushed open the car door, expecting the sudden blast of arctic wind on her face, not caring. She'd start carting in supplies in a minute, but first, she was dying to see the inside of the cottage.

She'd been dreaming about this for weeks. She couldn't see much of the surrounding area—the darkness and blustery snow blocked her view of the lake. Still, she could make out a huge cluster of white birch to the south. Spruce and pines bordered the north, making a nearly impenetrable privacy barrier. A quarter mile to the north was supposed to be a community "winter play" area—a skating rink, a start-up spot for cross-country skiers, that kind of thing.

But the isolation of her cottage was perfect. Exactly what she craved. Not forever—just until Christmas and the holidays were over. Much as Poppy loved her sisters, she *had* to have some alone time.

She couldn't pin down when her life had spun completely out of control—but she knew she'd let things go wrong for far too long. This wasn't about anyone else's choices, just her own. Maybe two weeks wasn't long enough to do a complete Life Reboot. But since she could only buy two weeks of freedom, it would have to be enough.

She scrabbled in her purse for the cabin key, which had been mailed to her last week, then high-stepped through the snow to the side door. Once inside, she flicked on a light switch and shook her head, almost laughing. For darn sure, it was nothing like her home in Madison. But for the same reason, it was absolutely perfect.

A vaulted ceiling framed the long room. On the lake side, huge windows reflected the gorgeous view of the slope down to the frozen lake. An old plaid couch and rustic chair faced the tall stone fireplace, with chopped wood in a bin on the hearth. Knotty pine covered the walls and ceiling.

She could smell the cedar, the drying wood chips, the fresh clean air. She could hear the silence.

Poppy turned around, found a separate light switch that illuminated the kitchen area. Appliances lined the far wall like soldiers—freezer, fridge, electric stove, microwave, and in the middle, an old-fashioned charmer of a porcelain sink. Nothing new, nothing fancy, but even the scratched plank floor was clean enough to eat on. The vintage oak table could easily function for both eating and computer space.

She kicked off her boots and parka, then slowly poked and prowled through the rest of her new nest. She discovered a bathroom smaller than a closet. A sliding door led to the main bedroom, which was just large enough for a double bed, an empty wardrobe, and a claw-footed bureau where blankets and towels and linens were stored.

Off the living area was one last room that she immediately named Girl Cave. A cracked leather chair and old futon were mounded with pillows. A TV and battered bookcase were the only other furnishings. It was clearly intended as a place to curl up and hide out.

Okay, so the whole place was old-fashioned and outdated. She should have seen the place before renting it, but when she talked to Mr. Bell . . . well, his voice was frail as a whisper, his heart obviously pure gold. He said it was clean, tidy, but he didn't know how to send photos—too newfangled for him. And he'd offered a rental price so cheap that she couldn't turn it down and didn't want to. Old-fashioned or not, the place was clean and comfortable, an easy place to just *be*.

Abruptly she spun around. Time to move. It was getting darker by the minute and she was already crazy tired, but the car had to be unloaded.

WITHIN AN HOUR, Poppy had carted in all the bags and boxes from the Subaru, refrigerated the perishables and stashed everything away, from clothes to food to supplies. Her laptop and cell were parked on the table, not plugged in yet—especially not the phone. It was running low on battery, but she had no desire to have contact with the outside world—not yet anyway.

The last thing she carried in was the big white box from the front seat of the car. She didn't open it. It wasn't time yet. Tomorrow, she'd let herself deal with the box . . . and with the memories of her mom that came with it. For now, she just set it on the table, and because her stomach was grumbling from starvation, she put together a snack-type meal of cheese and fruit and crackers.

And that was it. The last bite of food brought on an unstoppable yawn. She wasn't just out of gas; her energy tank was completely empty. She grabbed a pillow and the purple comforter she'd brought from home and curled up on the plaid couch. She didn't want to sleep yet. There was so much to do, so much to plan, so much to start working on.

Somehow, though, she snuggled into the soft old comforter and immediately crashed.

* * *

SAM COOPER ALMOST swerved the truck into a drift. "Bubbles! This is no time to kiss my neck!"

Bubbles had all the size and regal stature of a full-blooded Irish wolfhound. She'd just snoozed her way through obedience school. She'd gotten an A in "very loving," her only good grade. Which was to say—if she wanted to lick Sam's neck, she licked Sam's neck. If he'd raised her, she'd have better manners. He hadn't raised her. He hadn't even inherited her. She'd been forced on him by his six-year-old niece.

Sam tried a mean-sounding "*Lie down*." Which had the same effect as moving stone. He sighed. "We'll be home in less than five. Then one of us is going to get a steak—for good behavior. The other's going to get kibble. Let's see if you can figure out who's who."

She ignored that threat, the way she did all the others. The wind was still howling, but Sam caught a brief glimpse of Silver Lake. In the summer, the place was crammed with tourists and families—but at this time of year, on his side of the lake, only a few sturdy souls stuck it out during the snow months.

A few hours before, he'd put a blade on his Silverado and aimed for old man Olson's. Sam never minded helping a neighbor, and he'd promised that he'd keep the place plowed out after any big storm—there was nothing like a seemingly unoccupied cabin to attract partiers or wintertime squatters.

He was a curve away from home when abruptly he tapped his brake, then stopped, craning his neck to see through the windshield wipers. Even in the dark—especially because of the dark—he could see the lights shining from Cassius Bell's cottage.

Cassius hadn't used the cabin much in several years, not since his wife died, and as far as Sam knew, he'd moved in with his sister last summer, much closer to town. Surely, Cassius wouldn't risk driving in a snowstorm just to hang out in the old place, but you never knew. Maybe he drove here just to check the place and then got stuck when the storm started.

Sam hesitated, thinking he was too tired and hungry to go looking for trouble. But he could see a car parked in the driveway, too snow-covered to make out the size or make. It must have been parked there a couple hours, at least, judging from the billowy, pillowy beds of snow behind it.

Of course, the existence of the car didn't necessarily mean anything was wrong. It's just that no one was out and about in a storm like this—no one with any sense, anyway.

"This is all your fault," he told Bubbles. "If you weren't such a busybody, we could be home, defrosting that steak by now."

The dog took criticism well, he had to give her that. The minute he switched off the engine and jammed on a stocking cap, she was bumping her head, raring to get out. So that made two idiots inviting frostbite, and, damn, that wind was bitter sharp. Bubbles bounded through the snow faster than Sam could. He made it to the door, rapped hard, waited.

He knuckled the door again. Waited again. Called out, "Hey, Cassius? It's me, Sam Cooper. Just checking to make sure you're okay."

When there was still no answer, he tried the doorknob and discovered it was unlocked. Holding Bubbles's collar with one hand, he poked his head inside. "Hello? It's me, Sam—"

Bubbles nudged him aside and broke through the hold on her collar, aiming straight inside. Her ecstatic enthusiasm seemed over the top, even for a dog who had no sense of boundaries. She galloped for the couch, where a small body draped in purple popped in sight with a shocked gasp. Defying all logic, the loud gasp turned into something resembling a lover's croon. And then laughter.

"Good grief. I thought I was in a dream, and you were Rufus. He wasn't as pretty as you, but he was the wolfhound who lived next door where I grew up. He spent more time with us than he did with his owner. You're listening to every word, aren't you? Rufus was a vicious attack dog, just like you. I adored him. Stop. Stop, you goof. I can't take any more wet kisses! Okay. Okay, I'll rub your ears. You're just a big old baby, aren't you . . ."

Sam saw the woman half turn, as if assuming she'd find the dog's owner somewhere close by. He only had seconds to catch a look at her. Delicate bones, expressive eyes, glorious red hair all tousled. She obviously had no fear of huge, hairy, ruffian dogs. Yet when she finally spotted Sam in the doorway, her smile dropped flatter than a pancake. "You really startled me! I mean, obviously I knew the dog was attached to an owner, but you were so *quiet*."

She made *quiet* sound like a substantial sin. He had the uneasy feeling that conceivably he'd made a rotten first impression. "Wait, please. I'm sorry I scared you. It's just me. Sam Cooper. I live a quarter mile from here, and when I saw lights on, I worried something was wrong. Cassius Bell, the man who owns this place, hasn't been here in a blue moon. I couldn't imagine him driving here in this kind of blizzard unless something serious was wrong, but I thought maybe he'd gotten stuck—or even that a stranger had gotten stranded here . . ."

Talking didn't appear to be working. Her expression hadn't changed. Worse, Bubbles was looking at him the same cool way—except for the brief look of adoration directed toward his visitor. Darn dog acted as if she already knew that two females against a male never worked out well—at least for the man.

Well, he couldn't blame Bubbles totally, when he was having an equally stunning reaction to the lady, but for different reasons. Once he got a good look at her, every sane thought whisked from his mind faster than dandelion fluff.

She might be on the slight side—certainly Bubbles was bigger—but she was definitely a grown woman. Likely younger than him by a few years. Thirty, thirty-two? With a short, thick sweep of auburn hair, richer than dark honey, tumbled about from sleep. Classy arched brows, high cheekbones, slim lips, and deep blue eyes. Sea blue. Soft blue. Unforgettable blue.

Sam tried to mentally kick himself in the behind. Yeah, he'd been celibate for quite a while. Being left at the altar could do that to a man. Worse yet, he was the jerk who'd hurt his fiancée, which was the outstanding reason why he'd avoided women for a good long while.

Still, studying her, he noticed a spare sprinkling of freckles across her nose. It wasn't the freckles specifically, but something about her that—instantaneously—worried him this one could be serious trouble.

Her perspective was conceivably different, considering how she was wagging a finger at him.

"You do this a lot? Just walk in on a complete stranger, scare her half to death?!"

He wanted to swipe a hand over his face. Somehow she failed to recognize the obvious truth. He was the one standing at a polite distance away in the doorway. His dog had already leaped on the couch and was half mauling her to death with kisses. Yet who was she scolding for bad behavior? Was this fair?

"Bubbles, get *down*. And I didn't mean to scare you. Like I said, I thought Cassius had gotten stuck here, or that someone broke in here because of the storm, that they were in trouble . . ."

Sam's brain went stone-blank again. When she finally stood up to face him, he had to remind himself that he was turning thirty-five in a couple months. Obviously he was too mature to be falling this fast for a stranger. And he hadn't *fallen*. It's just everything about her was so . . . arresting.

She wasn't skinny, just fragile-boned. In stocking feet, she might be five two or five three—hard to tell when he was looking down at her from a six-foot-three height. Maybe six four with his boots.

She noticed the boots, too. "You're tracking in snow all over the place. I don't know you from Adam. You don't have any reason to know me from Adam." She took a step toward him, with her finger wagging even harder.

He could see why she didn't bother threatening him with a gun or weapon. That finger was shooting straight at him.

"Honestly, I told you the truth. I tend to look out for neighbors on this side of the lake, just because there aren't many of us here in the winter. And in a snowstorm like this, easy to understand how someone could pretty desperately need a place to shelter. You could have serious trouble . . ."

"I don't have trouble." But she lowered that killer finger. A little. "And if I'd needed help, obviously I'd have called 911. Not a stranger."

"I understand. But think about it, we're already not strangers," he said reassuringly. "I'm Sam, like I told you. And you've already met Bubbles."

"Bubbles? You named this stately wolfhound Bubbles?"

"I didn't, I didn't. It was my niece. She named her. It wasn't my fault."

Bubbles cocked her head, as if she were wondering why Sam

had somehow turned into a babbling lunatic. The dog was the one with the long tongue, dripping drool on her shoulder, not him. Still, he tried out his most calming tone. "I was just trying to say that you don't need to be worried. We don't have serial killers around here. At least none that I know of. And if one showed up, you'd be better off with me and Bubbles showing up than some idiot you didn't know."

She frowned, looking confused.

"You really are on the slight side," he tried to explain, meaning that it was reasonable she'd need help in a heavy-duty-type emergency.

"But that's exactly why you shouldn't be breaking into cottages and scaring a woman half to death."

"I didn't break in. I just opened the door," he said reasonably. "And you don't look half dead. Or even remotely scared."

"That's because I'm *not* scared."

"And that's good. Because I'd feel bad if I scared a woman, any woman. The last thing I'd want to do is worry you in any way."

A slim hand pushed at her hair. "I'm not sure whether you're nuts or I am, but somehow I'm almost positive this conversation doesn't make any sense."

He wasn't trying to have a logical conversation. He was trying to find a subtle way of pushing off his parka and heeling off his boots. Then, even more subtly, he yanked a chair from the oak table and straddled it. He couldn't tower over her forever. He was too damned tired.

Obviously she didn't want him here.

And he seriously didn't want to intrude on her. But something was wrong.

A delectably attractive woman shows up in the middle of a snowstorm, who looked like she belonged in a white-carpeted penthouse rather than an old man's hunting cabin. Alone. A few weeks before Christmas.

He couldn't just leave her. Not without having a clue why she was here, why she'd even want to be here of all places. Whether she had food and supplies to outlast the storm, whether she even knew how the furnace worked.

"Hey, you thirsty?" he asked her.

"It's my house. I wasn't offering a drink. You aren't a guest."

He nodded. "But I wasn't asking for me. I was asking for you."

She threw up her hands as if giving up trying to communicate with a bonehead. "Fine. I'd like a drink."

There. He had an excuse to move, instead of just staring at her. Bubbles, he noticed, still wasn't leaving her side.

"Anything special you have around? What are you thirsty for?"

"Truthfully, I don't know." For the first time she lost some of that testiness. She looked just plain tired. Almost woebegone tired.

"Well, we'll see." He crossed the room to the lustily humming fridge. The appliance had to be older than sin. Quickly, though, he verified that she'd brought supplies. Fresh vegetables, eggs, butter, milk, fresh stuff in general.

He snooped a little further, tracked down two bottles of wine in the cupboard, one shiraz, one malbec. "I'm pretty sure you brought this wine, since Cassius is a hard-core root beer addict, no alcohol for him at all. Anyway, I'm going to open the malbec unless you shout no." He didn't wait for the yes or no, just messed around until he found a water glass, and then a corkscrew.

By the time Sam turned around, she'd folded the comforter, hid the bed pillow, finger-straightened her hair, and was sitting down like a laced-up financial adviser. Bubbles was still leaned against her, offering adoring looks and taking up the rest of the space on the couch.

He handed her the wine, wishing a brick would fall on his head. Something needed to knock some sense into him. His hormones were more stirred up than they'd been in years. There was just something about her.

Now that she wasn't wrapped up in the comforter, he got a better look at her. She wore black leggings, huge boot socks, and a thick warm tunic in greens and cream. The drape of the tunic suggested she had no boobs. The leggings testified that she barely had a butt. So. She had no height, no weight, no figure, and she'd popped on some black-framed glasses—possibly intended to make him think she was smart and tough.

Sam suspected she was very smart—for real. And tough,

because she really showed no wariness of him at all. Just annoyance.

She took a short sip of wine. Then gulped almost the rest of the glass. "Looks like you were dehydrated," he said.

"I don't need . . ."

But it was too late to waste her time protesting now. He'd already sprung up and aimed for the bottle. This time he filled the water glass half full. "I know you want me out of your hair. And I will be. I'd just appreciate a little story, okay? Not all your sins and flaws. Just the good parts—like how you ended up here."

"Nosy on top of everything else?"

He nodded, as if she'd delivered a sage truth that he only wished he could deny. And she was gulping down that second glass as ferociously as the first.

"How about if I build a fire?

"Will you leave quicker if I say yes?"

"You know I will." There. He almost—almost—won a grin. She even started relaxing, once he turned around and quit paying attention to her. He hunkered down on the hearth, checked the flue, started building a serious fire. An arc of twigs. Then a grid of skinny logs, from the bin. Then the whisk of a match, to start it.

It took. A sharp candle-drip of flame, then a sizzle. Then a pop, as the spark took and sneakily spread. When the cradle of wood took on life, he added a short log, crisscrossed by another and another.

Bubbles started snoring. She knew about fire-building. It was code for time to snooze and veg out. And Sam had always taken his fire-building seriously. Doing something right was always worth the time. More relevant tonight, the longer it took him, the more questions this intriguing woman answered.

She clearly didn't appreciate his nosiness, and she didn't give up much—but he could still see a puzzle coming together.

She was in trouble. Just like he'd thought.

Chapter Two

POPPY COULDN'T STOP talking. It didn't make sense.

She couldn't remember a single time she'd spilled private information to a stranger. She'd always been friendly. Comfortable with people. She had women friends, loved chatting with her guys in the lab, could hold her own when she had to. Maybe she'd had a couple glasses of wine—possibly three?—but hardly enough to suddenly change personality.

She simply never aired her problems with anyone, even her sisters.

She had a vague memory of kicking Sam out, only he sort of talked her out of it. He didn't specifically insist on staying; he just went off on a different topic entirely, said it was odd that Cassius hadn't left her a note. He always had, for other renters, with Sam's name and number on it, so the renter would have a contact they could trust if anything went wrong.

Poppy claimed she'd never seen such a note. He asked if she'd looked in the first drawer by the back door. She hadn't.

He'd gotten up, opened the drawer, came back with the older man's scrawled note about Sam being someone she could ask for help, if she needed it, "without a qualm."

So fine. He had some credentials as a good guy. Only she was still talking, and he still showed no signs of leaving. Worse yet, the more malbec she sipped, the more Poppy kept thinking . . . who cared? Who really cared if she spilled her whole life story?

Sam didn't know her. She was only going to be here for two short weeks. Was the world going to end if she peeled off her emotional body armor for a few minutes?

And of course it was relevant to nothing, but he *was* handsome. Deep blue eyes and a scrub of whiskers, a mouth that was sin soft, and a slow, slow come-on grin. His shoulders filled a doorway, and likely two of her feet would fit in one of his boots.

His hair was almost black, with a crisp short cut that could fool a woman into believing he was a clean-cut kind of guy— but Poppy wasn't born yesterday. His voice was a bass, so low and so deep and so sexy that he could likely croon a woman into a coma.

There wasn't enough wine in the universe to put her into a coma over a man. His major character flaws were all out there, naked, not hidden. He was intrusive and manipulative and nosy. And *bossy*. He just took over like he owned her and the rest of the world.

Still, the dog made up for it. Bubbles was as tall as Poppy's shoulders and anyone who could baby-love a monster dog like that had to be a Good Man. "Tell me how you ended up with this oversize puppy again."

Sam was feeding more wood to the fire . . . after he'd gotten her some crackers with the last glass of wine and then the comforter so she'd curl up again. "You were just starting to tell me about your sisters."

"And I still will. But first I want to hear the Bubbles story again."

Sam sighed. "Okay, okay." He collapsed in the recliner across from her. "I have two brothers. They're both better looking than I am—but not as smart. Conan, now, he's the youngest, and his brain has always been soft."

"And he's married and has a daughter."

"Actually, he has two kids now. Kristin's the oldest, and when she was three, Conan wanted to get her a puppy. I don't know who on earth talked him into this breed—you could see from her paws that she was going to be huge. But the original owner conned Conan into thinking the dog had fancy heritage, not just AKC, but practically wolfhound royalty. I swear, you could sell Conan swampland in the Arctic. But the real problem was, right off, that Kristin and the dog bonded. They were practically inseparable. She slept on him. She spilled food on him. She gave the dog dolls, all her toys."

"And the name? Bubbles?"

"Originally I think she was trying to say Baby. Only it came out Boobie. That wasn't going over well with the ladies in the family, so we coaxed her into calling the dog Bubbles. Less than a year later, the dog was three feet tall. Taller than Kristin. Taller than the kitchen table. Taller than door handles—which Bubbles could and did open whenever she wanted. Everything was marginally okay, until Conan's wife got pregnant again."

Sam sighed. "Conan's wife—Karla—said the dog had to go. They had a small house. The dog already took up half of it. It just wasn't working, but Kristin was five by then and got hysterical at even the thought of giving her up."

"So you got conned into taking the darling?" Poppy said it in a croon, because she was looking straight into Bubbles's big brown eyes.

"I wasn't *conned*. My niece and I just made a deal. She's six now. Old enough to negotiate in a mature way."

"Right," Poppy murmured, trying not to laugh.

"The dog's hers and will always be hers. She can come over and be with Bubbles any time she wants. It's just that the dog stays at my house. That was our deal."

"And you got what out of the deal?"

Sam's eyebrows shot up, as if the answer should have been obvious. "My niece is happy."

"Ah. I get it now. What a negotiator you are. I'll bet your mom is so proud."

He rolled his eyes, but she could easily see he was used to being teased. "All right. You made me tell embarrassing family stories, so now it's your turn. Back to your sisters. First, though, I'm getting you something more to eat."

She considered mentioning that he was being bossy again,

that she wasn't hungry, that it wasn't up to him . . . but arguing took so much energy. When she closed her eyes, she heard the creaks and crinkles of fire, smelled the enticing, soothing odor of applewood. Sam had unfurled the comforter again, wrapped it around her, tucked in her toes. Bubbles, lying at Poppy's feet, let out a laid-back snore every once in a while, clearly happy.

So was Poppy. Not happy exactly. But unstressed, the way she hadn't felt unstressed since she could remember.

A peanut butter and honey sandwich was nudged into her hand. He said, "Sisters."

"Yeah, yeah." She took a bite, then another. "I'm thirty-three. Just had a birthday a couple weeks ago. Camille—Cam—is almost thirty. Marigold is almost twenty-eight. They're not just sisters. I'm closer to them than anyone in the world. But . . ."

"But?"

She finished the sandwich, dusted her hands, took one last sip of wine. "But we lost my mom early on. Mom was just driving to the grocery store, nothing special, nothing different—when the other car ran a red light, driving way too fast. The accident demolished our car . . . and our mom. And our lives."

"Man, that's tough. How old were you?"

"At the time, I'd just turned eleven. The next few months after that—well, everything changed. Our dad's an artist, and a really good one, but he completely lost it after Mom died. Maybe he was always common sense challenged, and we just hadn't realized it before. He loved us. No question about that.

But he couldn't remember to buy groceries. Or what time school started in the morning."

Sam didn't prod her this time. Bubbles did. The dog stretched, stood up, and put her head on Poppy's stomach. Just offering comfort. Poppy rubbed her ears, offering comfort right back.

"So . . . I was the oldest sister. Naturally stuff landed on me. No one was going to make breakfast unless I did. No one was going to have clothes ready for school, unless I figured out the washer and dryer. I didn't really know how to cook. But I could make scrambled eggs. And a lot of PB&J sandwiches. I could get Dad to drive me to the grocery store, but somehow I was the one going up and down the aisles, trying to manage what we were going to eat. If I didn't open the bills, I suspect they'd still be lying on his desk."

Mr. Restless was moving around again, turning off the lamp behind her head, switching off the bright overhead, tending to the fire. She kept talking, just to fill the silence.

"Don't think I'm complaining. Or feeling sorry for myself. It was nothing like that. I loved my sisters. We pulled together. We made it all work. We helped figure things out on our own. It was just that, once everyone got older . . ."

"Tell me."

"It's just . . . it never stopped. My taking care of them. Thankfully we lived in Madison. I could go to the university there, especially because I got a couple scholarships in chemistry and math. I could also still live at home, get my sisters through school, ready for proms, ready for college, all that kind of thing. They were used to my being there."

"Sounds like they completely depended on you."

"Yeah, they did. They needed to. But I lived at home until both of them were out of high school, just commuted from home for my first job. By the time Marigold was out of high school and headed for college, I had a different job—a good-paying job at the university—and I really wanted to be on my own. Bought a house. A little one. Not far from campus, not far from either sister or my dad, and I could walk to the lab where I worked."

"Sounds good?"

"It was good. It *is* good. Except that nothing consequential ever changed."

"Meaning?"

"Dad, for instance—he still calls me if a faucet is leaking. Or if it's tax time. Or if he can't make his computer work. And my sisters . . . one of them is always showing up at my door with a suitcase, never thinking to call, just assuming she can stay a few days. Or one'll call at three in the morning, just wanting to talk about a breakup or a problem. We're so connected, it's like we're glued at the hip. I just thought that once we were all adults, this would naturally be different. And the same thing happens to me at work."

"How so?"

"Okay. Long story short. I've had two jobs—the first was with an environmental firm. I loved it. I graduated with a double degree, biochemistry and environmental sciences. I know. That sounds like I'm an academic geek type. But reality is, I love to put on a pair of hip boots and wade in the mud." At his look of surprise, Poppy chuckled. "Wisconsin has so many wonderful lakes. And that's what I wanted to work with. Issues with clean water, pollutants, protecting the health of fish and balance of microorganisms and all that. It's a different world. We're threatened by invasive species like no one ever dreamed of fifty years ago . . ." She stopped abruptly. She didn't want to go on, bore him witless. Really she wanted to stop talking, but the darn stranger—Sam—kept encouraging her.

"Anyway, early on, I developed a couple new processes. They were ideas I'd started in college, never had a chance to finish, so they didn't just come out of thin air. Whatever. The company was delighted, immediately applied for patents—but then they claimed the patents belonged to them. Legally, they were certainly correct. I went back through the employee agreement I'd signed at the start. Somewhere in all that legal jargon, I clearly agreed to give away all rights for any patentworthy processes I came up with. It was all legal. I was the stupid one. It's just . . . I worked double the hours I had to, because I loved the work and honestly cared. But they made thousands—potentially millions, actually—and all I got out of it was a 'good girl' and a pat on the back. Honest to Pete, I just felt taken advantage of. So I quit."

"Good move."

"So . . . then I went to the university—because they knew me, especially in the chemistry and biology departments. We sat down together, came up with an agreement. I get use of a lab, for certain projects and problems we all agree on. They get a portion of the take if my work is successful—or I develop more patents. It's going great. Sort of. I've got a great staff—mostly grad students or kids working on papers for their major— which means cheap labor and a ton of dedication. Only I still seem to be working sixty hours a week, and I still jump if anyone asks me to help."

Poppy yawned, couldn't help it. Her head slipped a little deeper into the pillow. The fire was burning down now, a softer gold, a quieter flame. Sam, in the easy chair, was in shadow. She could feel his gaze on her, that he was listening.

No one listened to her. Possibly because she never talked about herself. But darn it, that made it harder to stop.

"I make plenty of money, Sam. And our dad isn't one of those starving-artist types—he's got plenty socked away. But I kicked in for my sisters because I could and I wanted to and because our dad would never think of how hard it was for them to get started on their own. So I made sure they had safe wheels and start-up expenses for wherever they wanted to live. Padded their first accounts with some survival cash if something went wrong. They got out of school looking the same way I did— wearing old jeans and older sweatshirts and even older jackets. They needed working clothes. We loved—absolutely *loved*— shopping together. None of that was a hardship for me. I haven't paid off the whole mortgage on my house, but I'm really close.

Yet with all that money, I barely buy myself a new lipstick. Because I don't have time. Or just don't have any energy left. And then the crowning blow came on my birthday."

"What happened?"

"An old school friend asked me to go out for a drink. We weren't 'great' friends, but we both enjoyed catching up once a year or so. That's what I thought this was, but no. She wanted to ask if I'd babysit her two Pomeranians for the week over Christmas." She pushed a strand of hair behind her ear. "Sam. You can probably tell that I love dogs. But I *know* these dogs. They're not just spoiled. They're miniature terrorists."

"I've heard that about Pomeranians." He let out a throaty chuckle.

"Still, I would have said yes. Because I always say yes. But this time, out of the blue, I said no. It was a first, hearing the sound of a no come out of my mouth. I went home and looked in the mirror. You know what I saw?"

"A gorgeous woman?"

"No, you goof. I saw a woman who hadn't had her hair cut in over a year. Who was wearing a sweater older than Methuselah. Who hadn't bought new makeup in a decade, maybe longer. And it just all clicked. What a mess I was."

He shook his head. "I'm staring right at you. I don't see anything remotely resembling a mess."

"You're biased. You know I love your dog. But that's the point. I don't have a dog. I have men friends, but no serious man in my life. I eat on the run. I don't have any kind of personal life. I'm not blaming anyone but myself for letting everything tumble out of control, but this all just has to stop. I need a reset button."

"You haven't had a boyfriend in a while?"

She rolled her eyes. Trust a guy to home in on a minor sexual point. "Anyway. I got my hair cut and styled—five inches off. New makeup, even if I haven't worn most of it yet. New clothes. And I researched a place—this place."

"You cut five inches off that gorgeous hair?"

She could hardly hold her head up. Undoubtedly she was mumbling. Her mouth was tired from talking. Her whole body was tired . . . from everything. Her whole nonlife.

Poppy sighed, from the gut, from the heart. "Something is really wrong with me, Sam. I cave in whenever anyone asks me for anything. I seem to lack some critical personality ingredient. I love caring for other people, but I have no life of my own. I'm either working or caretaking 100 percent of the time. So I found this cabin, and I bullied my work schedule into carving out two free weeks. Two weeks of isolation and quiet. So I can figure this out."

Possibly her eyes were closed, because she could feel his knuckles brush against her cheek as he tucked the comforter around her. She heard him move the grate tight around the dying fire. One click of his finger, and Bubbles rose, ambled over, and bent down to lick her cheek, then ambled to the back door.

"I want a life of my own. I've never even analyzed what I want, what I need. I'm happy to stand up for anyone who needs me, but I never seem to stand up for *me*. I can't keep going on this way. Does that sound completely selfish?"

* * *

NATURALLY SAM DIDN'T answer her. When Poppy finally opened her eyes, blazing bright sunlight poured through the east windows. The fire had completely died. The furnace was thrumming.

Sam was nowhere in sight—no surprise.

She climbed off the couch, stretched out the kinks, then ambled to the window. Snow swirled and curled and draped in every direction, so deep the whole world looked like an artist's canvas in white diamonds.

Poppy waited for embarrassment to hit. She must have bored the poor man half to death. She'd certainly bored herself. She told herself she should be cringing inside and out for babbling all her personal history to a complete stranger.

And she was cringing. A little. Yet as she stared at the peaceful, gorgeous view, she felt a smile coming from nowhere.

Okay. So she wished she hadn't yammered all night to the poor man. But it was his fault he was so easy to talk to, his fault that he'd listened. And right or wrong, she felt as if a lead weight had lifted from her shoulders, to get it all out, to say it out loud, what was wrong, what she was trying to change. Sam had made her feel incredibly better, whether he'd intended that or not.

Poppy spun around and aimed for the shower. She'd bought

some fancy shampoo when she had her hair cut—it was expensive and luxurious and smelled downright sexy. Unlike her, but then, that was why she'd splurged. Over the next few weeks, she hoped to try out a few more vices.

The hair dryer was hidden somewhere. While she waited for it to show itself, she pulled on skinny new cords and big socks and a Fair Isle wool sweater that still had its tags. Then she found the hair dryer under the counter, exactly where she'd put it, and discovered the bubblegum-popping hairdresser was right. Her hair was so much lighter that it dried in minutes and looked all thick and shiny. Not that it mattered, but it made her feel new. Not like her old self.

After that she prowled the kitchen, found a banana and blueberries and a granola bar. The rush of sugar, for completely unknown reasons, made her think of Sam.

Really, she mused, it was completely reasonable to behave weirdly around Sam—besides the fact that he was hot and she hadn't been near a Seriously Good Looker in forever, well, come on, he'd made that deal with his little niece about the dog. What a good heart. What a sucker. What a real man.

From the back windows, Poppy suddenly heard the roar of a snowplow—exactly what she'd been waiting for. Hustling now, she plugged in a laptop by the window. Then—regretfully—she plugged in her phone and immediately set it up to vibrate rather than ring. Still, she saw seven, ten, no, *sixteen* messages since she'd left yesterday.

She hesitated for an instant. This one time, maybe one of her sisters really needed her. Or her dad could have an honest crisis. Or something could have happened at the lab.

"No," she said aloud. It wasn't that hard, trying the no word in the privacy of the cabin. She tried yelling "NO!" at the top of her lungs, and that felt even better. Before she could be tempted to give in and read even one message, Poppy jogged into action.

A small shock waited for her outside. Sam had cleaned the snow off her car and bladed the driveway. He'd never asked! Or even got a big thank-you from her. Besides that, the snowplows had cleared the road early that morning, so driving was going to be almost normal. It's not as if she wanted to drive that far. A mile at most.

So she finished up preparing: pulling on ski pants, zipping a down vest over her heavy sweater, and jamming on a white hat and gloves. Then, at last, she picked up the white box on the kitchen table.

The box was old. Her mom had given it to her on her tenth birthday. Back then, the box had contained a new pair of Riedells—that fit her perfectly then. Maybe it was the same old box, but Poppy had splurged on a new pair of Riedells—that fit her perfectly now.

Today, she figured, was the first day of her new reckless life. Her mom would have approved. Her mom, in fact, would likely have kicked her out the door . . . with the sacred box.

Come hell or high water, she was about to alter the wrong course her life was on. And hopefully going to have a great time doing it.

Chapter Three

MINUTES LATER, POPPY turned in, thinking the church looked just like the picture on the website—only prettier. Actually, she'd researched this site even before searching for rental cottages.

The stone building was old and picturesque, with a white spire and gorgeous stained-glass windows. The website claimed it was a thriving church from April through September, and a thriving winter community center in the colder months.

Two ample parking lots framed the church. They'd both been turned into skating rinks. The one on the left had a sign— FOR HOCKEY PLAYERS ONLY—where a few grown-up guys were swinging a stick around. The lot on the right was the rink FOR FIGURE SKATERS . . . where Poppy picked a parking spot and turned off the engine.

She was still looking around as she reached for her skates. A side door to the church was marked open—the website claimed there was running water, as well as several rooms that were semiheated: bathrooms, a first aid station, a long closet that stored sports gear, and some generic benches to defrost cold hands and feet.

Perfect.

The figure skating rink was completely empty.

Which was even more perfect. Maybe she'd been good at skating once, but that was a mighty long time ago. She fully expected to fall on her butt, probably a dozen times and then some. She'd just as soon not disgrace herself in front of a crowd.

Poppy pushed off her boots and lifted the pair of Riedell skates with a treasuring touch. It wasn't the best brand in the universe, but it was darned good. Once, she'd given the Riedells credit for enabling her to skate like a dream.

She remembered the feeling of the soft white leather, the protective quilted lining. She pulled them on, worried that she'd forgotten how to lace them, but it was like riding a bike. Her mind remembered how as if she'd done it yesterday.

Naturally she kept the guards on until she climbed out of the car, snugged the white cap on her head, pulled on gloves. Once she reached the rink, she pulled off the guards, took a big breath, and then took a first step onto the ice.

Memories of her mom flooded her mind—and her heart. She'd never expected the skates for her tenth birthday. As her mom well knew, she was about as athletic as a baby moose in a china shop.

But even more special than the gift was that her mom set up

skating times for just the two of them. Not her little sisters, not Dad, not school friends. Just the two of them.

"I need this time with just you, Poppy," her mom had said. "Being ten is an in-between birthday. You're bored with the toys you loved as a child, but you look at the older girls at school, and you're just not there yet. Two years from now, you'll be bored at the idea of hanging out with your mother. But right now, I've still got you."

"That's just silly, Mom," Poppy remembered saying. Remembered thinking that there'd never be a time she wouldn't love being with her mom.

A brisk wind shined her cheeks as she took a first cautious step on the ice, then another—wobbling like a little kid. She'd wobbled back then, too.

"But that's the point, Poppy," her mom had said. "When I was ten, I was all arms and legs. I just hadn't grown into my body yet. I was so clumsy I had to laugh at myself."

Poppy recalled how loud she sighed. "Mom, you were never clumsy. I can't even imagine you crashing on your face like I'm going to."

Mom had taken her hand, helping her balance, protecting her from falling. "I want to help you find your grace, honey. The way my mom helped me. I want you to forget everyone else and whatever they think. This is about you. It's about you, finding joy inside yourself."

Poppy took a long breath now, put those precious memories aside, and started trying to skate. The ice was fresh. Smooth as glass. The sunlit morning was bright with cold—but not once she started moving. She took the risk and let go, letting the skates test some speed, test some rhythm.

She figured she'd fall. Break her nose. Bloody a knee. Get a bruise the size of Montana. But it was coming back . . . the smile that came with speed. The "lift" that came from soaring across the ice as if she owned it.

Her mom's voice came back again, softer than a whisper. "You can't find your grace, honey, without taking a risk. You can fly. You will fly. You'll feel so joyful you forget everything else. You can't bottle the feeling, Poppy, but you can remember that it's there, that being happy inside yourself. It's in you. You just have to take the risk to get there."

It was almost as if her mom were still right there with her . . . until she forgot how to turn—at least at the speed she was skating.

Down she went. Her hip skidded on ice, hurt like fire. A skating fall always hurt like hell. But slowly she pushed herself to her knees, then to standing again. It had been there for a moment. That crazy feeling of soaring. That crazy *fun*.

She never had the chance to compete in serious skating, but she'd naturally loved it from the start. She picked up jumping early on. Then she had to try pulling off an axel now and then. Stop on a dime, pull off a pretty toe pick. Flirt with a camel spin. Even dance on the ice—if the right music was on. Rock and roll was the best, the easiest, the most natural. She wasn't remotely sexy at ten. She'd die if anyone thought she was sexy.

But sharp skates could move to any music, if she let her heart hear it. If she let her body hear it.

Poppy took off again, owning speed, sharing the sunlight on the ice. She tried a turn. Then a twirl.

The problem with skating was that you couldn't really learn anything if you were cautious. Speed enabled the skater.

Her mom obviously wasn't here now. It wasn't the same. Yet she remembered all the things they'd tried. Failed. Mastered.

A figure eight was far easier than she remembered. Stopping via the toe pick took some practice, but then the technique came back to her. And then she figured she might as well go for it—a very, very careful camel spin, her back leg stretched behind her, parallel to the ice, with her arms spread wide as if they were wings, and then just soar.

Deep in her heart, she could hear her mom whispering, "There, my Poppy."

* * *

THE COOPER BROTHERS invariably could find an hour to kill on a weekend morning. The excuse was hockey. Pretty hard to play hockey without a goalie and only three players, but they'd invented their own kind of pickup game when they were kids.

After a couple hours—okay, so they'd never planned to play so long—they headed to the side door of the church, carrying their equipment, each claiming they'd won over the others. Inside it was a little musty and dim, but easy enough to see the closet where they stored hockey sticks and pucks. They shared a padlocked locker for their own gear—their own buckets, a change of gloves and socks. They all sat on a long bench, unlacing their skates and changing to boots, ribbing each other as mercilessly as possible.

"Sam owes me five bucks." Brer, the middle brother, was as big as an ox, his claims always the most imaginative.

"I beat you fair and square. Two scores to your one. But okay, if you're that desperate—"

"Desperate?!"

"Hey." Conan, ever the interceptor between brothers, aimed for the door. "Sam, you're still good to take Kristin day after tomorrow?"

"Always." Sam handed out bottled water, which they all gulped faster than river rats. Creaming one's brothers took a lot of energy.

But his attention was on Conan now. "How's Karla doing?"

"Okay."

Clearly Conan's wife was not okay. He exchanged a glance with Brer. "Need some help? I mean, besides on Monday."

"I don't know. Yet." Conan turned off the extra lights. "Haven't told anyone yet, but she's pregs with our third."

"Another baby so soon?" Brer might have gone on, but Sam cracked an elbow in his gut.

"We always wanted three. And we wanted them close together, you know, so we'd get all that baby stuff over with at once. Like no one sleeping, and diapers in every room, and toys that reproduce all over the house. Not counting the crying and the having to be patient all the time—"

"Quit sounding so happy," Brer ordered him. "You know darn well you're nuts for kids."

"I know. And Karla is, too. But maybe a third pregnancy this quick is a little too soon."

Sam delivered another subtle elbow to Brer so he wouldn't open his mouth. Not about this. "The two of us are crazy jealous of you, you know that? Kids. A family. Going home to a warm woman instead of a cold house."

Brer interjected, "Hey, I'm looking. So's Sam. You're the youngest, but you found the perfect woman early on."

Sam was still looking at Conan's face. Something was definitely wrong. He suspected Conan's wife wasn't doing so well, but this wasn't the time or place, with all of them hustling to get home now, to question Conan further.

They finished cleaning up, checking around. The church went out of its way to make the neighborhood family-friendly—like offering the church grounds in the winter to enable families to do snow sports. But behind the scenes, Sam and his brothers did their share of work. Just logical, when they all loved the ice rink—and they could clean the rink and pour fresh water on it for clear ice tomorrow. Just not that hard.

Sam pushed open the door into blinding bright light on snow.

And saw her.

Brer said to Conan, "I always thought you could go pro in

hockey. You're fast. I mean, not as good as your older brothers, but . . ." His sentence trailed off as he and his brothers glanced toward the figure skating rink.

At first Sam wasn't certain it was Poppy. No one else was on the rink but the one woman, and from the back, all he could really see was a white cap and a slim frame. But he knew. Even before she turned.

She looked . . . free. At home on the ice. Arms stretched out, one leg extended, graceful as a swan. Naturally sensual. Naturally owning the ice. She wasn't "performing." She didn't realize anyone was there yet. She was just being herself. The woman she didn't have time for.

"Who the hell is she?" Brer whispered, almost with reverence.

"That's my girl." Brer and Conan registered instant shock and then immediately tried to surge toward her. Sam stopped them, quiet and fast. "She doesn't know it yet. But I do. I'm just telling you ahead of time."

She was so darn gorgeous. He watched her try a turn, still working her camel spin. Perfect. He couldn't remember yearning for anything this fiercely. He wanted her to feel that way with him. Freedom. Sensuality. Joyful, not in a noisy way, but in a heart-filled way, embracing sunlight and confidence in everything she was and could be.

She caught his breath.

His brothers were utterly silent, watching him.

Poppy finished her turn—and then clearly spotted him—because she clutched on the last turn, almost fell. But she didn't.

She smiled again, waved—but once she noticed the two guys with him, she turned again, sped down the ice to the far end.

That woman was *fast*. Or she could be, Sam mused. When she was trying to avoid trouble.

"Brer, Conan . . ." He turned around, found no one there. If that wasn't just like his brothers, to disappear from sight if they thought they could leave him with trouble. Of course, they probably had the insane idea that he wanted trouble.

Which he did.

He didn't call her, just hiked to the safety fence surrounding the rink and leaned on the edge. She spun around—eventually—and likely noticed that he'd failed to leave. She skated toward him, but slowly, no fancy moves. For sure, no risky ones.

"I didn't realize it was you at first," she said. She pushed off her white cap, let her hair spring free.

"I was with my brothers—"

"I figured. All three of you are taller than trees."

He grinned. "We shoot around a puck when we can steal an hour or two. The guys were watching you skate. Wanted to know if you played hockey."

She shook her head. "I'm a great hockey watcher. Watching all those broken noses and violence is really fun—from the stands."

He had to grin again. "Looks to me like you're faster than all of us."

"Because I have figure skates, and you're stuck wearing those big clunkers."

"My feet are clunker size. It's not the skates."

"If you say so." Her eyes didn't twinkle, but she obviously felt comfortable teasing him.

"You doing okay? Settling in? Everything working okay?"

"Really well. Appreciated all the help last night. And really appreciated your cleaning up my driveway. Where's Bubbles?"

Always the dog. "I had to leave her home. She'll just chase us on the ice if we let her come." He pushed away from the fence. "But I do have to get back. She needs her run. And I need to pretend I do serious work sometimes, even in the winter."

"I was just about to pack up and get back to my place, too. Stuff I need to do."

Yup, he was being dismissed. But that was okay. He'd carved a little niche closer. Poppy was talking to him, teasing him. Sam dug a hand in his pocket, pulled out a bedraggled business card, offered it to her. "Almost forgot I had this. But that old note that Cassius leaves for new renters—I'm almost sure that was my old cell, and it doesn't have my business number either. You need something, give a shout."

"Thanks."

He turned away, hiked for his truck, made a point of not looking back. But he was thinking about how she looked on the ice, how she looked when she took off the white cap and shook her hair loose. Her smiles. Her sass.

He had to hope he was growing on her . . . because she was sure growing on him.

Chapter Four

SKATING HAD BEEN exhilarating. More than exhilarating. Poppy came home starving, feeling full of herself, and tickled she'd run into Sam. Getting a look at his brothers was like a free genealogy lesson. All three men looked like stars in a Superman movie—capable of leaping tall buildings in a single bound—*and* while they were appreciating a girl with those big blue eyes.

Well. She hadn't paid that much attention to the brothers. But they did look clearly like kin. And Sam *did* have those wicked blue eyes.

Poppy checked her phone, found dozens of texts and messages on email and voice mail and thought, *Nope, not yet.*

For just a short stretch of time, she wanted to revel in that grand feeling of freedom, of remembering who she used to be as a kid—carefree, safe, loving life. She'd fiercely wanted to be just like her mom, who never seemed to fear anything. That little girl had long grown up, but the morning of skating brought back some memories of those days of innocent laughter, those old joys and dreams.

Doing more things she hadn't done in years might help as well.

FOR AN EARLY dinner that night, because she couldn't wait any longer, Poppy made homemade mac and cheese, drizzled some honey on toast, and carted that less-than-perfect dinner into the TV room. She'd brought books with her—not nonfiction treatises like *Environmental Crises in the Lakes*, or *Unique Ways of Attacking Alien Species*, or *Vitamins for Clean Lakes*. Instead, she'd brought romances—books she'd never had a chance to read—and heaps more that the bookstore owner had insisted she try.

That lazy plan couldn't have worked better. She read. Snacked. Read some more. Found the ice-cream bars. Read some more, thinking she was never reading nonfiction again.

Then, she just felt like snuggling. Cleaned up the kitchen, kicked off her socks, and wrapped up in the purple comforter. Maybe she'd watch TV for a while, then go back to reading. That was the new plan.

She slept for eleven straight hours, no restless churning around, no waking up worried for no reason. Just . . . sleep.

* * *

THE NEXT MORNING, when Sam peeled out of the driveway, the truck—of its own accord—failed to turn right, toward the hardware store, his intended destination. The steering wheel turned left, toward Poppy's.

He wondered if there was a possibility that his brains had atrophied overnight.

He'd only known her two days and was already nuts about her. That was fourteen-year-old-boy thinking.

Reality was that there was no reason he couldn't knock on the door and say hi. But a grown man should have a reason for stopping by. A *real* reason.

If only he hadn't seen her skating yesterday, he wouldn't be having this problem. But he had, and the image was glued on his pitiful, atrophied brain. Her grace, her beauty, her confidence on the ice, how she'd glowed. Her skin, her eyes. She'd just been so happy and unlike that exhausted woman he'd met before.

How was he supposed to forget that?

It wasn't reasonable for even a grown man to forget that.

Bubbles insisted on the passenger window being open, which meant that the inside truck temperature reached maybe zero degrees. But the sky was a brilliant blue. No signs of the wild wind or ice pelts from the blizzard two nights ago. Sun poured down on rolls and mounds and artistic drifts of snow, studding the landscape with crystals.

Poppy's car was still in the driveway, so she was home. And though Sam expected she wanted—and needed—heaps of serious sleep, it was past ten in the morning, so she was likely up and about.

Time to fish or cut bait, as his dad used to say. He'd made some headway with her yesterday . . . they seemed to talk as easily as if they were already long friends. And he had Bubbles with him. She loved Bubbles.

So he pulled in, cut the engine. Bubbles almost killed him when she realized they were at Poppy's place and attempted to jump over his head. Her wagging tail alone tried to dislodge the truck mirror. He opened the door as fast as he could and let the hooligan loose.

Sam followed, noting Poppy's in-and-out footsteps in the snow. When he knocked on her door, there was no answer. A peek in the windows showed lights on, signs of activity and life. He knocked again, then tried the knob and discovered the door was unlocked.

"*You*. Be quiet. And you're not going in, this is not your house. I'm just going to call her name to see if she's home." Bubbles promptly sat, expressing perfect obedience. Sometimes there really were miracles.

Sam poked his head in, called Poppy's name a couple times, but still, he heard no sounds. He took another step inside, noticed the open bathroom door—she wasn't in there—the bed was empty and ditto for the couch in the TV room. He turned to leave and immediately saw that the hooks next to the door were empty—no jacket, no boots on the floor, no hat. So she was outside somewhere.

He headed back out, closed the door, and abruptly realized the dog had disappeared from sight—and fast. And that fast, he could hear a woman's peal of laughter from beyond a hefty drift toward the lake.

Now that he really looked, he could see an amazing lumpy shape that appeared to be rolling, slowly, downhill. Whatever was powering the misshaped dirigible seemed to have a purple stocking cap, snow-crusted, with a fringe of dark red hair peeking around the edges.

Her cheeks were redder than cherries, not surprising for a morning struggling to make the climb to twenty degrees. He caught the burst of another chuckle—but she was laughing at Bubbles, not him. She waved when she saw him, which seemed a pale welcome compared to her joy at seeing the dog again.

But that was okay. Since at least one of them had earned a welcome, Sam felt justified in hiking closer. By the time he'd negotiated the drifts, she'd added a much smaller lump on top of the bulbously fat bottom one.

He could be tactful. Not often, but sometimes. "Is that supposed to be a snowman?"

"Good morning, Sam."

"Good morning, Poppy."

"And of course it's not a snowman. It's a snowwoman. The snowball I started with didn't happen to be round, and the more I rolled it . . . well, it kind of took on an artistic curve. So I figured why not? I mean, it's *my* snowwoman."

"Snowwoman," he echoed. "And the little ball on top?"

"I don't know what happened there. In my head, I decided to

name her Agnes? And then she just seemed to look littler from the waist up."

"Agnes, huh?" Poppy was still talking to him, but mostly she was flat on her back, laughing while Bubbles lavished her cheek with a big soft tongue.

Eventually, the dog settled down and Poppy pushed up on her elbows. "When I went skating yesterday, I'd forgotten how much I used to love playing outside in the winter. That's how I came up with the idea of building a snowman. I think it's time I quit being a serious grown-up for a while. You know. Regress. Try being a kid again, when I knew how to play."

"I like the idea of playing . . . but how far did you want to go back? Are you talking the age of braces?"

"Ugh. Not that."

"Zits?"

"Bite your tongue, boy."

"That fun age when hormones yo-yoed up and down and were a constant menace in your life?"

"Okay, okay. I definitely don't want to go back *that* far."

He cocked his head. "When did you learn to skate?"

"When I was ten. My mom taught me." All good memories were in her eyes. Pretty clear her mom had been a peach and then some. But then she cocked her head. "Your mom and dad—are they still together?"

"More than together. I'm pretty sure they've been inseparable since high school."

"Hmm." Poppy uncurled, dusted the excess snow off her back. "Do you like their marriage, Sam? I mean, would you like to have a marriage the way they do?"

"That's a hard question," he admitted.

"Too personal?"

"No. You just made me think." He started packing snow, adding it to her snowwoman's scrawny chest. "I couldn't ask for a better family. My dad and I butted heads when I was a teenager. But that's because I was stupid and he was trying to save me."

"Your mom?"

"Mom would have taken a bullet for me. Sometimes that was embarrassing. I mean—when I was a teenager, I could stand up for myself. And did. But she was an active part of all our lives."

"She sounds wonderful."

"She is. But as far as their marriage . . . they were fighters. Not mean. Not physical. Ever. But they argued a lot. Loud. The three of us would scatter faster than wind once they got going."

Poppy waited, as if she clearly hoped he'd say more.

"My brothers were okay with it. The loud fights. The parents were okay with it, too. Nobody held grudges. It's just how they were."

"But . . ."

Again, he thought she wanted him to tell her more. "But everybody argues. You can't escape it. And I can be more bull-headed than an ox—which everyone in my family will tell you. But I don't like yelling."

She released a long breath. "Me either. Fights are okay. But clean fights. If you're really mad, get out of the room. I don't think anyone's really listening when both people are talking over each other."

He arched an eyebrow. He wasn't sure how they'd waded into personal subjects so fast, but he understood nosiness. "Your turn."

"My turn?"

"What about your parents? I mean, you told me your mom died. But before that, did you like their marriage, how they were together? Did they have the kind of relationship you'd want for yourself?"

"Now *you're* the one asking the hard questions."

"Hey, you started it."

"Okay, okay, I did. But I'm getting kind of cold—would you mind helping me finish the snowwoman? She still needs a head, a face, hair." She shot him a slow grin. "And after that, I'll answer the hard question—assuming either of us even remember it—while I heat up a couple mugs of hot chocolate."

"That sounds 100 percent ideal."

Well, it seemed 100 percent ideal, until she put him to work. He was assigned the task of finding arms for her snow lady, while Poppy went to work on the head. Her small project took longer than creating a snow husband for the snow lady.

Man, but she was picky. Everything had to be just right. She and the hooligan took off for a stand of fir trees; both of them disappeared from sight, and then Poppy emerged with treasures. The pine cones and pine needles created quite a hair style. Then she had to find two perfect sticks for eyebrows. Then she hesitated, unsure how she wanted to do the mouth and eyes.

"You're freezing," he pointed out reasonably.

"I know. But I can't leave until she's done."

"You want frostbite?"

Poppy took a breath, took on a dead serious tone. "Look, Sam. I'm stuck with certain character flaws. First, I'm an annoying overachiever. And second, I have an unrelenting sense of responsibility. In other people, those can be nice qualities. Not with me. I'm genetically wired to never give in. Which means I can't desert my snow lady until she has lipstick and some pretty eyes."

"Lipstick?"

But trust her, even with all the snow, she found some bushes with berries on the south side of the woods. She squished the berries into the snow. Made a quite expansive mouth for her snow lady. Then bounded back to the cabin, where she emerged with two chestnuts for the lady's eyes.

She donated her own scarf to drape around the snow lady's neck and then stood back. "Does she need anything else?"

He shook his head. "I hate to tell you this, but I'm afraid we'd be dangerous if we ever worked on a project together. I'm as bad as you are. I can't quit until everything's right. I don't care what anyone else says. Actually, my brothers are always claiming I don't listen to what anyone else says."

"Whew. What a relief to have those confessions out of the way—that we're both insufferable to be around."

He laughed, and the three of them aimed for the cabin. Bubbles barged in as soon as the door was open—intent on claiming the couch before either of the humans could get near it. Since both admitted to being half frozen, Sam started a fire, while Poppy did the hot chocolate thing.

"Hey. You promised you'd answer the same question you asked me. About your parents' marriage. Did you like how they were together? Or did you promise yourself you'd never be like them in a million years?"

She looked startled for a moment, held up a spoon dripping with chocolate. She jumped, swiped the gooey spill, then started stirring again. "I loved both parents, but differently. I loved my mom unconditionally and forever." The color of her voice seemed to fade. "And I love my dad. No question about that. But love just seems to shrink a little, if you discover that your loved one can't be trusted. For pretty much anything."

She'd just showed him a mental scrapbook of pictures about her childhood. Nothing filled out, but sure sounded like she had more sadness and troubles than a kid should have to go through.

"Anyway . . ." Poppy turned away, searched around in a cupboard for one giant bag of marshmallows and two blue mugs. Eventually she got around to her family again. "A short story. One time my mom was outside gardening, digging in the flower bed, and suddenly her knee hit this old rusty nail. Punctured her skin. Went in pretty deep. I got up and ran for my dad, who was naturally in his studio—he had the studio added on when I was really little. It was like a whole apartment separate from the rest of the house, which was great, but it was that far that I knew he couldn't have heard my mom cry out. So I told him he had to come, right now, that mom was hurt.

"He looked at me as if I'd sprouted wings. He said, 'Is she dying?' I said no. He said, 'Can she move?' I said yes, sort of. And he said my mother would tell him if she wanted his help. I should scoot. He was working."

Poppy shook her head. "We had to bundle up the two little ones, get them in the car; and my mom had to drive to the hospital herself. That incident has stuck in my mind to this day. I never said anything, until when she was teaching me to skate, and I had those hours alone with her. I told her how upset I'd been that Dad hadn't helped her. He should have.

"She said, 'Yes, he should have.' But then she just looked at me and said, 'I'll bet sometimes you wonder why your dad and I stay together, don't you?'

"And that was exactly what I'd wondered. It's not that I didn't love him. But he was always absentee. Never around when we needed him. Only showing up when he had time to play." Poppy sighed. "My mom told me that we can't help who we fall in love with. Yet it's a guarantee that person will have flaws because everyone has flaws. You can't know ahead of time whether you can survive his faults, or whether he can survive yours. Over time, each of you have to figure that out—whether his faults are going to drive you nuts, or whether you can accept who he is and love him anyway. Mom always said that a marriage was private. That no one else could judge what's right or wrong for those two people. So . . . back to the question."

She spun around, obviously looking for some kind of tray, not finding one. "I don't want a marriage like my parents had. But my mom made me think about what mattered . . . and what didn't." Now she smiled at him as she carried the steaming mugs of cocoa on a cookie sheet. She'd added napkins. And toast with melted butter.

"I'm warning you now," she said gravely. "I dunk my toast in the cocoa."

Obviously they were finished discussing lightweight subjects and on to serious issues, he thought wryly. "Some family traditions are unshakable," he agreed. "Like dunking toast in your cocoa. Or having to take the top of the Oreo before you eat the white part. But . . ." Sam glanced at his mug. "Are you positive there's actually cocoa in there?"

"Uh-oh. Don't tell me you don't like marshmallows."

"I do, I do. I just don't usually think of them as a major food group." He stole a couple of couch cushions from the dog, plopped them down on the hearth. Both cupped their red-cold hands on the mugs and stretched stockinged feet to the fire to warm up.

Sam couldn't believe how easy he felt with Poppy, how comfortable it was to tease and be teased, to just be next to her.

When she was relaxed like this, she seemed so comfortable—with him, with herself, with her world. She wasn't a secret keeper, a grudge holder. She'd been frank about her history, her issues. Not down deep at the gut level, but they didn't know each other that well yet.

He tried to stop looking at her. But she shot him a studying glance as often as he looked at her.

Of all the women he'd known, Sam couldn't remember anyone who pulled at his senses like this. He hungered to be with her, to know more about her. To help her fix the stresses she'd been under. She forced him to feel frightening thoughts about the future—about belonging, to her, with her. About how she'd be in bed. About how he'd be. About what kind of passions they could ignite in each other.

Which was all crazy. He didn't know her well enough to be thinking along such serious lines. But he wanted to.

When the mugs were drained, he forced himself to stand up, stretch. "Well, I've been in your hair long enough. I've got a heap of chores to do, and bet you'd like some space. But hey. You're here for a break, so why don't you come over for dinner?"

Her easy smile froze. "You mean . . . at your place?"

"Well, yeah. I see the roads are pretty well plowed out, but I doubt there's much in the way of restaurants on a Sunday night. And Bubbles will be with us, if you're worried about a chaperone."

She chuckled. "I wasn't."

But she was, Sam thought. Which was interesting. Truth to

tell, he was enticed by the possibilities of spending some private time together. But not at this second. He motioned toward the window.

"You can actually see my place from here—it's that big old monster at the crest of the hill. Normally it wouldn't be a long walk from here, if you could just stroll the lakeshore, but the snow would make that difficult right now. As the crow flies, it's less than a quarter mile. And we can make it an early dinner. Really early. Say five?"

Poppy thought. She seemed to think for quite a while, which told Sam she hadn't felt safe outside her own venue in quite a while.

"That sounds great," she said finally. "Especially the part about not having to cook for a change—although I'd be glad to whip up something for dessert or salad or something."

"Poppy"—Sam spoke as he grabbed his parka, woke his dog, found his boots—"from what you told me, you're always stuck 'whipping up something' for someone else. So I'm the cook tonight. You bring nothing. Just wear warm, comfortable clothes, so we can be outside for a stretch."

"Sure," she said.

"If you don't mind, I'll pick you up. Next time, you'll know the way, but it's dark so soon this time of year, and the driveway's not that easy to find. Once you've been there, it'll be a piece of cake."

"All right," she said, but she sounded less sure about being dependent on his driving her there and back.

He grinned, thinking he needed to take her worries down a notch. "Just think. You'll be home early enough that if my cooking is atrocious, you'll still have time to come back and raid your fridge here."

There. Her smile was back. "Whew. I appreciate you giving me an escape plan if I need one." They both chuckled.

He and Bubbles skedaddled pretty quick, after that. But Sam mused that Poppy would never need an escape plan with him. Life had trapped her enough. The only way he could start building trust was by spending more time together.

There was no way, no how, he ever wanted her feeling trapped by him. The only things he wanted to do with her, to her, together, were things they both wanted.

He hoped.

Chapter Five

POPPY WATCHED THE truck pull out of the drive and enjoyed a sweet shiver. That man was a *tall* drink of water for a woman who'd been parched as long as she had.

Still, a smart woman didn't dive off a pier without knowing how deep the water was. She wanted to get in trouble. With him. Terrible trouble. Lusty, risky, delicious trouble.

Only she needed to be a lot more sure of herself than she was right now.

A test seemed to be in order. She plunked down at the table with half a sandwich and signed on to her computer, and then her cell phone. It was an ideal way to take her inner strength out for a test drive.

The number of messages and texts was daunting—eleven more messages since yesterday, and eight more texts. On her computer, messages spilled over from email, WhatsApp, and Telegram.

Poppy searched first for work contacts—not that she didn't

care about family, but because her lab team had just finished the grant application project. She had one full-time biologist, four grad students, and a handful of biology or environmental science majors working with her. The grown-ups wouldn't contact her unless there was a fire. But the younger ones had given heart and soul—and long hours—to their latest project, between the ideas, the research, and all the gut background work. There was nothing else to do until after Christmas, but the youngest team members tended to worry. So if they'd contacted her, she would have quickly responded.

There were no work messages. So. So far so good.

But all the rest were from her sisters. In spite of impossible odds, she missed them. Cam—Camille—seemed to have a legion of men chasing her, all claiming to be in love. Cam always hid at Poppy's house after breaking up with the latest guy. Cam was smart and fun, and the two of them could sister-talk until they were both hoarse.

Marigold, the baby, was their free spirit—a little too much like their dad, Poppy had always worried—but it wasn't like Mari was irresponsible. More like she just couldn't be tethered. She could sing at the top of her lungs just for the joy of it . . . patch a roof on her own . . . wear bohemian skirts one day and a slinky black dress the next. She was the clown, the one who made all of them laugh, even on days they had nothing to laugh about.

Poppy clicked on a dozen messages, then a half dozen more, then stopped cold. She *did* miss them, but she had to stop enabling their dependence on her. They *knew* she loved them. They knew, if they really needed her, she'd be there faster than the speed of light.

But their dependence on her wasn't healthy—for them or for her.

She wanted it stopped. She had to believe her sisters knew that she'd never deliberately hurt them.

No matter how strong her resolve, the last texts made her hesitate.

From Cam: Poppy, we need to know where you are. What if something happened and you needed us? We don't want to bug you. We just need to know you're okay.

And then from Marigold: I wasn't worried at first. You can vacation all you want! I want you to have fun! I love you! I want you to do something wild and free. But I still need to know how to reach you, Poppy.

The taste of guilt was familiar, that horrible feeling that she was letting them down. Trying to shake it off, Poppy took a long hike around the house, which took all of five seconds. Then sat back down to answer two notes—one to each sister.

I'm fine. I love you. I've gotten all your messages and appreciate them. I just need some quiet time. Nothing to worry about.

Okay. Swiftly, Poppy shut down all the devices and thought, *Enough trials for one day.* She was going out to dinner with a special guy, and tarnation, she intended to enjoy preparing for it.

She washed her hair. Blow-dried it. Somewhere in all her new stuff was an apricot satin bra and matching thong. Somewhere in the bathroom drawers were heaps of new makeup.

The surface, though, was exactly as ordered. Leggings and snow pants. A Christmas green sweater with big boot socks. A couple dangly things at her wrist and neck because she just wanted to.

POPPY HURTLED OUT of the house the minute Sam's truck pulled in shortly before five. He opened his door and then just hung on it. "Wait. Wait. Where's my Poppy?"

"Say what?"

"What'd you do? You look . . ."

"Scruffy? Warm? Comfortable? Ready for the outdoors, as instructed?"

"Yeah, yeah. But your face is . . . I don't know." He swiped a hand over his face, which she was coming to know was a familiar way of his coping with confusion. "I was going to say beautiful, but I'll take that back right away. You'd think I was flirting instead of trying to make an objective evaluation. And I'm not flirting. I was just thrown off by the change in you."

She climbed into the truck on her side, not sure whether to laugh or roll her eyes. She ended up doing both. "Sam, you are so full of malarkey. It's just makeup. A lot of women wear it. I love to wear it. It's just that I haven't taken the time to buy new stuff in quite a while."

"That's probably because you didn't need it. Hey. What's in your hands? Didn't I give you express orders not to bring anything?"

"You did. But I don't obey anyone's orders, Sam. It's just something called spaghetti ice cream. Dessert. I brought it with me for the holiday, but it's something fun. When we get to your place, though, it has to go in the freezer pretty quick."

"Did you say spaghetti ice cream?"

"I'm not explaining. You'll see."

Maybe it was all Sam's nonsense, but somehow they were easily talking and teasing again. Poppy forgot her nerves, forgot being wary. The drive to his place was short, but she was glad he'd insisted on driving, because she'd never have found it. The driveway was in the middle of solid woods, and from there it curved around until his house finally came in sight.

"Sam, for heaven's sake!"

"What?"

"Wow. Just *wow*."

Poppy couldn't stop gaping. The last stretch of drive ended in a white stone archway—tall enough for a truck, wide enough to fit two. A keystone in the center had his last name carved in copper.

"I was expecting a house. Not a castle!"

"I know parts of it look a little on the fancy side, when I'm not a fancy kind of guy. But when I started working with stone, I had to have some things to practice on. Lots of customers like archways, so I started with this one. Then if it fell apart, it'd fall on me instead of a customer. Archways—at least the big ones—can be really challenging."

"Besides, you wouldn't have any fun if it was easy, right?"

He started to respond, but then they were both distracted. Bubbles had been left alone, and the instant the dog saw the truck, she started howling like a drama queen who'd been abandoned.

Poppy kept studying the place. On a late winter afternoon, it was already dark, but Sam had Christmas lights draped all over the place. He'd planted white pines in the front yard, not a tidy row but a slew of them, all lit up with the same white fairy lights.

A curved flagstone path led to the front door. The house was three stories, so naturally the entrance was big enough for a giant, with a shiny-red double door, framed by sidelights and a fanlight above. Fat red balls nestled in the spruce wreath.

Sam cleared his throat. "The thing is, I help with my brothers' and parents' decorations, so I have to get mine done way ahead. Everyone thinks I have nothing to do in the winter. It isn't remotely true. There might not be much outdoor work right now, but there's paperwork and taxes and planning."

"Sam, if you're trying to apologize for having such a big Christmas splash—"

"I am."

"Well, quit it. It's gorgeous." He led her around the house, rather than up to the front door. The building was old stone, built on a slope that faced the lake. Even in the dark, Poppy could see turrets and sloping dormers and mullioned windows. Character more than luxuries, she mused. Architecture that cherished the views of lake and woods. Sam being Sam, he had birdhouses and bird feeders all over the place. Wildlife was obviously welcomed here.

He ushered her in via a side door. "Kitchen's through here. If you'll pop that 'spaghetti ice cream' in the freezer, I'll grab your coat and get some dinner started. Feel free to snoop."

"Sam! I've never snooped in my life!"

"You will. Everyone does. I didn't build the place, so I'm not taking credit or criticism for its eccentricities. I'll catch up with you. I just need five or ten in the kitchen."

Well, he said she could snoop, so it wasn't her fault that she took him up on it. A curved staircase led to a balcony with a window seat and huge circular window that viewed the star-studded night. Poppy hesitated at the top of the stairs, realizing at a glance that there were at least five doors on the second floor—too much to explore for a cursory look around. At the end of the hall, though, was one open door, obviously leading to the master suite. If she craned her head just a little, she could catch the corner of a platform bed, windowed walls leading to a balcony, and a fireplace midwall. Well, she couldn't quite see the fireplace, but it looked blue—almost like sapphire. The stone was softer than a gemstone, though, richer, perhaps lapis.

She really wanted to see it closer, but she'd be guilty of snooping for sure, then—even if it was just her own conscience playing judge and jury. Still, she didn't want to leave Sam alone forever, so she skedaddled back downstairs, only took a quick round through the first floor.

Double French doors led to a dining room, with a massive breakfront and table in chestnut. She presumed that he'd inherited the table, because it had clawed feet, a zillion leaves, and looked well used and well loved. It had earned its scratches. No question that lots of people had shared dinners together here.

Near the front of the house, Sam had obviously set up an office. Built-in bookshelves dominated the walls, with the usual techno stuff and a desk that could and obviously had taken a beating. A playroom for a guy who likely came in with dirty boots and was headed for a sit-down with a computer and phone. Clearly Bubbles used the long Oriental rug as a place to nap when Sam worked inside, because there was a basket of balls and dog toys heaped there.

And the last room—a huge living room—was a major stunner. Naturally there was another fireplace; this one took up the entire corner, reaching to the ceiling, with a triangular hearth. Dramatic mullioned windows overlooked the woods. The opposite wall took her breath away; it was made of white and salmon quartz, natural opal, sodalite, moonstone, rough boulder stones veined with gold . . . who would think to make a wall with all those kinds of rocks? It wasn't show-off fancy. Just unique.

When she heard Sam's footsteps, she whirled around. "You realize this wall is completely magnificent?"

He grinned. "I didn't plan it. The problem was, every time I finished a project, I'd end up with spare rocks and stones that just piled in a corner of my shop. Some of them were too darned interesting to just leave there, so I started on the wall. Back then, I wanted to redo my life from investment banking into something physical, something personal. Started the Cooper Stone Company. I've got a storefront closer to Madison, but that's the window dressing side of things. I'll show you my shop here another time, my real workplace where I can mess with designs, masonry, tools. See if some stones want to work together or don't." He shook his head. "I love that darned wall. Even if it's goofy."

"It's not goofy! I could look at it all day. And then all night, with the fire on it."

"Okay. But you haven't seen the scary floor yet."

"Scary?"

"Well, it scares some people. It's sort of an overdone calculated guy cave. The thing is, my brothers come over a lot. We all hunt and fish. Kids and cousins in the family hang out, too. So that floor is all about . . ." He frowned, couldn't seem to find the right word.

So Poppy pelted down the back stairs ahead of him, and then had to laugh. Talk about a man haven. Big couches, big TV. Wall decorations included deer horns and fish, interspersed by sports apparel in Wisconsin Badgers' red and white. A serious kitchen had been designed for real work—like scaling fish and carving venison and other ghastly hunting things. The counter was long enough to sleep on, and the triple sink had hanging hoses.

An adjacent mudroom had heaps of hooks on one wall, a generous shower, and equipment of all kinds—fishing rods, snow gear, etc., etc. As far as Poppy could tell, the whole giant room could be hosed down for a massive cleanup—no matter what kind of messes the guys made.

Outside was an open patio, spacious enough to feed a crowd in the summer, including an outside brick fireplace. All of it was covered with heaps of snow now, but it was clearly a space where all ages could be outside or inside, just gathering together for the joy of it.

Poppy touched a long stuffed fish on the wall. "I saw this in a hardware store once. Does it sing if I press its tummy?" she asked.

"Ha ha. I saw that for sale one Christmas, too. But, hey, if you want to press *my* tummy, I'll sing for you any time."

Her heart kicked up an extra beat, but she tried to keep her voice demure. "Thank you, Sam. I may reserve that vital piece of information for another time."

He laughed again, but suddenly he was looking at her. Looking at her differently. And she couldn't seem to pull away from looking back at him the same way. His eyes turned serious, intent.

Maybe she'd guessed he was interested when they first met.

The spark was there. But she'd thought he was maybe a natural flirt, just basically interested. Not seriously. Not playing. But really wondering where they could go together.

And darn the man, but she was wondering the same thing.

Sam stepped closer, then another step closer. Poppy lifted her face, to meet the kiss she thought was coming.

But then he stopped, sighed. "Nah. We need to be sure you can survive dinner before anything else."

She didn't ask what "anything else" meant. But her heart was galloping a zillion beats per second. "You're worried I can't survive dinner?"

From a back closet, he pulled out a giant piece of fur. "This," he said, "was my mom's. Years ago, she found a size 24 raccoon coat in an army/navy store. It was so ratty we all thought she was nuts, but she bought it, cut it down. Looked like new. And since then everybody gets to use it when there's a problem with serious warmth. It'll probably still be big on you? I think Mom said it was more like a size 10 now. But the point is how unbeatably warm it is."

"You're suggesting I need that coat for dinner?"

He nodded. "We're cooking outside."

Maybe their love affair was going to be extremely short. It couldn't be ten degrees outside.

BUT AN HOUR later, Poppy changed her mind. Sam had everything prepared outside. She was parked on a heated seat, swallowed in her own winter gear plus the giant raccoon coat that could have kept anyone toasty. And that wasn't counting the mulled wine, which warmed her from the inside out.

"When are you going to tell me what that spaghetti ice cream is?" he asked.

"After dinner. Not before. First, you have plenty of time to tell me all about your past. I told you all my troubles. It's your turn."

"That sounds like a bribe. I don't get dessert unless I do the whole past history thing."

"Bribe. Blackmail. I haven't enough experience with criminal activity to have all the terms down. And in the meantime, don't look at me. I'm probably drooling. *When* is it going to be done? It smells over-the-moon fantastic."

It did. It was just a chicken, roasting on an iron spit. A brick circle defined the firepit, and this couldn't have been Sam's first cookout, because he'd rigged up a way to turn the spit, so he could baste the chicken with more butter. Or add a little crushed black pepper and salt. Potatoes, on the coals, were covered with foil. He claimed they were done.

"This is a guy meal," Sam warned her. "No vegetable."

"Like I care. You made mulled wine. *That*, I care about. Now. About the past women in your life."

"Huh."

Poppy told herself this couldn't be romantic. With the fur coat, she had to be wearing twenty pounds of clothes. For certain she couldn't move. Sam had forced her into another pair of socks—his—and UGGs gloves. She never had a chance to be cold, especially after he produced the thermoses with the hot mulled wine.

Sam, on the other hand, looked like the *GQ* caveman of all time. Hunched over the firepit, the flames burnished his face, adding an extra mystery to his eyes. He wore lumberjack boots along with the usual Guy Outdoor Gear. Just behind was a magic box—magic, because he kept producing supplies from it. Napkins. Butter. More mulled wine. Paprika. Silverware.

"Sam, you have a stupendous house. You're clearly a complete sucker for dogs and kids. You do things for your neighbors, for your family. So. It makes no sense that there's no woman in this picture. Divorced?"

"Nope."

"There had to be someone you were in love with."

He sighed. "Yeah. Thought she'd be the one true love of my life. But then she sacked me before the wedding. Which I deserved."

"Oh god. Finally, some dirt. Tell me, tell me."

"Well . . . let me start with our first kiss. Her name was Celeste. Long blond hair. Baby blue eyes. She'd flip that hair around all the time. And she wore a lot of shiny clothes back then. Shirts that had stars and hearts on them. Twirly skirts. Anyway, we were outside, in the woods, with a bunch of other people our age . . . when she started walking toward me. Almost knocked me over, to tell the truth. But Celeste, she closed her eyes and put her hands on my cheeks and kissed me." He sighed. "Blew my socks off. It was incredible. And then came the good stuff."

"I can't wait to hear."

"We went back inside, talked to our teacher, Mrs. Houston. We told her we were engaged to be married. She said that second grade seemed a little young to be engaged, but that was all right. We could put our desks together, if we wanted. But we couldn't be kissing or anything like that, not in school."

"Second grade. Did you hear that, Bubbles? Second grade."

"If you're going to interrupt—"

"I'm not, I'm not. It's a wonderful story. I can't wait to hear what happens next."

"Well, it was a really long engagement. Our parents were all for it. A lot of dating was involved in the first few years. I'd knock on her door; her parents would let her out and we'd swing on the swing set in her backyard. Or she'd come over and sit between my parents on the couch while we watched TV with my brothers. Occasionally she wore makeup. And lots of spangly stuff. I think she had a rhinestone purse, for a while. The lusty behavior didn't seem to progress, but we excelled at smooching."

"I don't doubt it for a minute."

"We were a couple for so long, I can't remember when we weren't. Did everything together in high school, then both applied to U of W—so it was easy for us to still be together. I wanted a degree, maybe a master's, in finance and econ. She wanted something in fashion. Neither of us saw trouble coming. Except that I loved the studies. Did an internship with an investment firm, who took me on the instant I graduated. Didn't even need the master's degree."

"It all sounds good."

"She thought it sounded good, too. She was planning the wedding. The place we'd live. The furniture and all that. She still really liked sparkly things, and that was okay, because I started making real money, amazingly fast. Company said I was a natural. I lapped it up, not the money, but the work. Only ate lunch and dinner, because I'd have starved otherwise. Fell asleep if we'd go out to a movie. Bought her a car for Christmas. A pretty little MG convertible. She really loved it. But she really didn't like my taking business phone calls on Christmas Eve or past ten at night."

"Aw, Sam." Poppy grieved for him even before she heard the unhappy ending.

"I don't remember exactly why it all exploded, but we were at dinner, something about finalizing wedding plans, and suddenly she threw the ring across the table. She said a bunch of things, like I was the most inconsiderate man on the planet, selfish, blind, cruel, insensitive. I'm sure I'm leaving some of it out, but that was the gist. She kept the car. The stuff. That was only right. Those were always just for her."

She hurt for him. "What a heartbreak," she said gently.

"It was. But no question—she was the good person and I was the idiot. Every label she threw at me was right on. Anyway, that was over three years ago. That was when I quit, moved here, started the stone company. Put my life together real, real differently, and real, real slowly."

"Tell me." Poppy watched Sam turn the chicken for maybe the last time, fill up both their mugs with more mulled wine, and start plating the potatoes. The fire spit and sparked, sharp and gold against the black velvet night.

He handed out paper towels. "Trust me. We're eating this with our hands." Then he went back to his story. "I never meant to hurt her. But I did. Afterward, I could see that we were together so long that it was just easy to go with the flow. Everyone assumed we'd get married. Both families liked us. And she didn't change. I did. I was caught up in the job. I was thinking about getting ahead, success, making my mark. The market fascinated me, so did people—how needs and families were all different, all complicated. Easy to see why some people made poor financial decisions. I thought I could help them figure it out."

"Sounds like you still love it."

"I could. But by then I associated the job—or my addiction to the job—as a factor in why I'd failed Celeste. To be honest, I don't think we'd have ended up happy together anyway. We never did value the same things. But I still recognized what I did wrong, and that I wanted to fix it. Not to win her back. That would have been like putting the pieces of a broken egg back together. Too much hurt. I saw her a year and a half ago—don't remember where—but she was with her husband; he was in a tux and she was dressed to the gills. That was the kind of guy she wanted. A man who liked to wear a tux, a guy who liked to be seen with the 'in people.' I'm afraid I have no interest whatsoever in whoever the 'in people' are. But . . ."

"But?" Poppy prompted him.

"But I did want to be a better man than I was then. I started by quitting that job, and vowing big-time that I'd be careful to avoid any career that took over my life. I could see I was prey to it"—Sam motioned at her with a fork—"the same way you are. I was hard-core responsible. A perfectionist. Had to have everything right or I couldn't sleep at night. But it was too much, Poppy. I stopped being me and started being the job. And the only reason I'm still rambling on about this is because, maybe, just maybe, there isn't another person in the universe who could understand how I fell into that existence. Except for you."

For a second she was startled. Then thoughtfully nodded. Maybe she'd never been as overdevoted to her job as he'd been—but it was close. And for certain she was overdevoted to her family; she'd stopped having time for herself or even thinking about dreams for herself. How could trying to do plain old good things turn out to be so self-destructive?

Poppy shook her head. "It's crazy. Finding someone else who really understands. Who'd think we were remotely alike? But I do know what you mean. You weren't aiming to do anything wrong—you were trying to do the right things, to build a life, a career. How could you know it was going to take you over? Or how hard it would be to break away."

"Yeah. I knew you'd get it. And that's why—when you shared what you were going through that first night—I wanted to share back. No reason we need to always dwell on serious subjects. I just wanted you to know that I'm not a complete stranger to what you've been going through."

She hunched up on her knees. Bubbles was so close to the fire she risked burning her nose, which didn't remotely worry the dog. "When you started the stone business . . . it seems obvious you really like it."

"I do. And it's a natural in the family. Back in the 1850s, my dad's side came from Cornish stock. That's where we all get the black hair, blue eyes gene. The men in my family all worked in the mines, but my great-great-grandfather didn't want to die in the mines the way his father did. So they immigrated here. Got into the stone business. Wisconsin's loaded with rocks. Good rocks for building, for making things. My grandfather passed it on to a couple of his sons, but when our generation came along, my brothers wanted nothing to do with it. But I'd always worked with my gramps and uncles. I knew masonry. Handled a chisel before I was in grade school. I always did like it."

"But you're not afraid it'll take over your life?"

"No. But because I needed to be sure of that, I didn't see anyone for a few years, beyond a casual date here and there. People tend to repeat their mistakes. And I didn't want to repeat mine. Working with stone is hard and physical and creative. Every project is one of a kind. I make darn good money, but I also earn it. Still, there's ample time to fish with my brothers, take the cousins and kids out kayaking. Be with family, make a feast, enjoy a beer, a game of cards. I want that free time. I'd never let work, any work, get in the way again."

Poppy saw something new in Sam's eyes. A warning. A challenge. Honesty, sharper than a blade. He was coming after her. He didn't say that. In fact, all he did was hand her the plates, then the chicken—which came free off the bone without even asking it twice.

The first bite tasted like nectar. The second was even better.

"Holy moly," she murmured.

"I know. Makes me want to cook outside every night. I haven't a clue why it's so good this way."

She did. He knew what he was doing, even if it was the unexpected skill of pulling together a dinner in the evening. Sam never shouted about anything he did well, but he had ways of giving, she thought, that made others look like amateurs in the love department.

How did all this get so dangerous? It was just dinner. Sharing her plate with Bubbles, until Sam put a stop to it. Savoring those sweet bites of white meat. Her fingers were sticky. She ate every morsel, it was all so delicious. So why did her gaze keep sliding toward his, meeting up, producing a heartbeat she'd never danced to before?

And dinner wasn't even over yet.

Chapter Six

SAM TURNED AROUND to forage yet again in the storage box behind him.

"I don't know what you're getting out of that magic box this time, but honestly, I couldn't eat another thing . . . oh."

Sam handed her two long sticks.

"Oh," she repeated. "Thank you so much. Those are exceptionally nice sticks."

He grinned. Then produced the bag of big marshmallows. "I know you brought dessert—but we have to have a couple of these. Can't waste a great bed of coals without roasting a few marshmallows, can we?"

"I love marshmallows."

He knew that.

"But I haven't roasted marshmallows since . . . since I can remember."

Her first one, of course, fell in the fire. The second one burned to a crisp.

Out of pity, Sam finally gave Poppy his stick with a perfectly cooked dark-gold marshmallow, much too hot to touch.

She touched. Bit into it. And there it was, right on her face. A look of lust. Pure lust. "Okay. That's a taste on a par with total perfection. The crusty top, scrumptious. The almost-liquid melty white inside, beyond scrumptious."

Sam stared at her the entire time she was slowly, slowly devouring the first one. "Sheesh," he said, sounding as if he were complaining. "All right, all right. You can have the next one, too."

"I can do it myself!"

"Never mind. I'll make 'em. It's more fun watching you eat 'em than eating them myself."

Poppy tried to turn back into her normal grown-up self. No more closing her eyes with groans and sighs of ecstasy. But it was hard to eat a roasted marshmallow like a lady. They were gooey. Messy. They stuck to lips and fingers and chin.

"I'm afraid I'm going to be sick," she mentioned after the fourth one.

"Okay." He made to scoop up the sticks—but she held him off with a panicked expression.

"Wait! One more."

"Where's your sense of self-discipline? Fear of dental bills? Restraint?"

"It's your fault. You're corrupting me," she teased. Sam laughed, but then his laughter faded. Hers did, too.

He wasn't corrupting her. But he was thinking about it. And

her expression conveyed that she was thinking about how much she wouldn't mind being corrupted. By him.

"Now I'm feeling guilty that we left your dessert in the freezer."

"It'll wait until tomorrow. It's frozen, no sweat. I couldn't eat another thing tonight."

"Well, it'll take a bit to get all this cleaned up—and if you remember, I promised to get you home early."

For an instant she looked crushed, as if she never dreamed he'd cut off the evening when they'd been having so much fun. But quick as a finger snap, she averted her face and simply started cleaning up with him.

The fire needed putting out, utensils and messes all put back in the box, the warm blanket she'd been sitting on folded up. Bubbles got in the middle of everything—which was one big body to interfere with any practical task—but that got Poppy chuckling again.

Eventually the dinner debris was all packed away, the raccoon coat stored back in the house—with Bubbles, who couldn't believe she was being deprived of a truck ride.

"She takes up the whole truck. And I'll be right back." Sam was partly talking to Poppy, partly to the dog. Either way, they were both installed in his truck all too fast, shivering until the heater started working, headlights beaming on the soft white landscape.

"So beautiful around here, Sam. Quiet. Peaceful. A little piece of heaven."

"That's how I think of it, too. In the summer, the lake's loaded with fishermen and tourists. That's good fun, too, to see all the kids and families enjoying the lake. But in the deep winter, I love the quiet time. Maybe everybody needs a stretch of solitude?"

"Sure agree. Think we all get too busy to just . . . look around, take a pulse for who we are and what we're doing."

"Good way of putting it."

It was an easy chat. She always seemed to easily talk with him, but Sam heard a careful note in Poppy's voice now. She'd been crazy happy. He'd pretty abruptly shut down the evening. She wasn't sure what was going on.

He pulled into her drive. Doused the lights.

"You don't have to walk me in—"

He was already out and closing his door, winding around to her side. Then he said, "Yeah, I have to."

"You think I can't walk five inches to the back door by myself?"

"No. Because the only thing missing from this evening was a good-night kiss. Just in case we've both been worried about it, let's get the darn thing over with."

At the cottage door, Sam swooped in, low and slow, not at all as if he were worrying about this. He was, though—worried if this was going to matter to her as much as it mattered to him. Worried she'd think he was just playing around. His cold hands pulled off her hat, let his fingers slide through her silky hair, ease closer. His eyes met hers for a millisecond.

He wasn't playing around.

Her lips were so smooth and warm. So soft. He tried a kiss that whispered and wooed. Her sweet taste made him forget about the ice-cold night, the sharp hiss of wind.

He deepened the kiss, until Poppy helplessly closed her eyes, her arms looping around his neck as if she'd fall if she couldn't hold on.

Sam held on for both of them, waging another kiss. Then another. He wanted to engulf her in tenderness, in longing, in needing. He'd never felt on such a tightrope. She was the first woman—in his life—who'd ever provoked this sense of belonging, of rightness. Yeah, she had troubles going on, changes she was struggling to make. But problems didn't define her.

She was strong and smart. Perceptive and giving. Her heart poured out love to those around her. She was a fierce protector. And she just happened to be all woman besides. Sensual. Vulnerable. Even demanding, when she really started kissing him back.

With five tons of winter gear between them, he couldn't feel her breasts, her body, any bare part of her. Yet he still felt a cleaving, a matching up of body parts, a drumbeat announcement of where his body naturally belonged. Where hers did.

Sam lifted his head, smiled slowly at Poppy—a smile full of devilment, and something more. "One more," he said.

She charged back for another kiss, as if hoping he'd change his mind. She made out like she needed. This. Him. His taste, his touch, his mouth. She sent out invitations bright as light-

Poppy sighed in exasperation. She needed something to get her mind off That Man.

And she knew exactly what would do it.

She plunked down at her computer, booted up, and began checking email. She also checked her phone messages. And there they were. Her sisters, everywhere, from texts to email to WhatsApp to Telegram.

From Cam. Poppy, we've never had a Christmas without you. You've never had one without us. Please think this through again. Then from Marigold. Come on sis. We have to do our ornaments. How can we have a holiday without making ornaments together? And I found the best kits this year.

From Cam. Dad is running around like a witless cat. Unpaid bills on the desk, and heaps of checks he forgot to deposit. He missed a dentist appointment. I can do this stuff but I didn't know you were doing it all. Is there a calendar or something for his appointments?

From Marigold. Hey sis. I'll get a ham if you just tell me how many lbs and how you buy it. No pressure.

From Cam. Poppy, I feel terrible that I've let you down. You're always there for us. Now you sound unhappy. Please give me a chance to be there for you.

From Marigold. Hey are you still unhappy? How about if we get together, share a drink. We'll just joke and laugh. No pressure.

From Cam. Dad says no reason we can't all skip Christmas this year. What's the big deal. But Poppy we all remember Mom on Christmas.

She sat in front of the computer for a while; that last one made her feel exactly what she'd expected to feel: the fierce desire to give in. The wave of love for her sisters that she always had, always would have. But she also felt the terror that she'd suck right back into old patterns if she gave in. She *needed* this space.

Did that make her the most terrible person in the universe? Obviously Christmas was an extra tough time to pull this on her family, but this was the only possible stretch of time in the year she could get extra time off.

And the truth was, there *was* no perfect time to drop out. There never would be.

It's just . . . she'd been gone less than a week. And already, it was so darned hard.

* * *

KRISTIN WAS PERFECTLY happy in the truck's back seat, as long as she could lean over and talk to Sam nonstop. Occasionally Bubbles leaned over to lick her face.

"Why does this lady have to be with us?"

"She doesn't have to. But she loves Bubbles. And she was hoping to meet you. And last night's fresh snow froze up, so it's icy on the roads and I'd rather pick her up than her risk driving herself. And I'll drive her back after lunch."

Kristin thought. She never thought for long. "She must be okay if she likes my dog."

"That's what I thought," Sam said.

"What's her name again?"

"Poppy."

"Like the big red flower?"

"Yup."

"Does my dad know her?"

"Nope. She usually lives in Madison. She just rented this cottage by the lake for a couple weeks."

"Well, I might not talk to her if I don't like her."

So far, Sam couldn't recall a stretch of three minutes when Kristin had ever been silent, but he considered that miracles could happen.

When they pulled in Poppy's driveway, Kristin and Bubbles leaped to get out almost faster than Sam could turn off the engine. Kristin was in her new purple snowsuit—which was only part of the ensemble. There were also purple boots. Purple hat. Purple scarf. Purple mittens. Sam was pretty sure there was a little purple purse involved, but he hadn't seen it in a while now.

"You can help me clean off her car, or you can knock on the door and say hello."

"That's silly, Uncle Sam. You know I can't talk to strangers."

"She's not a stranger, because I know her. But you can wait if you want to. I just want to clean the fresh snow off her car. No sweat."

Yeah. Maybe thirty seconds later, Kristin was pounding the door with her mitten, accompanied by Bubbles, who scratched the door when her sidekick pounded.

Sam watched the door open—Poppy's look of surprise . . . and something more when she saw him. *She'd liked those kisses*, he thought.

So had he.

But then she realized there were two beings trying to get her attention. "You must be Kristin," she said.

"Yeah. I heard you liked my dog."

"Yup. I love her." Over the little one's head, "You don't have to do that. I can clean it off!"

"I said I'd do it. I thought it would establish how good I am at keeping promises."

"But you didn't promise. And you invited me over for lunch. So I just figured I'd do it."

"Poppy," Kristin said delicately. "You probably shouldn't argue with Uncle Sam. You can't win. Nobody wins against Uncle Sam."

"Ah."

"OMG. OMG. You have a purple jacket! You like purple?"

That was the last Sam saw of the three of them for the next twenty minutes. When they disappeared inside, he swiped off the snow, then just took a look at Poppy's primary method of transportation. Close up, he guessed the Subaru was older than his great-aunt Mary, and Mary was close to ninety. The inside was spotless. The back seat had notebooks and books and work stuff contained in a tidy box. The outside had scrapes and scuffs and dents. The tires would make it until spring, but not much longer. Wipers needed replacing. Exhaust looked rusted—not all the way through—but that expense was coming sooner than later, for sure. It wasn't going to last much longer.

On the short ride back to his place, Sam got a better look at Poppy. Something was off. She'd gone quiet. She looked tired, instead of spunky and vibrant. She was clearly in love with Kristin—who wouldn't be?—but if she didn't have the dog and child trying to snare all her attention, she'd have run out of excuses to avoid looking at him.

He thought they were past the need to put up fences.

"Uncle Sam said you had spaghetti ice cream for us for dessert."

"True."

"He thought you made it up. But I knew you meant it. And you understand about mac and cheese. It has to come from the box. Not homemade. Not messed with. Just like it says on the box."

"I couldn't agree more," Poppy agreed.

"Well, none of the other grown-ups do. So. How do you feel about spangles and glitter?"

"Oh, I like them."

"Me, too. I like them on my nails sometimes, but Dad's not so great with nail polish."

"Does your mom like nail polish?"

Kristin abruptly took a big breath. "We're not talking about my mom today. Because she's not here. And Kristin misses her *very* much. She wants Mom to come *home*. But she's being a big girl about it. Bubbles, are you crying? No, Bubbles isn't crying. And Kristin isn't crying either."

Poppy glanced at him, but Sam could only mouth, *I'll explain later.*

So Poppy turned back to the squirt. "Hey, Kristin?"

"What?"

"If you don't mind, could you give me a hug? Because sometimes when I feel like crying, a hug can really help."

The squirt flew in Poppy's arms for a major body squish. A true eyes-closed, arms-wrapped-tight, body-to-body hug. Then her eyes shot up to Poppy's again. "You know what we're going to do this afternoon? I mean, after lunch."

"What?"

"We're going to cut down two Christmas trees. One for me. One for Uncle Sam. Uncle Sam, should we cut one down for Poppy, too?"

Poppy raised her hand. "That's okay. Two is plenty to cut down in one afternoon."

In the kitchen, Sam had two boxes of mac and cheese on the counter. Good thing, because his niece supervised every step and stir in making it. She was so serious about the job that Sam figured she just might be the best birth control in the universe. He'd never get to touch Poppy. He'd never get to have a private word with Poppy. He'd probably never get close enough to steal a kiss under this level of supervision.

But then came dessert. Poppy made both of them close their

eyes. She found the bowls in the cupboard, the spoons, took the covered package from the freezer, and filled the bowls. "Everybody still closing their eyes?"

"Yes, Poppy," Kristin said, but she wasn't.

"Yes, Poppy," Sam said, but he wasn't either.

She served the two bowls, and then said, "Voilà. You can open your eyes now."

Kristin's eyes were already wide open. "It's spaghetti for real!"

"It's supposed to look like spaghetti. But put your spoon in. You'll see it's ice cream."

"How on earth did you do this?" Sam asked.

"Like a woman's going to give away her trade secrets." But she did. "You know those manual devices you can get from a kitchen store to make pasta? Where you push the dough through and it comes out in long strings? Well, for this, you take vanilla ice cream, add a couple of ingredients, and refreeze it in a pan. Then scoop it up and put it through the device. Then you have the noodles." She motioned. "Then for the sauce, you use a dark cherry sauce, heated up, then chilled to mound over it."

"Spaghetti!" Kristin piped in. "Perfect. And I like spaghetti, too, but not as much as I like this. Uh-oh."

"What?"

"Bubbles wants some." Kristin looked at her uncle Sam. "She can't have things like ice cream because it would make her teeth go bad and bad teeth would really hurt her. But it's hard not to give her things she really really really wants."

"You're so right," Sam said.

"Even if it's a teensy spoonful. It would still be really bad."

"You're so right."

"Even if it was such a small bit on the spoon that you could hardly see it."

"You're so right," Poppy said and promptly tried to divert the little one. "But if you're finished, I'll bet Bubbles would love to play ball with you. Or fetch. Does she like to fetch?"

"She does, she does!" Dog and girl immediately bounded off, and for a whole four minutes the adults were free. They both got up to feed the dishwasher.

"The ice-cream thing was great, Poppy."

"So's your niece. Does she ever stop talking?"

"Never."

"What a charmer. And she sure loves her uncle Sam."

"I'm very lovable," he agreed and then said casually, "You okay? Something seems wrong."

"With me, nah. I'm having a great time. But I was worried about Kristin's mom . . ."

"I don't know what my brother told her, but yeah, there's something going on. Medical." Sam shot a look at the doorway, just in case Kristin was within listening distance. But the sound of the ball and giggling came from the stairway, a solid distance from them. "Think I already told you that Conan and Karla have two kids, but they'd like a couple more. Well, she just miscarried. Conan said she was around three months along. The doctor said she was fine, but he wanted to keep her in the hospital overnight, do a D&C, run a few tests. Anyway, the toddler's with Karla's mom. Kristin's hanging with me through this afternoon, and then I'll take her over to my mom's to spend the night."

"And your brother didn't want Kristin to hear the whole story."

"Right. He thinks she's too young to understand this. But I think making it a mystery wasn't his best choice. Kristin's too darned smart. She knows something's wrong."

"Sometimes having siblings is tough, isn't it? You don't get to tell them what to do, even if you're positive they're making a mistake."

He caught a flash of something in her eyes. "Have your sisters been calling you?"

She gave a short laugh. "All the time. It's okay. I expected it."

But it wasn't okay. That's what the shadowed eyes and quietness had been about. Kristin naturally opened Poppy up, and yeah, they'd all been having fun, but he could sense her avoiding being alone with him. Just then, though, Kristin and Monster Dog galloped back into the kitchen and proclaimed that it was now time to cut down Christmas trees.

"And we want two big ones. Bigger than you, Uncle Sam! BIG!"

"Was that an insult?" he asked Poppy.

"Nah. She thinks you're big and powerful."

"Uncle Sam? Maybe Poppy needs us to cut down a tree for her too?"

"Nope. No trees for me this year. But I'll come along and lie in the snow while you cut down both trees, okay?"

Kristin giggled. "I'm going to lie in the snow with Poppy."

"And make snow angels."

"*Yes!*"

"We'll supervise Uncle Sam, won't we, Kristin?"

"'Xactly. We're gonna supervise you, Uncle Sam."

"Hey. Cutting down trees will be the easy part. Having two females gang up on me all afternoon's going to be the tough part."

"*Three* females, Uncle Sam! Bubbles is a girl, too! And she's coming with us." A sudden look of horror. "She does get to come, doesn't she?"

"Hey." Sam scooched down to give her a hug. "Do we ever go anywhere without your dog?"

"No."

"So of course she's coming. And of course she's getting the front seat, because she's spoiled rotten. But I only spoiled her rotten because she's your dog and I try to love her like you do."

"I know." The skip went back in her step.

It took the usual hour to get everyone bundled up, mittens found, boots on tight, scarves snugged, the truck started. It was only a short drive to the woods Sam had picked. Then came the two females debating vociferously about which trees were best—which took forever. At least two hours later—two beautiful Christmas trees later—they all scrambled back in the truck, claiming to be dying of cold.

"Oh boy," Kristin suddenly said, "have we all turned into reindeer?"

"What?"

"We all have red noses! Just like Rudolph!"

That kind of nonsensical conversation went on until Sam pulled into Poppy's driveway. "Wish you didn't have to go," he said, but not in the teasing way they'd both been talking to the child. This wasn't teasing. This was trying to coax Poppy into remembering last night together.

"You both could come in," she said.

"I only wish. We can't. Kristin's grandma is expecting her for dinner, and then to spend the night, and she can't wait, right, honey?"

"Oh yeah. I love my grandma. She'll make some fudge cherry almond cookies. Just for me."

Sam added to Poppy, "They don't live far away—about a half hour—but then there'll be a visit I can't get out of, and the drive back. It'll all end up pretty late. So maybe see you tomorrow?"

"Sounds great," she said, but she shot out of the truck faster than a bird taking flight. Kristin got a kiss. The dog got a kiss. Poppy looked at Sam as if she was *thinking* about a kiss, but he didn't get one.

Maybe by tomorrow night, he could think up some way to change that around.

Chapter Seven

POPPY PLANNED FOR a long, lazy sleep, but she woke before dawn. She hadn't dreamed about Sam, but she'd thought about the darn man half the night.

He'd been so adorable and natural with his niece. A half-dozen times, he'd hunkered down to talk to Kristin at her level, always staying calm, ignoring any messes she created. The child piled all over him, neck, shoulders, lap. He kept up a conversation as if agile, acrobatic monkeys draped on his shoulders was a normal part of his day.

His family sounded so great, loving but more than that; they really enjoyed being together. She'd always loved being with her sisters, but it was different. It was no one's fault, but she was reminded again how, after losing their mom, her role had been caretaker and caregiver. She was the oldest daughter, and somehow they expected it of her—to just step into her mother's shoes.

Poppy expected it of herself.

She'd *always* expected it of herself.

That thought popped in her mind and lodged there. Not a good thing. Before anxiety could get a vise grip on her day, she hopped out of bed.

A few minutes later, she grabbed her skates, charged outside, and started the car. Naturally it was brutally cold this early in the morning, but there wasn't a single light on anywhere around the lake. No one was up, and that was exactly why this predawn time was so perfect. Normal people would still be sleeping. She'd have the world to herself for a little while.

Poppy parked in the empty church lot, laced on her skates. The sun wouldn't come up for a while yet, but a tinge of pearl gray brushed the skyline in the east and there was more than enough daylight to enjoy a skate. The hush of quiet was a joy in itself. The rink had a fresh coat of ice, and even in the dim light, was clear as a mirror. Poppy stepped out into the clean wintergreen air. It really was colder than a well digger's ankle—as her mom used to say—but skating was work. Once she started flying across the ice, she'd be warm in no time.

Eventually she wanted to practice more of the tricks and moves she used to do so easily, but the first skate three days ago had warned her how rusty she was. For a while she just wanted to circle and crisscross the ice. Find her speed. Find her grace, as her mom used to say. The feeling of joy came from the inside, and again as her mom often said, it was free. Poppy just had to let it in.

SLOWLY THE PEARL gray sky sifted into a soft pink—still not true daylight but the color of magic, she mused. Even in the dark days of December, it had to be close to nine by now. Sooner or later, kids and families were bound to show up, get out to enjoy the day. Poppy cruised into one last spin and abruptly saw the three guys hunched over the fence. She'd never heard a sound, much less the noise or car or truck doors slamming from the other side of the church.

Sam, she'd know anywhere. The three brothers together had the look of giant Vikings—particularly decked out in their hockey gear, helmets, sticks, and all. They were all wearing thick gloves—and when they realized she spotted them—all three curled their pointer fingers to urge her to come closer.

She did, half laughing. "You guys *almost* scared me half to death."

"No one wanted to say anything and startle you," Sam said. "Didn't want you to fall."

She toe-picked to a stop. "So . . . what's the story? Am I in trouble for something?"

Sam chuckled. "Just the opposite. We saw you skating . . . and we all had the same idea. Would you mind being part of our team for an hour or so?"

"You mean . . . play hockey?" Surely they were joking.

"Uh-huh." Brer and Conan nodded their heads exuberantly. Brer was easy to identify even if she hadn't formally met him. He was the size of a bear. And Conan was even easier to identify because his eyes had dark shadows, as if he hadn't slept at all. She remembered Sam telling her about his wife spending the night in the hospital.

Brer pushed his brothers aside to make his plea. "Here's the thing. It's hard to play, two against one. Two against two is a much better game." Then he added, "Oh, by the way, I'm Brer and that's Conan," pointing to his brother.

Conan added, "We couldn't help but notice that you're faster than all three of us put together."

As if guessing she wanted to be filled in about Conan, Sam said, "Conan can't pick up his wife for another hour and a half. The kids are both with grandparents. He knows she's okay. But we had to find some way to keep him busy. He was so restless he was probably going to start tearing the bark off trees. So we decided on a short hockey game."

Poppy's eyes met his for a second and a half, but there was no possibility of having a private conversation. All three of them kept talking.

She tried to get a word in edgewise, filling in the obvious reasons this was a terrible idea, like "I don't have the right skates" and "I've been to hockey games, but I've never played and I don't know the rules," and the most obvious reason why she'd never do this. "You guys. Did you happen to notice that I'm smaller than you all by a *lot*? You'll kill me."

Sam seriously frowned. "Hey. Would I have gotten you into this if there was risk for you?"

"I don't know."

Wrong answer. He looked so hurt she felt she had to backtrack. "Look, Sam, honestly, I'm game. I just don't think—"

"There. See, you don't have to think. We're going to pair off. You're with me—"

Brer firmly interrupted. "No, no, no. She'll partner with me." And then looked at her square. "I promise, we'll make it easy. All I want you to do is take that stick and skate toward the goal with the puck. No one is going to get near you, because I'd kill 'em if they tried. And Sam would kill us all if you even got a scratch. So you're safe. Just skate the puck down close to the goal, and then scoot over to the side. I'll take it from there."

"All right, all right." Obviously she couldn't have Sam's brothers thinking she was a poor sport. But she had a bad feeling she wasn't going to survive this. And she shot Sam several looks to let him know that he was responsible if she let everybody down.

But it wasn't like that. Yeah, they were all dressed differently than she was, different skates, different sizes, and all that. But it all was so much simpler than Poppy expected. She experimented with using the stick to move the puck a couple times. It didn't seem all that hard, so then she just "went for it" as instructed.

With ice this fresh, it was easy to fly. She skated the rink to the goal and then—well, she intended to get out of the way, but she was right there? So she figured she might as well slap in the puck on her own.

Easy peasy. Nothing to it.

But when she turned around, she found Brer, bent over, guffawing with laughter and the other two men staring at her with rock-hard expressions.

"What? What? What's going on? Did I do it wrong?"

"No," Sam assured her. "You did everything right. You scored. You did really great. But we need to immediately change the rules. Brer can't be your partner all the time. We're going to share you."

"Excuse me?"

"I get her next." Conan held up his hand.

She looked at Sam, expecting him to either explain or, more likely, insist on partnering with her himself. But no. He passed her on to Conan as if he valued her on a par with last week's newspaper.

Later, they would have words. Poppy wouldn't need many words to express her opinion of his behavior. But right then, apparently, she and Conan were competing for the next score. She was anxious to hear how his wife was, but probably she wasn't supposed to know his private business—besides which, they were all lined up ready to go. The puck came her way.

She did the same thing she did last time. Skate as fast as she could, her concentration focused only on the puck and the goal basket ahead. The stick was easier to control this time, now that she'd gotten the feel of it. It was easier to keep her balance and maintain speed at the same time.

Poppy wasn't exactly sure where the three guys were located, but she knew Conan had her back. Once close to the goal—well, it was the same situation as last time. She was so close to the net that it was pretty silly not to punch the puck in, so she did.

She turned around. Same result—sort of. Conan was cheering and skating toward her—actually aiming a gorilla hug toward her. "I don't know how my brother found you, but don't shake him, okay? I have no idea how my big brother finally learned judgment in great women. And I can't wait for Karla to meet you."

Sam skated up behind them. "Speaking of which . . ."

Conan pushed up a glove to see his watch. "I know. I'll be a little early if I leave now, but I don't want Karla to have to wait for me. Sorry, guys, but I need to hustle and pick up my better half."

"Either of you need help, give a shout," Sam said, and Brer echoed the same sentiment. She got two major thumps on the back from Brer and Conan for being a great skater, for winning, for being a good sport, for being a beautiful woman no matter how Sam had privately described her.

The whole family was full of malarkey. But then Poppy had Sam alone, at least for a few minutes. Skates were off, put away, hockey gear stashed, all the obvious cleanup and lockup. When he finally came out of the side church door, she was waiting—but he got in the first words.

"I owe you big-time."

"You do," she agreed. "But mostly—I just didn't quite understand what was going on. You wanted me to play when you knew I couldn't. And then how could it be a fair game when everyone lets the girl win?"

"Now . . . no one was trying to throw the game your way. It's that Cooper guys are raised to not let girls get hurt."

She threw up her hands. Which didn't seem to deter him from ambling closer, dropping a kiss on her cheek, and then leaning on the fence post close to her.

"Here's the thing. Conan heard last night that Karla had had that procedure thing; she did fine, was feeling fine—but they still wouldn't let her go home until this morning. And they won't let you pick up a patient until eleven o'clock. Too much paperwork. So. Both kids were at grandparents'; he was alone last night, couldn't sleep a wink. When I called him this morning, he was a wreck. Brer and I figured we needed to get him out of the house for an hour."

"Well, that's all good. But I couldn't add anything to that—"

"Oh, yeah, you did." Sam had that look in his eyes again. Like he wanted to steal another Silly Kiss. "You did what we guys couldn't. Adding a female to the team added plain old fun. Plus he really did get his mind off Karla and worries for that little while. We're just brothers. We couldn't do that."

Poppy was pretty sure she'd been annoyed with him about

something, but now she couldn't remember what it was. "Quit it, Sam. You're giving me too much credit."

He hunched his shoulders, the best he could do to look helpless. "Okay. I'll take the credit back. I like taking credit for everything, anyway—"

"You goof." She gathered up her gear. "I'm headed home. Have a couple things I really want to get done today."

She didn't say what. Because there wasn't a "what." But she paused before breezing past him, lifted up, and gave him a Silly Kiss exactly like he'd given her.

He just grinned, and then called after her as she walked away, "You had fun."

"Of course I had fun. Your brothers are adorable."

"Me, too?"

She didn't answer that. But she was still chuckling when she got back to the cottage.

POPPY'S FIRST PRIORITY was food—all that skating had revved up an appetite. While she scrambled a couple eggs and brewed a fresh mug of hazelnut coffee, she planned the day.

Before putting her skates away, she wanted to sharpen the blades, rub conditioner into the soft white leather. But that was the only serious chore on her mind. After that, her most pressing ambition was to curl up with a book and a couple of Oreos. This time she picked the book from the bottom of her satchel, because it looked thick and long and the librarian claimed it was "criminal" she hadn't read it by now. Well, she'd known the title forever. Everyone did. She'd ducked it before, for the obvious reasons. She rarely had free reading time, and she never figured a sad story about the Civil War and a spoiled brat heroine could possibly be that interesting.

Good or bad, she figured the book could be a real test if she could lower her heart rate from a nonstop racing horse gallop to a nice, lazy hum. Maybe sloth could be an acquired skill? If she just practiced enough?

But after grabbing the book and the Oreos, Poppy hesitated. If she were going to seriously relax, she needed one more chore off her table. So she booted up the computer and turned on her cell.

It wasn't that big a deal this time. She was ready for the family. She felt so much stronger.

Something mysterious kept happening when she was around Sam. The goofy hockey game this morning sparked so much simple, happy energy. She loved how the brothers took care of each other. How they teased each other mercilessly. But they also relaxed together—which seemed to be something missing between her and her sisters.

The thought kept sinking in. That Sam and his brothers behaved like equals, all of an age. Poppy never had that with her sisters. She'd had the mom role from the time she was eleven. That wasn't a choice for any of them. But it's part of what was wrong. Cam and Marigold were still treating her as a mom figure, counting on her judgment, her support, her protection.

But she could change that, surely. It wasn't like there was

blame or fault involved. Her sisters had simply kept the same comfortable roles they'd had for years. She was the one who wanted to yank off the mom apron and just be a sister with them. There was no real reason to fear upsetting them. She didn't love them any less. She just wanted them less dependent on her.

Yet it didn't seem that easy to get that across. Last night, she'd sent both of them reassuring notes. Yet already today there was a new barrage of messages waiting for her.

The first one was from Cam, who started by enclosing a selfie. Cam was so darned beautiful. All three of them were auburn haired if not true redheads, but Cam's skin was pure cream, her eyes a striking green blue. Her hair was long and lustrous, so naturally she was the one who played Rapunzel when they were little. Every year at school, the kids told her that she was the meanest, strictest teacher they'd ever had—but every year, when kids passed on to the next grade, they hung back to spend time with Cam. She was fabulous with difficult kids, troubled kids, challenging kids.

Cam was so great with children. But so terrible with men. For once, her email note was short—Broke up with Steve. We almost lasted three months, imagine! I'm totally okay. Just wanted you to know it was over.

Nothing else. Poppy heard all the things Cam hadn't said—all the triggers Poppy would normally respond to. There were unspoken rules that both sisters understood. Poppy was supposed to know that Cam was brokenhearted, feeling guilty and unsure. She was supposed to pop over, insist on taking Cam for a shopping spree—after which, they'd pick up a pizza and head back to Poppy's to talk until the wee hours of the morning.

Poppy almost picked up the phone. Almost. She wanted to be there for Cam. She always wanted Cam to know she'd be there for her. But just this once, possibly they could postpone their traditional Cam-break-up-support marathon for a couple weeks?

She had to *try* changing. And start by not assuming things would go terribly if she didn't always behave in the same old patterns. Resolutely Poppy moved on to a long email message from Marigold. With every word, Poppy could picture her youngest sister's face, the bounce of hopelessly happy curls, the exuberant effervescence that Marigold had been born with.

Mari was born a free spirit, Poppy thought, but sometimes she worried that her little sister was secretly lost. All that bubbling energy and silliness and fun were wonderful. But something was missing. And this long message sounded so like her.

> Dad and I had a pretty loud fight. I told him I was thinking about moving again. I said, Dad, living with three other women is just too much estrogen in one apartment. Too many tampons, too many girl spats, too much drama. You get it, don't you, Poppy? I know you do. You always understand.

Moving is no big deal. When things are wrong, you try to fix them, right? But Dad said I was being irresponsible. ME? Dad, who has an IQ of a zillion, but who can't pay a bill or put gas in his own car? As kids we would have starved if you hadn't made food for us, sis. Remember when I had chickenpox? Dad was doing an important sculpture. I had a fever. You did everything. He never even showed up to see if I was okay.

Anyway, we're all calmed down now. I'm okay. He's okay. You don't have to call. Don't worry about me.

Ah. The classic end from Marigold—"Don't worry about me." That was the clue that her sister really wanted her to worry. To assume that Marigold wasn't okay and that she needed something, someone. Not to spill out sad stories, but just to do something silly with. To cuddle with over an old movie. To walk in the rain. To be with. But the truth was Marigold did this sort of thing time and time again, and she was always fine.

Again, Poppy almost picked up the phone. Almost. She wanted to be there for Marigold—for both her sisters. Only that's how it had always been. Her time had always been gobbled up by what her sisters needed, what their dad needed. She'd never planned to be a surrogate mom—she was only a few years older than they were. But no one else had volunteered for the job, and then the years kept slipping away. Same patterns. Same needs. Same actions and reactions.

She loved them. But loving them wasn't helping her figure out a better balance in her life. And so, for the first time in a long time, she didn't jump to their rescue—just maybe, conceivably, they could discover that they were both totally capable of rescuing themselves.

* * *

THE NEXT MORNING, Poppy pulled on warm clothes and headed for her Subaru. She was tempted, too tempted, to find Sam, to talk with him. He'd help her—she didn't doubt it—but she'd created her own problems. She needed to figure out the solutions herself, which meant she wanted to get out of sight and sound for a few hours.

Her car needed a fill-up and a wash. The gas station had a rocking Santa in a window, sparkling lights framing the roof. Inside, a clerk wore a Santa hat with snowflake earrings that twinkled. Chocolate marshmallow Santas were sold up front . . . peppermint candies with red and green stripes.

By the time she left, she'd bought banana-cream-pie ice cream—a Wisconsin favorite—and was humming her old favorite Christmas songs.

The roads were cleared so well, Poppy explored the neighborhood around the lake. It was cold, so with the ice cream in the trunk, she knew it wasn't likely to start melting anytime soon. Houses were draped with Christmas lights, yards with mangers, front doors with festive wreaths. That started her humming again.

It wasn't a shopping kind of neighborhood, but she found a store that sold all things relating to the Wisconsin Badgers team, a cheese and beer hangout, a miniature Mike's Donuts with Skittle twists in the window. A half mile later she came across a nursery—a huge place, loaded with trees and greenery and houseplants—one she was sure would have a lot of options for spring planting. She stopped, ambling inside without any specific thing on her mind—until she saw something for Sam. Something she wanted to give him.

Of course she didn't buy it. How could she? There was no reason to think they were exchanging presents. She'd made it more than clear that she wasn't—couldn't—do Christmas this year.

Yet as she headed back to the cottage, she felt as if an invisible hand from the sky had given her a good shake. All this time, she hadn't recognized the obvious. She *did* know what she wanted in her life. She *did* know what she needed. And although she didn't know *how* to accomplish those things quite yet . . . she was getting there.

She hoped.

Chapter Eight

LATE AFTERNOON, WHEN Sam pulled into Poppy's driveway, Bubbles immediately stood up, her tail wagging so hard she almost rocked the truck. "Okay, Bubbles, I want you to go find Poppy. Woof at the door." The dog let out a wolf howl of approval. "*Wait* a minute. Listen. I'm counting on you to be well behaved and charming, you hear me? Don't mess this up."

Aw, well. The dog leaped over Sam's lap and hurtled toward the back door, barking like a mad fiend. It took Sam longer to pick up three sacks, a computer, a smaller bag, and some breakables protected in a small box.

Poppy opened the door. He caught a fast picture of her—mussed-up hair, warm socks, leggings, and a big copper-colored sweater that almost reached her knees. He wanted to say hello, but temporarily he had one bag—the smallest one—between his teeth.

She took one look and had to bite her lip not to laugh. Still, she took the bag from his mouth before he dropped it, thank heavens.

"Did I know you were coming?"

"No," he admitted. "But don't say no yet. I have a plan."

"I can see that. You're running away from home for the next six months?"

"Nope." He handed her the heavier sack.

"You started a life of crime, and you want a place to hide the stolen goods until you can fence them?"

"Nope." Once inside, Sam aimed for the kitchen and started unpacking and organizing. Some stuff belonged on the table, some on the counter. "Now just let me explain before you kick me out."

Since he was shedding his gloves and boots and she hadn't objected yet, he figured there was a chance he and Bubbles were staying. At least for a while.

"I figured I owed you. First I got you into the Kristin thing. She talked your ears off. Dragged you into the tree-cutting deal with us. Then I badgered you into the hockey game with my brothers. And here you told me, really clearly, that you came here to rest. So . . ." He turned around. "Okay with you if I set up something in your TV room?"

"You don't owe me anything, Sam. I loved meeting Kristin and had a blast with your brothers. But . . ." It seemed a reasonable question. "What exactly are you setting up?"

Like he was going to tell her. The computer and small sack

went on the table in the TV room. Then, on the coffee table—which required protecting from Bubbles so everything had lids on it—White Russian cupcakes. Skittle twists from Mike's Donuts. Cheeses and crackers and dips. Snickerdoodles.

By then Poppy was shaking her head and laughing. He coaxed her into planting herself on the futon, turned on the computer, and camped next to her with the controls. "Ready?" he asked, and then snapped his fingers. "Of course we're not ready. We need drinks. I brought hot tea, brandy, beer—you already have wine and it's too late for coffee. So pick whatever—"

"I can get it."

"No, you cannot. You—sit. Bubbles—sit next to Poppy." Bubbles showed off how she could instantly obey—when she wanted to—and leaped right on the futon and snuggled next to Poppy. Sam returned from the kitchen with filled glasses, plunked down next to her, and then got around to explaining.

"I brought my computer over because I have Amazon Prime and a Fire TV Stick that works with it—which means I have access to a heap of movies. Which I figured you didn't, because the TV set here is older than Mammoth Cave. So . . ." He laid out her choices. *American President. Air Force One. Father Goose. A Christmas Story.*

"*Father Goose?!* That was my mom's favorite. We watched it every Christmas. I'll bet she even watched it when she was a kid, too."

"That's what I was looking for. Movies we've seen a million

times—but have also made us smile a million times. No stress. No thinking about serious problems. No making serious decisions. No sadness or worry allowed. Those are the rules."

"Man, you're tough," she said. "Mean to the bone. Alpha male all the way."

"Uh-huh. So. I'll pass out the snacks, and you pick the movie."

"*Father Goose.* Hands down."

So that was it. Sam left on one small lamp, clicked off the rest, and had a drunk Cary Grant on the screen in two minutes flat. If he said so himself, his plan was brilliant. Granted, he'd been afraid she'd say no, but it wasn't—after all—a *terrible* idea. Just kind of trite and silly.

From the night he'd met her, he hadn't been able to stop thinking about Poppy. She'd been low that first night. Tense. Anxious. Exhausted. Often enough, the next times he'd seen her, she'd started out on the quiet side—and ended up, more or less, full of the devil. There was a heap of joy in her. It came out so naturally, when she just had a chance to forget all the burdens taking her down.

He heard her first chuckle—when she saw Cary Grant's look of horror when he saw all the children. Sam coaxed her into taking a White Russian cupcake—a Wisconsin favorite— followed by a glass of cola. She snuggled a little closer.

Minutes later, she broke out in an outright giggle. Same issue. Cary Grant's look of terror when he discovered the kids had hidden all his whiskey.

Sam pulled an arm around her then, offering her the crook of his shoulder to use as a pillow. She snugged her legs under her, never took her eyes off the screen.

It hit him hard—that just being here for her was all he wanted. This was a clear test of how deep he'd fallen. This was no fancy candlelight dinner or a seduction type of date. He'd like to do both those things with her. But not yet.

Poppy was dealing with serious issues, and he kept grappling with how to help. It wasn't like he could leap in and fix a fuse or solve some gruesome plumbing leak. She needed protection from those who manipulated or took advantage of her, but that wasn't remotely possible when he'd never even laid eyes on her family. Maybe all Sam could do at this second was temporarily stand between her and stress—which wasn't hard. All he had to do was put up with *Father Goose*.

Cuddled close, he could smell her fresh washed hair, that exotic shampoo she liked, the softness against his chin. The copper sweater she wore drooped at the neck, was obviously well worn, had a hole near the shoulder. Clearly comfort clothes. No makeup or jewelry today, just Poppy, no stress in sight, just being herself.

Sam felt exactly the same. Being with her, relaxing, the ease of just being himself for the first time in heaven knew when.

Her giggle was so joyful.

Sam couldn't remember any woman who ever made him feel . . . joyful.

He pressed his lips against the crown of her head. Not a kiss.

Just something he had to do. Her head tilted up, a little startled surprise in her eyes, and then something else. Something warm and aware and vulnerable.

But then she was distracted again by the movie. For the third time Cary Grant showed his classic look of comic horror, when the littlest child finds him hiding on his boat and tries to bribe him with his own whiskey.

Poppy snuggled closer then. Laughing. When she half turned, her hand had relocated to his chest. Possibly, conceivably, her lips pressed a swift, soft kiss on his neck. It was dark. It could have been unintentional, just body parts that unexpectedly met when she shifted positions again. But he didn't think her lips unintentionally kissed a guy's neck very often. Maybe never.

He figured they could rewatch *Father Goose* any time. Maybe even once a week for the rest of their lives.

It only took a tiny amount of shifting to relocate her on his lap. Her eyes closed even before his mouth swooped down, slow, slower than silver and softer than a whisper. Coaxing. Wooing. Her fingers climbed his neck, cautiously, carefully, then held tight. Holding on when he came back for another kiss. And then another.

A whoosh of a sigh escaped her. But then Poppy took her turn. Not just kissing Sam back . . . but offering him a kiss of her own. Her lips were luscious, luxurious. Warming his mouth, warming some place inside him that had been hollow for a long time. Maybe forever. It felt as if he hadn't found her in forever. As if he'd looked and looked and finally, suddenly, she was right there. After all this time.

Her tongue found his. Her fingers reached up, combed through his hair, asking for a tighter kiss. A longer kiss. A daring kiss. His left hand was trapped, supporting her, but his right hand was free to stroke her back, to find bare skin beneath the loose sweater. She didn't stop him. He couldn't stop himself from savoring the texture of her skin, her back, her sides. He rained more kisses on her—midnight kisses, sunlit kisses, promising kisses.

He imagined the feeling of her bare breasts.

Unfortunately, a baseball bat hit his head. It was only a virtual bat. But it stopped him fast all the same.

He didn't have to imagine the feeling of her bare breasts, because he discovered she wasn't wearing a bra. No reason she should have been wearing one under that soft, bulky sweater. No reason for it to matter. But it did.

Beneath his palm, he could just feel the swell of her breast. He picked up the heat of her heartbeat. At some primal level he understood if he cupped her breast, cherished it, owned it, he'd know her in an entirely different way. It was what he wanted— not just feeling her bare breasts. But of her bare everything. Of risks bared and vulnerability exposed completely.

But not tonight. He'd promised himself. No pressure, no stress for her. No adding anything on her plate that she didn't completely volunteer for. It just plain wouldn't be right.

Still, it ached not to go further. He wasn't a boy. He had

no interest in playing games. In this case, he was trying his damnedest to play for all the stakes that really mattered. Not him. Not her. But her and him.

"Sam," she murmured.

"Hmmm?"

"I'm afraid we're in trouble."

"Believe me. I know," he agreed.

"Um. I meant a different kind of trouble."

"What?"

"Bubbles just finished off the cracker dip."

"Bubb—" He startled awake. Bubbles wagged her tail so hard she almost knocked over the futon. And then the dog turned her head to face the rest of the White Russian cupcakes—which she'd already taken the cover off.

"This," he said to Poppy, "is not fair."

"I so agree."

"We're going home. We'll just take the messes we made and come back another time."

She started to protest, but then simply went quiet.

"But," Sam said, as he divested himself from her and crumbs and got ahold of the dog's collar. "Promise me. I mean, a real swear, cross your heart and hope to die. You'll never watch *Father Goose* again with anyone but me."

"I promise."

* * *

THE NEXT AFTERNOON, Poppy had just finished lunch when she heard a knock on the door. Sam poked his head in. Actually, a platter of cookies showed up before his face did. "Made 'em myself. I can't stay more than a half hour, too much work today—and I won't even stay that long if you're busy."

Since waking that morning, she'd been reliving the movie, the old-fashioned necking, the dog eating the best cupcake . . . and the way Sam had looked at her. The way he'd touched her.

For the first time in hours, her mind glued on something else. The cookies. "Come in . . . and who did you say made these?"

"Okay, okay. I admit to the fib. Kristin's mom made them— Karla's up and around and making Christmas cookies—which means she fills up enough tins to feed the family and the neighborhood and probably all of Wisconsin.

"These were her grandma's grandma's recipe. Forgot the name. She just calls them black walnut cookies. Anyway . . . she said Kristin was totally happy to meet you, happy you love her Bubbles, happy you loved her. Kristin also informed her mom that she wants hair like yours when she grows up, and heck, there was something about purple, but I can't remember the whole list of accolades the squirt told her mother."

As if proving he couldn't stay, Sam sloughed off his boots, but only unzipped his parka. So . . . maybe he hadn't been thinking about last night. The making out. Bubbles stealing the cupcake. The way Poppy had looked at him. Well, obviously she didn't know how she'd looked, since she didn't have a mirror—but she knew how she *felt* when she looked at him. When he kissed her, touched her.

Only now . . . he was munching on a cookie.

So maybe his mind hadn't been replaying every second of the night before, the way hers had been.

"You could have let me have the first cookie," she said mildly.

His thick eyebrows shot up. "Wow. Were those the rules in your family? In my family it was boys first."

"Your poor mother. Three boys. Your poor, poor mother."

"That's what she used to say all the time. And not to change the subject, but who was the first boy who kissed you?"

Thank heavens her mind was still fast. She could almost keep up with the devil. "It was a nightmare."

"Oh, good. I love nightmare stories. What happened?"

"His name was Robbie Fleck. Age six. His birthday party. He lived down the street, less than a block, and he was the bane of my life. Followed me to kindergarten. Then first grade."

"What was so bad about him?"

"His shoes were about ten times bigger than the rest of him, so he clomped when he walked. And he couldn't keep a shirt tucked in. And sometimes spit bubbled in the corners of his mouth when he talked."

"Wow. I'm grateful I didn't have to kiss him."

"You should be grateful. It was awful. My mom *made* me go, said it'd be rude if I didn't go to the party when I was invited. Only when I got there, all the other kids were boys. I was the only girl. I was supposed to sit next to him while he gobbled down ice cream and cake, and I do mean 'gobbled.' Then he opened my present and that's when he kissed me."

"Oh no."

"He was all sticky with cake crumbs. And he kissed me so hard he practically knocked me off the chair."

"Hey, we could make a Hitchcock movie out of this, without even trying hard."

Poppy grabbed the plate of scrumptious black walnut cookies. Sam had already had two. And he'd almost been here a half hour. "You can have one more. After you tell me about the most embarrassing thing that ever happened to you in middle school."

He looked at her. "Just one story, right? If I tell you, I don't have to tell you any more."

"That depends on how many cookies you want."

"All right. I'll tell you a story. But you need to remember that blackmail goes both ways."

She waved off this objection, then lifted a cookie—the biggest in the tin—in front of him.

Sam snatched it. "Well, pretty sure I told you my mom's terrific. But it could be that three boys in the summer could tip her patience level. When she threw us outside to play, we all knew not to come back unless we were either bleeding, half dead, or it was almost lunchtime. I think she was having a bunch of women over for a shower or a coffee get-together. Can't remember exactly.

"Anyway. It was hot and we were bored. I was the oldest—nine, maybe. So Brer was almost eight and Conan around six or so. Our place had a lot of land in the back, mostly just woods, with a creek running through it. But down near the creek, there was this old shed. Hadn't been used for anything in years. We weren't supposed to go near it, but hey, like I said, it was hot and we were bored." He frowned at her. "This is *not* a funny story. It's a mortifying story."

"I got that." She made a motion, to wipe the smile off her face. "Keep going."

"So. We did what boys do. We broke in. Found heaps of cobwebs, scraps of wood, a petrified mouse. Or we thought it was a petrified mouse. That's what we told Conan anyway. It occurred to me, because I was the oldest and someone had to be the boss, that we could do something really helpful for Mom."

"I can't wait."

"We could burn it down. It was just an eyesore. No one wanted it. Mom had been a little crabby that morning and we all thought doing something helpful would cheer her up."

"O. M. G."

"I had matches in my pocket. Because I was nine. And when you're nine, you never know when you're going to need matches or a flashlight. The wood came down in nothing flat—it was all half-rotten and dried out. We had a blast pulling it down, piling it together, getting twigs and little stuff to get a fire going. I lit the match. And poof."

"O. M. G.," Poppy said again.

"It went up in a big, beautiful blaze. Smoke billowed everywhere. The fire shot sparks everywhere. We were so proud of ourselves, we could hardly stand it. It was fantastic. But then Mom and all these women came running from the house in their fancy dresses and heels, all screaming. And that was before the firetrucks came. And then, unfortunately, my dad came home from work, shot out of his car, leaving the door wide open and the engine still running."

Sam sighed. Took a bite of his cookie. "It seems our fire had taken off. Not many hardwoods along the creek line, but a lot of scrub, and it was all dry. A few sparks is all it took to bring on a blaze." At her expression, he motioned that it was all okay. "The blaze was out within a half hour. No good trees harmed. Just some of the scrub. Everyone went home. Except for family. Conan immediately claimed credit for the whole idea. Conan, being the youngest, never got in trouble for anything. Which was why he always owned up to anything we guys did. And also why the parents never believed him."

"Good grief, Sam . . ." Poppy didn't know what she wanted to say. Good thing, because he was already rounding up the story.

"My dad never hit us. Neither did my mom. Brer was the next one in line, and he was told to get to the house, get out of his sooty clothes, take a shower, and that they'd talk later to him. Then it was my turn. I was the oldest. I was always the one who was responsible. My dad . . . he never pulled the mean card. Never. Never heard him say an angry word either. But when he was disappointed in me, I invariably felt lower than a worm. A worthless worm. A worm who'd let him down. This time was worse . . . oh, darn."

"*Darn?*"

"I just saw the clock." Sam shot to his feet, started zipping up.

"Sam, you can't just *leave*. You have to finish the story—"

"I can't. Honest to Pete. I'm already five minutes late for a meeting with the bank, and it's all your fault. Not that I care—the banker'll still be there—and besides, glad we got all that past history out of the way so we don't have to bring it up again." He leaned forward, stole another cookie, then stole a kiss—a direct, soft landing on her startled lips—and he was gone.

Poppy stood in the window, watching his truck pull out, thinking she wanted to kill him. Shake him to sugar with her bare hands. Drown him in a bucket of purple Kool-Aid. Viciously thrash him with a wet towel. Sam knew perfectly well she was dying to know what his punishment was, what his dad had said and done.

He'd left her hanging and he'd done it deliberately. He was a horrible man. Insufferable. Sneaky. Unpredictable.

She tried to think up alternative terrible fates—all of which he deserved—yet in spite of herself, Poppy wanted to laugh. She was still standing at the window, watching his truck lights until they disappeared, and grinning like a goofball. Half laughing . . . and half feeling like warm butter, deep down on the inside.

Her feelings for him were exploding. And it was all his fault.

Chapter Nine

THE NEXT MORNING Poppy headed out to the skating rink. Sam didn't show up this time, nor his brothers, but that was just as well. She vented heaps of energy just skating and swirling around ... until she realized there was a handful of girls poking their fingers through the fence, all decked out in skating gear.

"Hey. Come on in. I don't need the whole rink. I was just playing."

"You really skate good," said one.

"We were wondering if you'd skate with us. Or help us learn some things."

"I don't know. What would you like to learn?"

She wasn't sure who they were, but obviously they lived around the lake and were used to skating here. It wasn't hard to pick up their names. Amelia was ten, had the jazziest skating outfit. Josie was six, wanted to know how to skate backward. Heather was nine, had a full mouth of braces, claimed that she fell a lot and wanted to know how to fall so you couldn't hurt yourself. Petra was nine, like Heather, but she'd been skating for a couple years and wanted to know how to do a camel.

Poppy had a blast with the kids. All of them fell but then they got right back up again. After an hour passed, she figured they were getting tired, and for sure she was . . . but she suggested they make a slow figure-eight snake. She led the crew, but everyone held on to the next girl's hand, then the next girl's, forming a slow-moving snake that curled into an eight. No one fell. They all screamed—about how much they loved it.

When it was over, she realized there was a row of neighborhood moms, hanging over the fence, watching the skating. "You're Poppy, aren't you?" one called out.

Another said she'd heard that Poppy could skate like the wind. Another mentioned that Sam Cooper was the lake catch that never got caught, but gossip had it he was interested in someone now. Someone who skated.

The kids piled off the ice, took off skates, headed for the bathroom, piled back out again. Poppy enjoyed the exchanges—and for sure, the kids—but was a little startled how much the adults knew about her. And how much they were assuming.

Everyone was cold, though, and eventually they all headed to their cars, Poppy included.

She barely made it back to the cottage, though, before hearing an alert beep on her cell. A Madison neighbor had called—the lady who lived two doors down from her—said they'd lost power the night before for several hours. She knew Poppy had a spare freezer that she usually kept filled, so the neighbor thought Poppy would want to know.

She did want to know. Her extra freezer was filled with peaches and blueberries and apples and strawberries from the summer, not counting the corn and beans and veggies. Dripping ice cream wouldn't be pretty either.

Poppy wanted to waste the afternoon driving to and from Madison like she wanted a case of hives, but it wouldn't kill her. She changed clothes, poured a mug of coffee, and aimed for the highway. Annoying or not, it was probably a good idea to make sure the snowplow folks she'd hired had done the job, that no pipes were broken and that the blizzard hadn't caused other damage.

TRAFFIC WAS RAMBUNCTIOUS, but it wasn't that long before Poppy was turning in to her driveway. At first glance, nothing seemed amiss. Her neighbors had their Christmas decorations out and trees in their windows—obviously she hadn't done decorations this year—but her drive and walkways were neatly shoveled. The neighborhood looked like a traditional college town, not where the students lived, but where profs and other university people wanted a shaded, quiet street. Location was perfect, she could walk to work, pretty much anywhere on campus, and take advantage of easy shopping as well.

Every home had its own character, and at this time of year, with snow snuggled on every roof and windowsill, it looked fairy-tale charming. Her house was a small redbrick bungalow, with a tall arched gable over the front porch, and a pretty arched door. Poppy remembered the first time she saw it—and fell in love—and still remembered that incredible feeling of accomplishment when the deal was signed and sealed. She'd actually done it. Bought her own home.

Yet when she unlocked the front door, went in, and switched on the lights, her heart felt an odd thud.

No matter how tired she was after a long day's work, she'd always loved turning the key, walking in, closing the door on all the day's pressures.

Today she just heard the echo of emptiness. Dusty silence. Granted, she'd never had spare time to think about serious decorating, yet now the smoke-gray couch in the living room seemed downright austere. The hearth was cold. When she'd bought the wall paintings, she thought the pale blues and grays looked dreamy. Now they just looked bland. Not her character. Not anyone's character.

Maybe it should have occurred to her before that it was her house, but she wasn't really living there.

Trying to shake that troublesome thought, Poppy surged into the task she came for—checking on the freezer first, then the thermostats. She ran water in the kitchen, checked the fridge, found no problems anywhere. The stainless steel appliances were sterilized clean, the walls a cheerful pale green, nothing wrong, nothing bad. Just nothing personal.

The downstairs bathroom had so much character that it never needed any of hers. Or so she'd thought. A toilet "room" hid behind a closed door; the shower and claw-foot tub were separate; a stained-glass window provided both light and privacy. An ample linen closet held shelves of tissue, bath products, neatly folded towels in rainbow colors—why not, when the room was tiled in white? Only she'd thought the bathroom was adorable. Still did. Only now it seemed obvious that the architect had been creative and interesting. She hadn't really added anything to make it "more." To make it hers.

Her bedroom, at least, showed some life. A slipper peeked out of the closet. A mirrored tray of jewelry was a splash of favorite colors and treasures. Her bedcovers were too fluffy to be tidy—she loved down, so had both a down mattress and down comforter, both in the deepest of purple, all billowy and warm. She'd found an old wardrobe at a rummage sale, finished it in a polished pecan, added a plush rug in furry white. The faint scent of Chanel's "Chance" seemed part of the room—she'd never spent much money on herself, but she loved that scent. It was an odd relief to find something of herself, something that mattered, when the rest of the house seemed so . . . lonely.

Poppy hiked the stairs to the last room—the only room under the gable—that she'd made into her home office. The slanted ceiling would make it impossible for Sam to walk in here without ducking—not that she was thinking about Sam. But this room, she figured he'd like. A real person lived and worked here. The bookshelves were stuffed. A C-shaped desk nestled under the gable, so she could see outside and yet still have a big workspace. The file cabinets were covered with doodads, photos, sayings. Framed pics of family and lake projects and awards filled up the wall space. She regularly did work reading in the oversize monster chair, chintzy and old—but comfortable enough to curl up in. A Tiffany lamp had been her grandmother's; she'd started a collection of interesting stones she'd found somewhere, and various mugs seemed to reproduce on the shelves. A violet throw on her desk chair was a threadbare velvet but still a treasure, because it was so drafty up here in the winter months.

She jumped when she heard a doorbell from downstairs. For certain, she wasn't expecting anyone, but she was also done checking the house and hot to get back to the cottage. And Sam.

"Coming!" she called out when the doorbell rang a second time and reached the front door out of breath, opening it quickly. Her jaw dropped when she recognized an old friend from high school. "Gary Pruitt!! I haven't seen you in ages! Come in—what a surprise!"

Poppy hadn't seen that familiar grin in a blue moon. And yeah, she was antsy to lock up and get on the road, but it seemed rude to just kick him out. It wasn't as if a few minutes' visit was going to make any big difference.

She directed Gary toward the kitchen, popped a pod in the Keurig, and then sat across from him at the glass table. "I'm sorry—I don't have more time than a quick cup of coffee. I'm headed upstate for a couple weeks, just came home to check the house after the blizzard. But you're here—so tell me what you can. How're you doing? What have you been up to? How did you even know I lived here?"

"Just like old times. You get me talking about myself before I even get my coat off."

She grinned, as she retrieved his mug of French roast from the machine and carried it to him. "I remember our crossing paths sometime in college? But I thought you left Wisconsin after you graduated. I had no idea you were back in town."

"It's a long story."

"Well, just give me the short version for now, okay?"

Gary was built like a barrel, all muscle and brawn. He'd been the heartthrob of the high school—which was how they'd gotten to be friends. He was the football star with the big brown eyes, the good student who was adored by the teachers. And every girl—except for her—had shamelessly chased after him.

They'd never gone out. She always figured he found her when he was hiding from all the cheerleaders trying to hunt him down. He'd find her sitting on a cool spot of grass in the summer, or in the upstairs balcony of the library in winter. He'd talk her ear off.

"Well, here's the thing. A couple months ago, my brother bought the house on the corner. He's getting married in June, and he had the crazy idea that getting that house ready to live in was going to be a piece of cake. When he figured out it was going to be a nightmare, he pulled me in to help. My place is on the other side of town, so easy enough for me to show up with tools and swing a hammer with him." He took a long slug of coffee.

"That's going okay?"

"Hard for one guy. Easy enough for two." He scratched his chin, an old gesture she vaguely remembered. "I knew where your dad lived, but I didn't know you'd bought a house on this block until a neighbor mentioned it a couple weeks ago. It's not like my brother and I have been out and about. We've been trapped inside every hour we can get, painting, putting in new counters, laying floors, stuff like that. But once I heard you lived here, I stopped by a couple times, just to say hey, but never found you home. When I just saw the car in the driveway, figured I finally caught up with you."

"So what have you been up to?"

"Well. The first plan started with the football college scholarship. I was doing great until senior year, when halfway through the season I blew my knee out. Really blew it out. Had to have a knee replacement. So that ended any hope for going pro. Have to admit, I fumbled around for a while, finished up college but just couldn't seem to find something I really wanted to do. Just by chance I heard there was a job back at the high school here, and well, it was coaching. That clicked for me, more than anything else had."

She cocked her head. "I'll bet the kids love you. Are you happy to be back in town? Happy with coaching?"

"It's okay. I like working with the kids, like being around

sports again. Truth is, I never planned on anything beyond playing football. You were the big planner and worker. I was just sailing through life."

"Hey, you got a degree."

"Yeah. I got a degree, but never had any ambition. Pretty much lucky. The coach thing's working out okay."

Just seeing him brought back memories—not so much of him but of those school years. Poppy had loved school. Loved being with kids her own age.

She had rarely gone out with any guys—not because she didn't want to, but because there just wasn't time. Her sisters needed her home at night. It took time to manage the household and caretake her sisters, and she had needed outstanding grades to get a serious academic scholarship.

Gary had turned into a completely unexpected friend. She wasn't a talker like he was, but he'd made her feel comfortable around him. They'd just chitchat. Grouse about calculus and trig. Tell stupid jokes. Analyze teachers. And, of course, discuss all the girls chasing after him. He had an exhausting love life, or so he'd complained.

Which naturally made her ask, "So . . . by now, have you got a wife and family in tow?"

"No kids. But I had a wife. Eloped the end of our junior year, got an apartment. Everything was going good, until my knee got busted and she figured out there was never going to be big money coming in."

Her face creased in sympathy. "Yikes."

"That's what I said."

"The bad girls always seemed to go for you."

"I know. And I swear I loved them all. But you're the only female I could ever really talk to."

Out of nowhere Poppy felt a weird vibe. Since he'd walked in she'd been happy enough to catch up with him, glad to share that old history—but suddenly everything about his visit felt different.

Gary used to be wonderfully comfortable to be around. They had a lot in common. They both had friends, but not "best" friends, not people they easily confided in. They'd both had the same rating in the high school yearbook—Most Likely to Succeed. They'd both had the heavy-hitter teachers, headed to college with honors. Maybe Poppy had the highest grades, but Gary pulled his weight in a classroom.

But the way he was looking at her now wasn't just different, but unexpected. She couldn't define it. Couldn't even imagine why she suddenly felt uneasy.

With a startled glance at the clock, Poppy jumped to her feet, took Gary's empty mug to rinse out and plunk in the dishwasher. "Darn it, I hate kicking you out, but I really, really need to get on the road. Normally a two-hour drive wouldn't be a big deal, but I really hate driving in the dark, especially with all the snow and ice."

"But I need a chance to hear what you're up to, what happened after you left school and all that."

She nodded briskly. "And I'm sure we'll have another chance. Just not today. Hey, I'm glad about your brother being engaged and the coach job and all."

Poppy didn't race. She just kept moving, turned off the lights, found her jacket, and slowly but surely aimed for the door. "Say hi to your brother, okay? And give him a hug from me."

"Wait a sec. If you have to take off like this, I need a big hug goodbye first."

Gary had yanked on his jacket, kept up with her pace, watched her lock the door. It was downright freezing in the overhang of the porch. Snow was dripping down in silvery ribbons. He opened his arms, like he might have done when they were in high school, for a big old brotherly hug.

She hesitated for a second—told herself to quit being ridiculous—and then stepped closer with a smile. She felt his arms go around her, accepted and returned the hug. But when she tried to edge back, his arms tightened around her.

She shot him a startled glance. His face was close. Too close.

"Poppy." His voice was slow. Quiet. "I was always hoping I'd see you again. Didn't you ever wonder? How good it might be between us?"

She thought about making a joke. Saying something, anything light, to lessen the awkwardness. But his expression was too serious. He'd wanted to kiss her. Still might try, unless she handled this. And handled it clearly.

"The truth?" Poppy stepped back. "No. Very seriously, no.

I thought we were good friends back then. For me, that was special. I mean it. I don't think good friends are that easy to find."

"That's exactly what I felt. But then a lot of life passed. And I remembered all the time I wasted on the wrong girls. And how easily you and I always talked together."

"We did," she agreed. Although if she really thought about, he did most of the talking. He needed to be able to talk, she'd always believed. To someone who listened. To someone who didn't care if he was a football star or not.

His arms dropped. "So you're married? Or with someone?"

What an easy out, she thought. To think of Sam. To bring up Sam's name. Unfortunately that fish wouldn't swim. First of all, because she'd never *use* Sam. And more than that, this was her problem to solve, not anyone else's.

"Gary, it wouldn't matter whether I was married or a three-time bigamist. I'm not in the market." She took another step toward the porch edge. "I appreciated you as a friend, but never had romantic feelings for you. For me, that's just a plain non-starter."

He opened his mouth to say something more, but she shook her head. "I hope you find someone who's right for you. But right now, I really have to go."

She angled away from him, took the porch steps, and aimed for her car. It didn't take more than a minute to climb in her Subaru, strap in, and turn the key.

After waving goodbye to Gary and a half-dozen turns later,

Poppy merged onto the interstate. Every mile toward the cottage, she felt freer. Lighter. She stopped for a burger and Coke, but otherwise zoned straight north.

Tension eased from her shoulders that she hadn't been aware of. Gary hadn't really upset her. She was sorry an old friendship had turned awkward, but whether she'd handled him well or badly, she'd said no. Clearly. Surely that was progress? Not just getting sucked into what someone else wanted or needed from her.

If there wasn't so much traffic, she'd have been inclined to sing along to the radio. She really was gaining ground. Getting smarter, stronger, and on her own terms.

Traffic picked up as Poppy got closer to the cottage. Snow started coming down, nothing worrisome, just a slow drift of crystal flakes, a splash of white magic. Her heart lifted and she couldn't seem to shake a smile. One more turn and she'd be there. Back to her wonderful refuge.

SAM WASN'T THERE. But he'd stopped by. As Poppy pulled into the driveway, she could see a slip of white paper Scotch-taped to the door. She dug for her cottage key, hustled to the door to read it.

MISSED YOU. HAD TO FEND OFF VULTURES FOR ENDLESS HOURS. TAX PEOPLE. BANK PEOPLE. LAWYERS.
    BUBBLES WAS VERY BRAVE. WE HAVE TO GO THROUGH THIS BUSINESS NONSENSE EVERY YEAR.

KEPT THINKING I'D HAVE TIME TO STOP OVER, BUT
COULDN'T MAKE IT HAPPEN.

I CAN SEE YOUR FACE IN MY MIND'S EYE. YOUR FACE,
YOUR SMILE. YOU.

I'LL BE AROUND TO CAUSE YOU TROUBLE JUST AS SOON
AS I CAN.

Poppy plucked the paper from the window, unlocked the
door, shook her head . . . and let loose an outright laugh as she
went inside.

Maybe she should be worried that he'd already come to
mean so much to her.

But just maybe, she'd give *him* more trouble than he was expecting, too.

* * *

POPPY DIDN'T SEE Sam for a couple more days, but she understood. He did his business planning this time of year, met
with companies where he was bidding on bigger projects for the
coming year. No sweat, she thought—but still appreciated that
he explained why he hadn't been around, that he'd been stuck
doing work things.

She skated. Explored around the lake, where she could find
paths through the snow that were penetrable. She discovered a
country grocery store. She didn't immediately need food, just
some ingredients to make a few different things.

But she had super curl-up time, too.

It snowed all afternoon on Sunday, a good thing, since she'd barely budged from the couch in two days. When she heard the rap on the door, she finally grudgingly put the book down.

She forgot about books and reading and everything else when Sam stomped in.

"Well, if it isn't Father Christmas." Just walking from the truck, his hat was covered with snow, his red parka dusted with the white stuff, too. Only a week until Christmas now, and he so looked the part.

"You comparing me to Claus?"

"No, no. You're way cuter." She threw a big towel on Bubbles, draped Sam's jacket and hat near the furnace. When she turned around, she realized he'd brought goodies. Cherries and chocolate syrup and nuts and marshmallows.

He expressed shock and pity when she looked doubtful at his plans.

"What? You never made a snow sundae? What kind of guys did you go out with, just people who took you to movies or out to dinner or concerts and stuff like that? Didn't anyone excel in the art of a cheap date?"

Poppy heard him. She just wasn't positive if she'd *mis*heard him. "We're really going to eat snow?"

"Not *old* snow. Brand-new fresh snow. Snow that's just fallen. No one's walked on it or peed on it or put chemicals on it. It's okay. Trust me."

Naturally it took both of them—and Bubbles—to fill up a

bowl of fresh snow outside. Inside, he promptly made the fancy sundaes—which both of them devoured. After that he started a fire and carried in a bag of chestnuts from his truck. "So. Did you ever roast chestnuts before? You know. On an open fire. Jack Frost nipping at your nose."

"Stop. Until now I didn't realize you were going to sing."

"Uh-oh. When my brothers and I get together—and have a beer or two—we've been known to belt out some college fight songs." On top of the fire, Sam set up a small rack, and then came through with a long pair of tongs to turn the nuts. "Now, we're stuck waiting for a while. They just don't taste as sweet unless they're roasted real slow. So. I wonder what we could think up to do in the meantime?"

Poppy figured it was about time she took charge. He was only going to keep flirting with her if she didn't. He was still hunkered by the fire when she knee-walked closer. Then closer still. Then turned her head to angle a kiss on him.

Aha.

This time, for darn sure, she'd surprised him.

Maybe she'd surprised herself. She hadn't planned to kiss him, much less seduce him. But the terrifying idea had gotten hold of her and refused to let go.

Slowly Poppy wound her arms around his neck and pressed closer. Sam was in jeans and a big sweater, his cheeks still cold from being outside, his chin on the stubbled side and his hair unbrushed. She pushed her fingers through his hair, back around his neck, trying another kiss. A slow kiss. A soft kiss. A kiss of longing and yearning and a whole lot of terror.

Almost two weeks were already gone. The day after Christmas, she had to head back to Madison, to her job, to her annoyingly cold house, to her life. She'd started coming to some conclusions, some ideas, about who she really was and what she needed in her life. None of them were glued down yet. But it wasn't as hard as she'd thought to pin down things that mattered.

Sam really mattered.

Poppy couldn't swear that she was right for him. Or that she could be sure of herself quite yet. But this moment was about right now. Whatever happened, she wanted him to know he mattered. She wanted him to *feel* how much she cared.

She wanted him, and this should have been easy. She was old friends with risk, had never feared trying and failing. But she really hated being naked. From a young age she'd learned to be tough and strong and capable. But to risk loving a man? Loving, as in really laying herself bare, inside and out?

She told herself to think about him instead of terror. His skin, his touch, his smell, his textures. She told herself to quit *thinking*, for heaven's sake. She'd been thinking her whole darned life. This moment, she just wanted to feel.

Him.

"Hey," he murmured, his voice thicker than dark honey.

"Don't talk, Sam. I'm trying to concentrate."

"I didn't come here to push you."

"I *know* that."

"I'm interested. More than interested. I can't get my mind off touching you."

"Would you please be quiet? For just a little bit."

He was quiet. For just a little bit.

She parted her lips, inviting a more intimate kiss, savoring the wicked-soft sweep of his tongue. She pushed at his sweater, willing it to disappear.

Sam handily made that happen. She wanted to explore his bare chest. All that sleek muscle, the shoulders bigger than her fists, so much strength.

That was the thing about Sam. All that strength. All that gentleness.

Her pulse started hammering, her heart beating double time, a burst of ruby-red desire seeping all the way up from her toes.

When had she ever wanted like this? Never. Nothing in her life had ever felt this right. This petrifying. This perfect.

She sank into him, loving his bare chest with her fingertips, loving his hands, roaming over her back, her arms. His fingers sieved into her hair when he dipped for another kiss, this one urging her up and against him. She felt the surge of his heartbeat. Felt his big calloused hands turn fire-warm. Felt him shift, to accommodate the growing potential between them.

Falling in lust with him was almost—almost—as soul-opening as falling in love with him. Giving wasn't hard. Giving had always come naturally to her; it was who she was, what she did. But this was so different. This was giving to someone who'd never asked her for anything. This was giving where there was no return obligation. No have-to involved.

Except for risk.

Her own risk, but, she was coming to feel, his, too.

His hands slid down, under her sweater, around her back again. His fingers discovered her bra, didn't seem to care for it, unlatched it. And the next kiss he offered took her breath.

"Sam?" Her voice was husky, not by choice. It was all she could manage. "You can still say no, but your chances are running out."

"If you're waiting for me to say no, that'll be never. But I was thinking . . . you might be a whole lot more comfortable at my place, my bedroom, a serious bed . . . this hearth is crazy hard."

"Hmm. I like the idea of going to your place. But not tonight. Tonight . . . I don't want to separate from you, for even minutes, even moments. It's too cold outside. And just-right warm right here."

"Okay. I have a challenge for you."

"Uh-oh."

"Trust me. This isn't an uh-oh. Here's the challenge. We start a kiss. And see how long we can keep kissing, until one of us has to come up for air."

"I like challenges like that. Where no one has to lose, and both sides win no matter wh—"

He didn't cut her off. His mouth just sealed hers, his taste alluring and tender, promising danger, promising belonging, promising that everything and anything could work out. With him. With them. With Poppy's arms still hooked around his neck, Sam lifted her—a definite measure he was a ton stronger than she was. He either knew where the bedroom was or navigated there by luck . . . or need.

The bathroom light was on because she'd never turned it off. The bedroom was dark, because she'd never turned a light on. There was just enough ambient light for him to locate the bed, for him to balance a knee on it, and then slower than molasses lower her flat.

Their lips were still glued. It just might be the longest kiss in recorded history. She planned to be impressed, when she had time. Right now she only had time for him.

She'd wanted him her whole life. A man who kissed her as if she were his sun and his stars . . . as if he couldn't cherish her enough.

The more he touched, the more she longed for more. The more she responded, the more she felt hopelessly, helplessly powerful. She loved this man. She loved his nose. The smell of his skin. The calluses on his hands, the rust in his voice when he was talking low. The scruffy black hair, how it folded around her fingers. The sexy darkness in his eyes, the wickedness, the promises. His humor. The way he walked with those big, long strides. The way he catered to the darned dog, the way his niece had him wrapped around her finger. The way he could cook. The way he so easily laughed, so readily enjoyed life. The way he created a fire, as if it were artwork. The way he was self-sufficient, able to do so many things, and yet. The way he was vulnerable. Like now. When she stroked him, just so. When she rubbed against him, and heard him suck in a breath. When her hand reached for his belt buckle.

"Hey," he murmured.

"Just what I was thinking. Hey back," she whispered.

"When you make up your mind . . . you really make up your mind."

"Oh yeah. I've made up my mind. About wanting you."

"Poppy. I'd shoot myself if I've done anything to make you feel pressured—"

"Who started this?"

"You did."

"So pay attention." Poppy took her hands off Sam's belt buckle, grabbed the bottom of her sweater, and yanked it over her head. Her hair tumbled and spun, tangling around her eyes, her cheeks. "Now if *you* feel pressured . . ."

Her bra was unhooked, but still dangling loose. She pushed it off.

"I feel pressured. I feel pressured."

She laughed, but not for long. Her chuckle turned into a wide smile that slowly turned into something else. The curve of her lips met the curve of his. Together, their kiss ignited a tangle of discoveries and promises and whispers, and finally, a joyous coming together.

SOMETIME LATER, POPPY was snoozing in the cradle of Sam's shoulder, when a sequence of loud popping sounds startled her. It sounded as if a gun were going off. His eyes shot open, too.

"Uh-oh. The chestnuts."

Bubbles woke up from her nap on the couch and let out a good, loud howl. Then, despite her breed's reputation for stalwart fearlessness, the dog galloped into the bedroom, leaped on the bed, and tried to hide under Sam.

"Hey, girl. Hey, Bubbs. It's not a gun. There's no danger, no trouble." He glanced at Poppy. "But I had in mind giving you a lot more trouble. There were a lot of things I could do better."

"Not that I can imagine in a zillion years," she promised him, as she grabbed a robe.

What a mess. She had no idea how long chestnuts normally roasted before they were "done," but once they exploded, apparently they *really* exploded. At least the disaster was contained inside the fireplace.

Sam spread out the logs—not that there was much fire left, but still, he wanted it positively out before he cleaned out the chestnut debris.

"This just isn't fair," he muttered. "I should be sleeping beside you right now. Or not sleeping at all. We could be doing anything but housekeeping a fireplace."

"I see soot on your nose."

"I'm going to ignore that insult. Do you have a bowl? And tinfoil you could line the bowl with? Tongs? Hot pads? Pliers?"

Heaven knew why both of them started chuckling. Even craziness like this was fun with him. But naturally, she thought they'd both completely shaken off their earlier mood.

But it seemed nothing shook Sam off the mood for more of

her. Once the hearth was cleaned up, the dog let out, then back in, and the door locked, he looked at Poppy with that dark glint in his eyes again. "The first time was a practice run," he said. "I think I almost remember how to do it now."

HE REMEMBERED MORE than she'd ever known. Eventually they both crashed. She fell asleep curled in his arms—not just because of lust or love but because the old bed was miserably narrow. She woke up on Monday morning with a sleepy smile—and Sam woke up with the same lusty gleam he'd had last night.

He reached for her, then pulled back with a heavy sigh. "Darn, Poppy. But I really need to get Bubbles out for a run, get her home and fed. I'm stuck with a couple callbacks. My youngest brother said he was coming by early this morning. But later today—"

Carefully Poppy kept any hint of disappointment from her voice. "Who was it who said to me, no pressure, no stress? I'm the one who's on a break, but you're still in the middle of your regular life. Come back when you're free."

"I feel badly about this—just taking off."

"You're not just taking off. You're doing stuff you have to do. Oh. You're an extraordinary lover. Or did I tell you that already?"

"I can't remember. Maybe you should tell me again."

The devil. He made her shake her head. Then wag a finger at him. "No pressure, no strings. Every part of last night was wonderful. The wonderfulest night since I can remember. Maybe even before I can remember. I'm going to spend all morning basking in how wicked I felt. How free. How gorgeous. And don't try to talk me out of it."

He leaned over, kissed her witless. "You are so much trouble."

"Thank you."

"Way more trouble than I could possibly have guessed."

"Thank you again. Go. Take your dog."

Sam didn't want to go, which warmed Poppy's heart. She had to kick him out, then spent an insane amount of time singing in the shower, making coffee and curling up in the monster-size chair by the window. A cardinal soared toward the woods, its cheerful red the only color in a fresh white world. Or no. On the ground was a fluffy rabbit, searching for who knows what, truthfully just seemed to be having a joyful morning.

So was she.

She got around to making herself a serious breakfast, putting on fresh cords and a Fair Isle sweater and then settling at the computer. Her fingers itched to work. Not exactly work—the lab projects were all on hold until after the holidays.

But after one sleepless night, she had more energy and enthusiasm than she'd had in years. It was Sam's fault, no question. He hadn't solved her problems—no one could solve her problems but herself.

She just felt . . . as if she had herself back. The Poppy before all the years of responsibility had compressed her spirit. The girl who could skate her heart out, the woman who her mom had hoped she would be. She'd risked. She'd dared. She'd done something that didn't have a have-to as part of it. She'd done something for herself—but hopefully that was good for Sam, too.

IT WAS AFTER two before Poppy heard the knock on the door. Usually it'd be Bubbles scratching to get in before Sam had even climbed out of the truck. Still, she bounced from the chair with anticipation and sprang to open the door.

Only it wasn't Sam.

It was two redheads, with her own startling blue eyes. Both of them were prettier than her. Both were standing shoulder to shoulder, like when they were little girls and full of anticipation about giving her a delightful surprise.

For a moment, Poppy couldn't speak for the sudden thick knot in her throat.

She'd anticipated seeing them after Christmas. Anticipated giving them warm hugs and all of them chattering and laughing at the same time, the way they always did. But it wasn't after Christmas now.

And she could have sworn she'd clearly explained that she needed time alone. Just another week. Not forever. But she so seriously craved that one more week.

As if recognizing she wasn't as happy to see them as they'd hoped, her sisters fell on her like butter on bread. "Oh, Poppy, don't be mad at us. You have no idea what we went through to find you! And then once we did, we had to come." Cam, her cap falling off, pulled Poppy into a fierce, loving hug.

Marigold, typically, started strewing clothes right and left. "Look, sis, we both realized that it was our turn to be there for you. The way you've always been there for us. You don't have to talk to us or share anything you don't want to share."

Cam finished the thought. "But we just couldn't stand the thought of your spending Christmas alone. You don't have to do anything. Not one little thing! We'll put everything together. You can just rest."

"It's been killing us both. Knowing you were troubled about something. Not feeling you could tell us. Not letting us help you. We're not *kids* anymore, Poppy. So just sit down," Marigold ordered, as she showed off her red-and-green-striped nails. "We're bringing in a few things from the car."

Until then, Poppy hadn't glanced behind her sisters. Now, from the window she could see the tail end of Cam's red Ford. And typical of Cam, the car had just been washed, every window gleaming, and the back seat loaded to the gills.

The knot in her throat tightened. Obviously the plan wasn't for a quick visit. The packed car looked more like an army showing up, prepared to bivouac indefinitely. An army of two who would need feeding, watering, cleaning up after, caretaking, attention.

"Cam. Marigold. Didn't you two get any of my notes? That I wasn't doing Christmas? That I needed some quiet retreat time?"

"Of course we got your notes." Marigold pushed off her boots. "That's exactly why we determined that you needed someone to spoil you for a change. No matter how much we all love Christmas, it takes a lot of work to put together—but not this year. Not for you. We'll do everything."

"And that's a serious promise," Cam said with a smile. "We'll guard you from any kind of stress. Don't you worry."

It was all so wrong Poppy couldn't seem to speak. She loved them. But she'd carefully told them, over and over, that she needed private time. They'd ignored her. Not heard her. Not tried to hear her.

Maybe someone else could have yelled at them to just STOP, turn around, get back in the car, and go back to Madison.

She wanted to do just that. But she just couldn't look at those two faces—so full of hope and worry and caring and love—and kick them out. Wreck their Christmases. Hurt them.

She just couldn't do it.

Chapter Ten

WHEN SAM ZOOMED into her driveway after three, he was startled to see a red car parked behind Poppy's.

Startled—and immediately wary.

Bubbles let out a woof, as if asking why he was suddenly backing out of the driveway, when both of them wanted to see Poppy.

"If we park behind the red car, we'll be boxing it in," he explained to the dog. "So we're going to back out and park on the street. Sit down."

Bubbles didn't want to sit down or settle down. Neither did Sam. He felt unexpectedly nervous about seeing Poppy this afternoon. He'd even done the rare spit-and-shine preparing for this visit—a decent navy-blue sweater, jeans with no holes, even shaved twice. He wanted her to know that he hadn't taken last night lightly. He wanted to be with her. Really with her.

All morning, while he helped Conan string Christmas lights, he thought of last night. The yearning in her eyes, the shyness—

and then her wild, sweet yielding when they came together. He still remembered her shush of a sigh after. Her moonlit smile.

But now, he was counting on seeing her again, after an interminably long morning. The red car in her driveway quelled all that anticipation and replaced it with plain old worry.

Poppy wasn't expecting visitors. No one was supposed to know where she was. She didn't know anyone here. No one knew her, except for his brothers.

"Come on, Bubb." He didn't need to ask. Bubbles vaulted over his lap as soon as the door opened. They hiked up her drive.

If someone—anyone—had tracked down Poppy to take advantage of her again, they were about to get a rude awakening.

Another look at the stranger's car was slightly—*slightly*—reassuring. The sturdy red Ford looked more like a teacher's car than a troublemaker's, but looks could be deceiving. He couldn't claim to guess what kind of a car a varmint or criminal or troublemaker might drive. It did seem slightly iffy that a serial killer would have gone to the trouble of washing and waxing the car in snowy, slushy weather.

Still. That was common sense thinking. Sam wasn't into common sense just then. He was into Poppy. No one was going to hurt her again. Not if he could help it.

He thumped on the back door, Bubbles standing at attention next to him.

When the door opened, he took one look and instantly realized that his odds of making love to Poppy today were about a zillion to one. If that high.

Without question, the two women who'd scrambled to answer the door were Poppy's sisters. They didn't look exactly like her, but they had the same thick dark-copper hair, the same small bones, the same pretty skin and sassy eyes, the same explosive feminine energy. They greeted him with huge welcoming smiles—as if they couldn't be more delighted to see him.

He wanted to swipe a hand over his face. It was downright impossible to think of them as anyone's enemy—but he told himself to toughen up. These were the two key people who demanded more from Poppy than she could possibly give. The ones who'd worn her down until she desperately needed rest. The ones she'd had to hide out from, to escape the constant stress.

Sam had no problem toughening up. If he had to kick these two to the curb to help Poppy, he was revved up and ready.

It was just going to take him a bit of time to concoct a war plan with all this instant commotion. The two women were as friendly as puppies—they fell on Bubbles with the same affection that Poppy had. Bubbles surged toward them, tail thwapping joyously, thrilled to circle two more females.

Sam had a second to analyze the war zone. Somehow the cabin had been destroyed. Boxes and debris cluttered every surface. Something bubbled in the oven—something that smelled like lasagna. Dirty bowls and mixing stuff took out one entire counter. Wine had been opened. Panini and cheese and stuffed celery and other assorted small eats had been arranged on a platter—which, of course, Bubbles homed in on faster than an ant at a picnic.

Sam searched for Poppy—saw the closed bedroom door—but initially he had no chance to pursue her. The sisters were simultaneously asking him questions and offering him drinks and food, but the immediate crisis was herding the dog from the plate of hoover doovers. He freed the plate from the dog, stashed it on the mantel with a *"No!"* to Bubbles, then almost crashed into an overflowing basket, loaded with sequins and glue and satin ribbons and stuff like that. He'd have had a heart attack if he'd spilled it.

The shortest sister told the tallest one to give "him" a chance, but she spun around to get in his face anyway. "So you're with Poppy? You're the reason she's been hiding from us?" Her tone was delighted. Shriekingly delighted. "You have no idea how happy we are to meet you. Cam!"

The shorter one—he was pretty sure she owned the impeccably kept car—finally edged past her sister. "I'm Cam. Short for Camille, but no one calls me anything but Cam. Glad to meet you . . . ?"

"I'm Sam. Sam Cooper. A neighbor of Poppy's—"

The taller one spoke to her sister as if he were deaf. "Isn't he adorable?"

"Um—" The other sister rolled her eyes, which pretty much explained that no one was likely to control the effervescent youngest of the family. "Don't worry, Sam. We all know how to behave. We just don't do it very often." A slim hand reached out to shake his, but then she hung on. "Our youngest sister, the tallest, is Marigold. I know we must sound a little off the wall, but you can't imagine how happy we are to see Poppy with someone."

"I don't know that she would characterize us quite that—"

"Don't fight it. We know Poppy. She hasn't looked this happy in a blue moon. We've been so afraid she was ill. Either downright sick or downright depressed. But now—"

"Would you two let the man breathe?" Finally Poppy showed up in the bedroom doorway. Someone explained how a half gallon of mulled cider had somehow spilled on Poppy—no guilty party named—but apparently that was why Poppy had to pop in the shower and why she still had wet hair.

For a few seconds, Sam forgot anyone else was in the room. Poppy's eyes met his, almost as fast as his met hers. He inhaled everything about her—her face, her hair, her oversize Santa sweatshirt and matching socks. But more than anything else, just her expression. Her eyes shied from him, and then met. Last night was suddenly between them like liquid gold. She remembered yielding. She remembered the size of him, the touch of him, his textures, her textures, the wealth of vulnerability they'd recklessly shared.

Yeah. He remembered that wonder, too. He hadn't expected it. There was no "expecting" something that precious. He'd loved before. But not like this. Maybe she hadn't felt that kind of splendor before. But she had now.

It was just that one instant that passed between them—that belonged to them—and then the noise came back. Her sisters. The clutter and busyness and action around the cabin. His pulse eased off the intimate throttle, kicked back to reality.

Making love wasn't conceivably on the immediate agenda. How she was surviving the sudden arrival of her sisters was.

On the surface, Poppy looked okay. No scars, no sign of bloodshed. No symptoms of panicked stress. But the minute she turned toward the kitchen, Sam took the chance to follow, throw an arm around her shoulder, and lean in. "You okay, Red?"

She didn't answer, at least with a yes or no. She just hugged in closer, her face tilted to his. "I didn't know they were coming. Total surprise."

Total shock, he interpreted. "They didn't call? Text that they were coming?"

She shook her head. "I don't even know, yet, how they tracked me down. But they're dead set on doing Christmas together."

Sam frowned, not sure what to say. What to think. Obviously this wasn't what she'd wanted, but they were here. A done deal. He'd only gotten a few looks, some conversation, but he'd picked up on something he wasn't expecting. If two puppies showed up at Poppy's back door, he couldn't imagine her turning them away.

That didn't mean anything about this was right. He needed to know a lot more to figure out how this was going to work out for her—or how it needed to work out. But temporarily, there was no chance for more private conversation.

"Hey, Sam?" One of the sisters—he was still getting them a little confused—tapped him on the shoulder to snare his attention. "Want some wine, cider, coffee, soda?"

The shorter sister clearly didn't want to be left out. "More to the point . . . since you're here, Sam, maybe you could help us?"

Of course he'd help. He wasn't about to leave Poppy alone. Besides, he really wanted to understand more about their family dynamics, see how the women talked, how they related together. His brothers, for sure, would create a get-together on a whim—but not without calling first. They wouldn't presume he could or would drop everything because they wanted to do something.

Still, every family had their own dynamic. His clan wasn't perfect by a long shot. But Poppy had told her sisters that she needed a retreat. And for sure, there wasn't much of a "quiet retreat" going on now.

A HALF HOUR later, his nerves were downright jittery. Sam didn't have nerves. He just wasn't a jittery kind of guy.

But it seemed the McGuire sisters had an annual Christmas tradition of making individual ornaments for the tree. He saw the kit pictures. They were pretty stupendous. Only the job they gave him was to separate spangles. By color. They gave him a bunch of little bowls to keep the colors straight.

That didn't sound tough, except that five spangles could fit on his thumb. Picking up a single one required crossing his eyes. His neck was already killing him from bending over to see the tiny things. Sam tried to make eye contact with Poppy, to get her attention, only she was running around and the instant he lost focus, the silly spangles spilled.

The two sisters flanked him on the couch—they just laughed at the spill, picked them all up for him. They seemed happy to have the time with him, wanted to get to know him. And they were hugely and undeniably happy to be with their sister.

"Poppy's the one who started this ornament tradition, Sam." Cam showed him the finished picture of the kit they were working on. "She thought up the idea after Mom died. We were too little to do fancy ones like this, back then. But we always made something. A memory ornament of some kind."

"And this time we brought a big pan of lasagna—Poppy's recipe because hers is the best. And we figured she'd never make it for herself. It should be almost done—you're welcome to stay; they'll be more than enough—and we should be done with the ornaments in another hour, easy."

His jaw dropped. "Another hour? Hey. Don't you need me to do something else? Carry something heavy? Fix computers? Leaky sinks?"

The women laughed. Both sisters patted his back. "You're a good sport."

Maybe. But Camille got to play with the velvet ribbon—that was the easy job. Marigold had it tough, though. She was stabbing pins into beads and crystal thingies. Then adding spangles. Then poking the pin into the base satin ornament.

"Now that we found Poppy, we figure we'll bring a tree

Wednesday. Just a small one. There isn't room for anything big, and besides, we don't want Pops to have a big mess to clean up after the holiday. We figured we'd put the lights on ahead of time. And just bring one box of ornaments."

"Two," Cam corrected her.

"Or three. But—"

Poppy did try to interrupt, but it never seemed to work out. "Would you two quit talking to Sam? Can't you talk to me, too?"

Two stricken faces looked at Poppy. "Good grief. Did we hurt your feelings?"

Poppy took a step toward them, her change in expression instantaneous. "No." Her tone turned soothing. "Of course not, you two. I'm glad you're getting to know him. Talk away."

Now Sam saw it. It wasn't some big "tell." It was just the way her expression changed—the way she suddenly moved toward them with an instinctively protective gesture.

He had a sudden mental picture of Poppy as a little girl, right after losing her mother, facing her two small sisters. She was way too young to take on a mother's role, but there it was. The lioness side of her. The lioness determined to protect her cubs come hell or high water.

It didn't matter if she'd just been a kid. She was the only lioness in their town. In their house. In their lives.

He'd been thinking that she needed to confront the sisters. Initially that had seemed like the next obvious step: to confront that they'd been overdependent on her, that they needed to set new boundaries. Now Sam recognized it wouldn't be that simple. Not for her. Not for her sisters either.

Their mom dying had been devastating. They'd all been so young. But Poppy had done everything in her power to make sure her sisters were cared for and loved and protected. She provided all the emotional support their father couldn't. She couldn't fail them. For Poppy, failing them would be like letting her mom down.

Nobody could tear down that big a mountain in a day—much less in a single conversation. Sam wanted to mull that further, but it was almost impossible to think with everyone talking at the same time.

"Hold up for a second?" Sam raised a hand, realizing that a trail of spangles seemed oddly attached to him. "If I could just interrupt to ask a question . . . how did you two figure out where Poppy was staying?"

Marigold happily deferred to Cam to do the answering. "Initially we didn't plan to track her down. But we kept worrying that something traumatic could have happened to her. Maybe she said over and over that she was okay, nothing wrong—but something had to be serious for her to take off like that. We *had* to know if she needed help."

"Wait a minute." Poppy interrupted in the firmest voice Sam had ever heard her use. So far. "I left you both notes and messages. I told you I needed some rest, some quiet time. The only way I could arrange work time off was if I used Christmas break."

"I get it, that you meant to sound reasonable, Poppy. But see it from our shoes. You've never disappeared like this, ever. You always loved Christmas. You're the one who created all our traditions and recipes and everything we did. We never had a holiday without you. How could we possibly think you were okay?"

Poppy leaned over the couch, just behind him, her voice turning defensive. "Because I told you I needed some time away? Because you know I've never lied to either of you? Doesn't everyone sometimes need some time off now and then? And I told you I'd have presents right after Christmas. And I also let Dad know I was away, because I was afraid he'd bug you two—but I couldn't totally stop that. We all know he's not as helpless as he makes out. He could lift a finger if he wanted to."

Both sisters nodded emphatically.

"I felt really guilty about leaving you with him—but we all know he's plenty smart. He's brilliant when it comes to his art, so he'd surely learn to pay the electric bill if the lights went out. All these years it's just been easier—for him—if we took everything on."

"We didn't take everything on for Dad, Pops. *You* did."

"I know, I know. That's totally on me. But when Mom died, he just seemed so lost, bumbling around as if he didn't know where he was or where he was going. I didn't know what else to do but try to help. But I never wanted either of you to feel obligated to do all the stuff that I always did. I really don't think it would kill Dad to figure a few things out for himself."

Sam raised his hand again, spraying more spangles. "Listen,

okay? I understand the three of you can all talk simultaneously, and somehow it makes sense to you all. But could you just go back to the one question I asked? About how you figured out where Poppy was?"

He got another couple empathetic pats on his back. Marigold said to Poppy, "He's just darling. Let's keep him."

Camille interrupted by responding to his question. "I'll answer you, Sam. After our mom died, well, let's just say that Poppy taught us a lot of survival skills. One of them was lying—when to fib and when not to fib. Like if one of us asks, 'Do you like my hair?' The answer is yes, always yes. Having integrity matters, but being able to lie sometimes matters, too. Anyway. Bribery is like that. Sometimes it comes in handy in real life. So. We called one of the deans at the university. Told him we had an emergency and somehow lost the paper where Poppy had written down the address where she was staying."

"Naturally he told us," Marigold said. "He's known Pops since forever. He knows the whole family. And we know Poppy would have given him an emergency contact address because she's, well, Poppy. He'd never dreamed we'd fib to him, so don't be mad at him, okay?"

"I'm not mad," Poppy said.

"Don't be mad at us either," Marigold said.

"I'm not mad at either of you either." Poppy wove around the crowded room to give each sister a hug, then took her big spoon and spatula back to the kitchen. "Dinner's only two shakes from being done. Barely time to wash hands."

Sam watched and kept watching, becoming more silent all the time. The darn spangles were finally all sorted. The first "breathtaking" ornaments were finished. A fabulous golden brown lasagna was served, with crusty garlic bread and a cranberry salad.

The sisters persisted in sneaking pieces of bread and bits of lasagna to Bubbles, brazenly encouraging the dog to become even more of a monster than she already was.

Sam kept waiting for a sign from Poppy that she needed rescuing, but he was starting to feel like a fully armed James Bond at a tea party. Near the end of dinner, the sisters wandered into some obviously stressful family issues. He went on automatic red alert, thinking she'd need him *then*. Only it was Poppy who did most of the diving for trouble, not avoiding it.

"So who's this latest guy you sent to the dating graveyard?" she asked Cam.

Her sister scowled. "Don't tease. I feel terrible about it."

"You always feel terrible after you break up."

"Steve was an especially good guy. There's nothing wrong with him. It was all me, as usual. I feel guilty and cruddy about it. As usual. But this time I decided I'm just never going through this again."

"And how're you going to avoid that?"

"I'm going to permanently take up celibacy." This announcement caused bits of bread to be thrown across the table—until Poppy put an end to it. "Okay, enough picking on you. Marigold's turn."

"What? What? There's nothing to pick on. My life's going smooth as silk."

Camille told the bigger truth. "Marigold. You've moved five times in two years, and now you're talking about moving *again*."

"But every time there's been something wrong. Really wrong. When something's wrong, you don't just sit in the mud, do you? You pull yourself up and get out of the mess. Didn't you drill that message into our heads a zillion times, Pops?"

Poppy rolled her eyes at the obvious dodge. "What's wrong this time?"

"What's wrong is three women are living in an apartment with one bathroom. Doesn't that say it all? Someone's always arguing. Someone always has a guy over that the others don't like. One picks up. The other leaves her crud all over. Clothes are hanging all over the furniture. No one wants to watch the same movies."

"A serious list."

"Yeah, it is," Marigold said defensively. "The last straw this time was Abigail. She doesn't want to have kids. Her boyfriend doesn't want to have kids. That's fine; it's their business. Until she wanted to give him a Vasectomy Reveal Party at the apartment."

Sam almost spit out a bit of garlic bread, and the ladies cracked up just as exuberantly. Poppy laughed, too, but she was the first to bring her youngest sister back to earth.

"I have a feeling we're all going to be laughing about that for weeks, but Marigold . . . come on. We all see you've had a tough time settling into a good place for you. I mean, you tried living solo. Then you tried a guy for a roommate. Then two women. You thought an old house with character was just the thing . . . then you tried a brand-new building . . ."

"So you're saying there's something wrong with me?" Marigold's voice turned soft and plaintive, unlike the wildly effervescent girl who'd first opened the door.

"Marigold, you dolt. You know perfectly well I love you no matter what. There's nothing wrong with you. You're wonderful."

"Well, that's a relief. I thought you were going to tell me I'm flaky."

"No one in this family would ever call you flaky and live to tell it," Poppy promised her. "You're our free spirit. We love you just as you are. You can move ten times a week, if that's what you want. I'm just asking if all this moving isn't getting you down."

By then, Sam had found dessert—a pan of apple kuchen—brought it back to the table, and exchanged dinner plates for smaller ones. He was used to pitching in—his family always had big feeds. Besides, conversation with the sisters was still flowing. A heap more issues were raised. Poppy asked the questions, clearly not afraid to put a problem out there, encouraging both of them to have their chance to air something out if they needed to.

"Okay, you've pried more than enough, Poppy. Now it's your turn," Cam finally said. "Tell us more about you and Sam."

"Sam is right here," Sam mentioned, not expecting that anyone would listen to his interruption. They didn't.

"Hey, you two had him to yourselves for almost an hour. If you failed to pry while you had him cornered, you lost out. Besides. Sam can answer for himself."

"We didn't pry, did we, Sam? We were just trying to get to know you."

"And having fun," Marigold added. "You like us, don't you, Sam?"

Any man who'd survived teenage girls in high school knew how to answer those questions. It was all good fun. Teasing, but caring teasing. Eventually the three women leaped from the table to do the dishes.

"It's okay, I can do these later," Poppy insisted.

"Give it up, Poppy. We're not leaving you with the whole mess," Cam corrected her. "But we do need to get them done because we still have the long drive back to Madison. We both have a couple half days of work left before the holiday."

All of them chipped in, including Sam. Dishes were only part of the cleanup. Both sisters did a haphazard job of straightening and gathering up their varied messes, then spent more time searching for coats and gloves—and kissing the dog. "Now that we've found you, Poppy, we've already planned how to pull together a last minute *easy* Christmas. *No* presents and no worrying about presents. We'll bring a *small* tree Wednesday afternoon. Still lots of time to grocery shop and do the food prep before Christmas Eve."

"We've always done the bigger dinner on the eve," Camille told Sam. "Then we could just spend Christmas being together. Relaxing."

Poppy heard the schedule planned. Her smile didn't disappear, but Sam saw her close her eyes tight for the breadth of a second. Quickly, though, she grabbed a big sweater, wrapped it around her, and walked them both out into the snow-peppered night. Effusive hugs had to be repeated. Both women ran back to give Sam an extra hug as well.

Darn, but they were cute. Cute as fresh air and real as sunshine. Really special, really engaging—but challenging in ways he'd never anticipated.

Their car started, the lights went on, and Cam backed out of the driveway. Sam finally had two seconds to grab Poppy and pull her into his arms. She'd been standing out there with no covering but a sweater. She was freezing. Less so when he tugged her closer. Tight closer. He blessed her forehead with a kiss, and then her lips.

She melted into him, releasing a fifty-pound sigh. "Sam. I'm so tired I can't see straight."

"Which is why I'm going home tonight. Definitely not what I'd planned or hoped for, but I'm about positive you'll be asleep as soon as your head hits a pillow. Any pillow."

"You thought they were going to be evil, didn't you?" She lifted her head.

"No. Well. Maybe a little. Maybe I thought they were going

to be bratty divas, constantly drawing attention to themselves, manipulative, conniving, selfish, demanding—"

"Stop." Her face was wan from tiredness, but she still let out a laugh. A short one. "I was afraid I gave you that impression. I never meant to. They're wonderful. I love them so much. But I can well imagine that you felt thrown into a swimming pool of pure estrogen."

"Poppy. I liked them both. Really."

She lifted up on tiptoe and kissed him again. "I did try to tell you. They're not the problem. I'm the problem. I'm the one who needs fixing."

He'd known her how long? Long enough to fall in love, but apparently not long enough to understand her situation. Seeing the three women together was unexpectedly illuminating. Poppy fit back into her family dynamic like pulling on a snug kid glove. Her sisters adored her, counted on her to be their mentor in chief, their supporter through thick and thin. She was the glue who held them together.

Sam couldn't think of a single reason why the two sisters would want the pattern to change. It worked well for them when they were kids, and it still worked now. It was only Poppy who looked as if she'd just survived a tornado, as exhausted as the woman he'd met on that first night.

"You know what? There are answers for this, Red. But it's too late tonight to get into all that—and you need to get inside where it's warm."

She nodded, but still said, "Really? Do you have some ideas?"

Hell, no. His best idea was riding in on a white charger—or with his wolf dog sidekick—and chasing away anyone who tried to use her. That would have been fun. That, he would have known how to do.

Right now, Sam wanted nothing more than to go inside with her, and make love until dawn. But . . . he needed to think.

Love had power. He believed that. Just maybe, though, they loved her too much. Poppy was the only caretaker the sisters had ever known. She'd slipped into the role of a mom before she'd even hit puberty. They saw her as strong as stone—because she *was* strong as stone.

Sam got it. He just wasn't sure how to help someone who was actually even more stone-headed than he was.

And Christmas Eve was only a couple days away now. Poppy's free time disappeared after the holiday. That didn't mean they had to stop seeing each other—but together time would be harder to manage. And she so obviously didn't want to go back to her "regular" life—and regular patterns—without getting a handle on how things could change for the better.

Sam wanted to input something that mattered to her. To show her that he could be a partner through even tough times.

"Bubbles." He snapped his fingers. The wolfhound took one look at his face and bounded for the truck. She knew when it was time to go home.

Chapter Eleven

POPPY SLEPT DEEPER than a tired puppy, but she woke with a start. Watery sunlight peeked through the old curtain, but there wasn't a peep of wind. She couldn't fathom what wakened her.

But then her ears picked up sounds. Whispers and tiptoes emanated from the living room. A giggle, quickly hushed. Something weighty was being pushed on casters—old casters, that squeaked. Overlying the sounds were smells—fresh coffee, cinnamon, bacon.

She peeled out of bed and grabbed a robe as she aimed for the doorway.

"Poppy! Darn it, did we wake you? We were trying to be quieter than mice!"

"You didn't wake me, but . . ." Her sisters both showed guilty expressions, but behind the fake remorse was plain-as-day excitement. They wanted her to be happy, happy they'd found her, happy at the Christmas they were putting together for her.

"Didn't you both tell me that you weren't coming back until tomorrow afternoon?"

"That's what we thought. But when we got home, Cam got a message that her school was closing early for the holidays because of some furnace crisis. And nobody minded if I took an extra day off."

"We both figured our coming early would help you," Cam said. "We can get more Christmas prep done. You can just curl up on the couch."

They both looked expectant. Hopeful. They wanted her to be happy so much that Poppy already felt exhausted. For a moment she was too overwhelmed to even speak.

The cottage had been taken over. How they'd brought in a tree without her hearing was a mystery. It was artificial, already dancing with lights. On the floor were three open boxes of their handmade ornaments, ready to dress the tree.

The kitchen counter space was crammed solid with holiday debris. Their mom's sacred serving dishes had become part of the sisters' traditions—like the Santa Claus cookie tray, the cut-glass salad bowls, the peace-on-earth mugs. And squished on the table were the cookie-making supplies—bowls, cookie sheets, colored sprinkles, butter, cinnamon, sugar, mixing spoons. Not counting what had already fallen on the floor.

Ten pounds of potatoes sat lonely by the back door. There was no space for them anywhere else.

When Poppy still hadn't said anything, Marigold said softly, "Are you angry with us, Poppy?"

"Not angry." Her voice came out thick and rusty. "But carrying all this stuff here—it would have made so much more sense to just do it at home. My house. Cam's house. Dad's house. Anywhere but here."

Marigold's eyes welled up. So did Cam's. No one moved. And no tears spilled, but they were close.

Poppy was so close to just . . . letting it all out. Getting mad. Getting it over with. She did *not* want this messy, noisy, exhausting Christmas they were putting together. Not this year. She loved the mess, the noise, the post-Christmas crash. But all these years, she'd tried hard to hear what her sisters needed, to come through for them. But she wanted to believe, needed to believe, that they'd try to hear her and what she needed.

Yet somehow it all clogged in her throat, the way it had before. It just refused to come out. Their faces looked just like, years ago, when she'd had to tell them there was no Santa Claus.

She couldn't do it. Wreck their Christmas. Make them feel guilty for all this effort and work they'd gone to, so they could give her a special holiday.

"You know what?" Poppy said gently. "Right now, let's just put everything aside and just create a Christmas together. But maybe, all three of us could think about how all this became so upsetting—for all of us. Think about it. And then come up with some ideas about how to fix this so it doesn't happen like this again. Okay?"

Cam piped up. "Okay. I'll take charge of dinner! I figured we'd do the recipe with the brown sugar coating the ham?

Unless you want to do the one with root beer. I bought root beer, just in case."

Marigold followed up. "We figured we'd do the tree and cookies today. And the planning for specifics. Then do the last grocery run and other prep stuff tomorrow. We can do everything much simpler than we usually do." Marigold was already opening the ornament boxes, taking out her favorites—the bright, splashy ones.

"We've been arguing about the salad. Marigold always wants the same old fresh-strawberry and sour cream one with the marshmallows. I'm thinking we should go with the seven-layer salad. Maybe the colors aren't as Christmasy, but the tastes are fresh? Where everything else is cooked, so it's nice to have a contrast with colors and textures." Camille, predictably, had cornered her favorite ornaments. She liked the tasteful ones— the ruby and emerald velvet balls, the Victorian ones with lace and satin ribbons. She could spend long minutes placing them just so on the tree.

"We both think we should have sweet potato pie for dessert. The recipe with the condensed milk. You know. Where we made it by mistake the first time and have loved it that way ever since?" Marigold found an old favorite, a Santa ball, and placed it center-tree.

"But we could make a lemon meringue pie for dessert, too. Just for fun. Or a red velvet cake—one pie, one cake. That's a better balance?"

"We keep debating about the vegetable. I think it should

be fresh beans with the cranberries and bacon. *She* thinks we should have the same old ancient beans and French fried onions—"

"Because everyone always loves it," Cam said. "No matter how many times we have it, nobody ever gets tired of it. And then there's potatoes. We can do the traditional cheesy potatoes? Or we could do scalloped potatoes, but the apple/scalloped recipe, not the usual one."

"Or we could do the dish where we slice the potatoes really thin, put it in a glass pie pan, layer it with cheese and herbs and butter and stuff, then turn it over when it's done? It really looks terrific—"

They both stopped talking abruptly. Looked at Poppy.

Cam finally said slowly, "Do you want us to disappear, Poppy? Just call it quits for this year?"

Poppy wanted to kick a wall. Or kick herself. Or run outside and hide under a giant snowball.

She didn't want to hurt her family. She never wanted to hurt her darn family. That's how all this had started. Mom dying. Mom, who was everything to all of them. Her, stepping up because there was no one else who could. Because she wanted to be like her mom. Because she wanted to protect them all. Because she wanted them to know that they could count on her no matter what.

She didn't want anything to change any more than they did. But she'd started to worry she was too darned tired these days . . . to count on herself.

* * *

AS SAM TURNED into Poppy's drive, he was whistling. Some dumb old song about Mama kissing Santa Claus, but only Bubbles could hear him and she hadn't started howling. Yet. She did better with Sam's whistling than his actual singing, but she still sensed something good was up.

And it was. He had two pairs of snowshoes in the back, subzero warm mittens for Poppy, and ski poles for both. His sister-in-law had pitched in a pair of boots and three pairs of ski socks—since he didn't know Poppy's shoe size, they figured the choice of socks would enable her to fit in the snowshoes no matter what.

She was going to love it. Exploring the snowy woods. Enjoying the day, the winter, the bright sunshine. After yesterday, he determined that a break was called for—an emotional rest time—a rejuice-the-heart time. A day plastered with smiles was what he had in mind . . .

Until he abruptly saw the red car.

They were back. The sisters. The sisters who'd claimed they weren't coming back until tomorrow afternoon.

He left the snowshoes and gear in the truck, guessing there'd be no way to use them, not today. The tallest sister, Marigold, must have spotted him from the window, because both sisters opened the door before he and Bubbles got close enough to knock. Bubbles got the first round of hugs and kisses, but the magpies drew him in with the same exuberant affection.

Apparently the sisters had been sharing old funny holiday stories, and once they wrapped his hands around a mug of coffee, they regaled him with more of the holiday tales.

They started with the first year Poppy made a turkey. No one told her there was a bag inside the turkey. The bird was still edible, but the sisters considered it a family obligation to tease her about it every year.

Then there was the year the mashed potatoes turned into rocks.

And then there was a year they didn't have a tree, so the girls went out to find one. They ran across a fallen tree in the woods—a little one that was straggly and saggy and clearly had no future of anyone appreciating it. But they did. They filled every hole with dolls and toys and stuffed animals.

Poppy finally surfaced—she was right there, in the kitchen area—but she'd been bending over the oven. When she stood up, she was carrying two cookie sheets with hot pads. "I've been *trying* to say hello! But as you can see, we're in the middle of bedlam!"

Yes, he could see the chaos. See the flour streaks on her face. See her private smile for him—and yet both frustration and anxiety in her eyes. "Hey, I'm good with bedlam. My mother always said that three boys meant constant bedlam. We just thought it was normal."

"Can I get you two to deal with the cookies? The ones that are cool go in the tins. Except for the ones you sample. I'd just like a break for a couple seconds."

That was exactly what Sam thought. That she needed a break. He announced, "Poppy and I are taking out the trash."

Poppy's jaw dropped—but then she grinned. "That's what I was thinking. We keep accumulating bags of trash around here."

"So I'll do the brawn. And Poppy'll tell me where to go."

"Exactly," Poppy affirmed. "We'll be right back."

Bubbles glanced their way but made no attempt to follow them. There was food in sight, after all, and two extra females to fawn over her. The dog clearly had her priorities. Poppy grabbed her parka, Sam grabbed his.

She charged out the door, spun to the left, did a quick turn at the end of the house.

"There's no trash back here," he noticed.

"No windows either. We're out of sight." She swooped on him. Small as she was, she knew her way around swooping. She framed his face with her freezing cold hands. "My sisters are like taffy. They stick."

"I can see that."

"We'll never get a chance to talk if we don't create one."

For once, Sam really wanted to talk. That long stretch of time yesterday he'd spent with her sisters had troubled him. Questions started to itch in his mind, questions that he really wanted to ask her about. But right then he was positive that talking was the last thing on her mind.

Poppy was pretty persuasive. Or possibly he was entranced at finding himself being persuaded so easily.

She whispered his name, calling him like a siren in the wind, snaring him with her lips, the tilt of her face, those gorgeous sassy eyes. She went up on tiptoe to kiss the tip of his nose, each cheek, lick his lower lip—slowly—then nuzzle more schmoozy kisses on his neck.

Then she wanted to talk. "Don't let this scare you, Sam. I don't want you to worry about it. But I still want to tell you that I feel . . . lit up . . . when I'm around you. Higher than champagne and starlight. It sounds nuts, but I keep feeling this downright tingle all the way down to my toes. You think I'm coming down with something?"

"I do. I think it's a serious illness. And I'm having some of the same symptoms. Getting a little worried about it." She started it. But if she was going to kiss him all over, Sam figured he was justified in turning her ideas on her—with one exception. He lifted her up, laid her against the back wall of the cabin, homed in for a honey soft kiss. To start with.

"Sam! Poppy! Sam! Can you hear me? I think we blew a fuse! We lost power. I don't know where the box is in this place!"

"Wow," Sam whispered. "That peace sure lasted a long time. Poppy?"

She turned quickly.

"Why on earth are they here so early? Did they call you?"

She shook her head, her bright smile fading. "They came early to help put together Christmas. To help me any way they could."

He cocked his head. "I don't suppose you could just put on your Scrooge hat and tell them to flake off?"

She gulped. "Whew. Sometimes you're pretty blunt."

"I know. It's one of my character flaws."

"Actually, I like it. Straight honesty works better for me than candy-wrapped sweet talk." She hesitated. "Besides which, I think you had a good idea. A really good idea. Only I don't seem to have a Scrooge hat, Sam. I don't even know where to buy one."

"Aw, Red." His hand was cold, but he still had to touch her. Her cheek, the side of her head, slide his fingers into her hair. "You're tough, you know that? You're strong. You just don't seem to have a mean bone in your entire body. Sometimes there's just no way to solve something *nicely*."

There. He'd coaxed a smile from her again. "Honest to Pete, I think I could handle a serial killer. A snake in a closet. A bear in the kitchen. But I just can't seem to be mean to my sisters. And you know what? I *do* know that's what I have to do. And I will. As soon as I figure out how."

He scooped an arm around her. "I guess we could enroll you in a meanness class, but I'm afraid you'd just flunk. But maybe it could help if we figure this out together."

They hiked back inside. Sam took on the blown fuse. In the dark, the sisters discussed whether they'd turned on too many appliances—the stove, the fridge, the coffee maker, the washing machine, the dryer, the microwave, the Christmas lights.

"You think?" Poppy asked wryly—but Sam had the problem fixed so fast they were back to the Christmas-creation projects in no time. Orange cinnamon cookies showed up on the counter to cool. Then sugar cookies heaped with sprinkles and frosting and about everything else.

Sam was the elected taste tester. A tough job, but he was man enough to do it.

Cam elected herself the list maker for the serious grocery trip. Sam and Marigold set up the table and chairs, just to see where it was all going to fit. Poppy made hot cider, did several loads of dishes, made decisions—sweet potato pie and a small red velvet cake, the ham crusted in brown sugar and tea, the apple/scalloped potato casserole that their grandmother used to make. Then they needed an inventory of dishes, bowls, silverware.

"I'll be darned," Poppy said suddenly. "We need to take out the trash again, Sam."

"I'll say. I can't believe we loaded up so much this fast."

"I can't either. Come on, we'll get it done lickety-split."

This time, they actually took out the trash. Beyond the cabin was a shed that stored tools, rakes, shovels, and that kind of thing. Bins for trash were obviously kept there. That chore took all of two seconds.

Poppy beat Sam to the back of the cabin with her arms already raised to take him on . . . to take him in.

He'd never guessed she was a wicked, wicked woman. Or

maybe he had. Something about her had captivated him from their first meeting. She had this streak of mischief. He loved it.

She had another streak of risking things she was afraid of. Like him.

And she made him want to risk the things he was afraid of. Like her. How much she'd come to mean to him, how unreasonably fast, how foolishly huge for two people who still barely knew each other. But he knew her fear. He knew her yearning. He knew he wanted to be there for her, more than any man ever had or could.

"You're asking for trouble, Poppy," he whispered to her.

"I know. But I've never asked for trouble in my entire life, Sam. I don't want to put you at a disadvantage. I could bungle this. I'm not sure what I'm doing."

He started to reply, but then heard two familiar female voices call from the back door. "Hey, you two. We're all about you two being together, but you don't have to catch pneumonia to do it. It's freezing out there."

They exchanged exasperated looks, but then gave up and joined back in.

EVENTUALLY THE DAY'S projects were finally done, the plans for the holiday feast organized. They all sat by the Christmas tree for a few minutes—just to ooh and aah over the lights and ornaments—and to bring up a few more plans.

Sam kept an eye throughout on Poppy, but she seemed in good shape. Christmas chaos had a rhythm to it. No matter how tiring, everyone had done the same chores and jobs every year. And Poppy'd managed this crew for years. It showed.

"We haven't talked about Dad. We all know he'll come for dinner," Poppy said. "I have no idea if he'll bring anyone, but it doesn't matter. We'll just add an extra chair if he does. Sam, can you come for Christmas Eve? Or have any family you'd like to include with us?"

"My clan does Christmas on Christmas, but I'll definitely join you on Christmas Eve." He hesitated. "Do you three have any other family that lives nearby? Aunts, uncles? Cousins? Grandparents?"

"We did when we were little," Poppy said. "Mom's mom lived close by. Gramps died young, but Grandma was in great health—until she went on a trip to the Far East, picked up a bug, seemed okay until she got home. But she wasn't. She died awfully quickly after that."

"Dad has a sister who lives in England," Cam mentioned.

"And there are a couple cousins on Dad's side, but they live on the other side of the country. It's hard to stay close."

Sam kept thinking an echo of the same song. These three had been alone, really alone, since their mom died. And most of the stories they'd told about past Christmases had been fun and funny—but never seemed to include their father.

Poppy suddenly jumped to her feet. "I just looked at the clock. Everybody has to be starving. I didn't really plan for anything ahead of time, but I'll think of something."

"You don't have to feed us, Poppy."

"I'm not thinking about a feast. Just something easy."

Poppy came through with omelets. Sam hung close, willing to take orders. She kept putting things in the bowl—sausage and three kinds of cheese and a little spinach and cinnamon and other stuff Sam had never seen served with eggs before. It was delicious. And easy.

By the time they sat down to eat, Sam offered some Christmas stories of his own. When his brothers were small, they had to make breakfast for his mom before they could open presents. They opted to make scrambled eggs in the microwave. The eggs were so tough they could probably have bounced upstairs by themselves. And there was enough jam on the toast to feed a family of five.

Marigold was a born giggler—easy to entertain her—but it took a few more embarrassing stories to get Cam going. She liked his story about the year Sam got his first two-wheeler and had to immediately try it out in the living room. Unfortunately he ran into the tree. More unfortunately, the tree fell over, and Sam got buried in all the debris.

Then there was the Christmas they had Irish wolfhound puppies who were supposed to be in a protected shed outside with their mama and instead ended up "somehow" in the house in the middle of everything.

Everyone was laughing and talking through dinner, but Sam could see Poppy was starting to flag. It hadn't been a hard day. Just an endlessly active day. It was so clear to Sam that her sisters wanted her to have a fun, stressless holiday. But at this point, even if everyone was over-the-top happy, there was such a thing as relentlessly happy.

SOMEHOW IT WAS eight at night by the time the dishes were done. Even Bubbles was sacked out like the dead. Since no one showed any signs of leaving, Sam took on the role of bad cop and stood up.

"I'm kicking you two beautiful ladies out," he said, with deep regret in his voice. "I enjoyed every minute of the day with all of you. But the three of us know that Poppy's never going to admit she's tired. She isn't as exhausted as when she first got here. But I think we all want to coax her to rest a little more."

The sisters stepped up faster than if there was a fire. "Poppy, we didn't think."

"Of course we're going, sis. We want you to rest. We'll do the rest of the work tomorrow—"

"Afraid Poppy can't do anything tomorrow," Sam said regretfully. "If either of you need help with the grocery run or getting things ready, give a shout, and I'll chip in. But Poppy needs one complete day off—and look at her. She's about to protest. But, Poppy, your sisters are on my side. You're getting a totally quiet day tomorrow and that's that."

"Hey," Poppy interrupted. "Believe it or not, I can vote for myself."

But she didn't, Sam thought. She never voted for herself. She swung her weight around, when it was for the ones she cared about, so it was her own fault if he was taking a page from her playbook. He had significantly more weight to swing around when it was for someone *he* cared about.

She shot him a dark glance, but he knew he'd already won. The sisters allied with him.

"We're voting for you. And you're getting the day off. Like Sam said," Cam told her.

"Nothing tomorrow at all." Still, Marigold looked back at him. "So . . . are you going, too, Sam, or staying here?"

"I'm leaving when you two ladies do," Sam said firmly. Which was not what he wanted at all.

Chapter Twelve

POPPY TURNED ON the windshield wipers full blast. The sky had just belched out another heap of snow and, from the look of darkening clouds in the west, intended to bring on more. For the most part, she didn't care. She was headed out, come hell or high water.

She may not have planned to participate in Christmas this year, but obviously she was neck-deep in holiday preparations now. That meant she needed presents under the tree. Her sisters were doing the grocery trip and food prep in Madison—she wasn't certain when they were coming back, either late today or tomorrow, Christmas Eve. It really didn't matter. The only chance she had to shop was today.

Madison was wonderful for shopping, but there was no way she wanted to drive that far. Google had given her an endless choice of stores and opportunities closer to the cottage—"closer" being less than an hour away.

The snow didn't bother Poppy, nor did the rushed shopping.

But the sudden upheaval was definitely throwing her off-balance. She'd never intended to neglect her family at Christmas—she'd just planned to buy their presents after the holiday. That plan obviously wasn't going to work now.

At least gifts for her sisters were easy. For Cam, she'd get a copper pan—because she loved to cook on copper—and for Marigold, one of those "forever pans"—for the cook who could ruin any and everything. Both of them loved candles—cinnamon and apple scented for Cam, a saucy lemon scent for Marigold. She'd also get a gift certificate for facials, which both girls loved. And then sweaters. Cam loved a cardigan she could layer; Marigold loved something soft and slouchy.

Her dad always wanted something exotic, but reality was, he needed shirts and socks. No matter how many he had—and could certainly afford—his clothes inevitably got paint or clay or solvents on them. He only noticed when he needed to go out in public, which meant he always needed a fresh stash.

So that shopping would take time, but it wasn't that challenging. Choosing a gift for Sam—now *that* was a challenge.

She'd been recklessly, deliciously sure about making love with him three nights ago. But he'd downgraded to smooches ever since then. Those smooches were potent and creative and alarmingly enticing. But still. What guy put on the brakes when the lights were all green?

Of course, maybe the event hadn't been as reckless and delicious as it'd been for her. And of course, they'd both had two ultrafull busy days.

But now Sam had met her sisters, spent time with them, saw what her family was like. Maybe that could make a guy instinctively put on the brakes until he was a lot more sure this was all a good idea?

If he was unsure where they were going—Poppy felt exactly the same way. Her life was temporarily a jumble. He knew that; she'd been honest. But the absolutely last thing she wanted to do was hurt him.

Still, for a woman who'd never done anything impulsively, she knew how different Sam was. He was the first man, the only man, she'd willingly jump off a cliff for. The only man she'd instinctively trusted. This was too special—*he* was too special—for her to stall. She wanted every minute with him that she could get. She wanted to explore everything it was possible to explore in the short time they had together. To never feel this way again?

She refused to throw away this chance.

BY NOON THE roads were all slushy and crushy. People were in a hurry to get their Christmas shopping done and were zooming out of parking spaces with only a harried glance at any cars behind them.

Poppy still hadn't found the right gift for Sam. It had to check all the boxes—something personal, but not presumptuous. Nothing too expensive, too practical, too ordinary. It had to reflect that she cared enough to know what he'd like.

She left the last store around two, wishing she could be a

whole lot less OCD. There was no perfect present. Obviously she knew that, but it wasn't helping her solve the problem. She had to have something for him. By then, another fresh four inches of new snow had fallen, all thick and heavy and intrusive, and the darned radio kept insisting there was more coming. Her trunk was filled with stuff, including wrapping paper and ribbons and tape.

Everything she needed, except something for Sam. She wanted something that showed she *knew* him. Deep down. The man he wanted to be, the man he was, the man who always stood up for the right things, the things that mattered.

Easy to figure *that* out. So for heaven's sake. Why was that so hard to translate into a gift?

But then, by accident—or desperation—she noticed a different type of business, isolated from the usual retail stores, and stared at the potential of it so long that the driver behind her honked. She turned in . . . and didn't come out for a good hour.

She didn't make it back to the cottage until five, wiped out from head to toe. Still, she easily laughed when she turned in the drive.

Sam had plowed her out. He'd also turned on lights for her, both inside and out. And there was a piece of paper, scrawled in his hasty handwriting, taped on the back door window.

YES, THEY'VE BEEN HERE. WE DID A FEW THINGS, LIKE PUT AWAY FOOD AND STUFF, BUT THEN I SENT THEM HOME (WITH BUBBLES'S HELP). I CAN'T COME OVER TONIGHT . . .

ACCORDING TO KRISTIN, HER MOM AND DAD ARE BUSY SO
SHE AND I ARE HAVING "A DATE NIGHT." SHE THINKS WE
SHOULD GIVE BUBBLES A BATH AND DRESS HIM UP FOR
CHRISTMAS.
   PRAY FOR ME.
   IF YOU'VE WORN YOURSELF OUT, YOU'LL BE IN
TROUBLE WITH ME. CHINESE IN THE FRIDGE, NOTHING TO
DO BUT HEAT UP.

                                                    LOVE, SAM

A smaller note, obviously written later than the first, was
scrawled beneath the big one.

   POPPY—I NEVER ASKED FOR YOUR CELL NUMBER.
THOUGHT YOU WERE TRYING TO AVOID CALLS. BUT IF
YOU HAVE TIME, PLEASE GIVE ME A QUICK CALL (OR
TEXT). KRISTIN AND I ARE HAVING AN ARGUMENT ABOUT
DIAMONDS. I NEED YOUR ADVICE.

By the time Poppy carted in the trunk full of presents and
packages inside, she was out of breath and laughing. First, because of that "Love, Sam." See? It wasn't all *her* fault that she'd
fallen so hard for him. He kept doing things and saying things
that forced her to laugh. Or forced her to love him.

He persisted in being the kind of man she'd never believed
existed.

Even shopping-tired, she microwaved the war su gai and rice, poured a tall glass of water, and slouched on the couch with her cell. She texted the number he'd scrawled on the second note.

You're having a problem with diamonds?

He answered immediately. She wants a diamond collar and diamond leash for Bubbles's Christmas present.

Hmm. I'm with her.

Poppy.

He texted her name, not said it aloud, but she could still mentally see him rolling his eyes. Well . . . I suspect she means rhinestones rather than diamonds.

The dog traipses in the woods. Digs in snow. Dives in the lake. Rolls in mud.

Okay, okay. First tell Kristin that a glitzy collar would make other dogs jealous, so jealous they might not want to play with her. And that could hurt Bubbles's feelings.

Say what?

Just do it, Sam. Then tell her that because Bubbles is such a girly dog, she'd probably want something really soft next to her neck. I've seen dog collars that are padded—like for serious hiking dogs—so it doesn't chafe? But Kristin could see that it felt soft.

DO NOT GO AWAY. I'll be right back.

She finished her dinner, was just about to trade in her glass of water for a short glass of wine, when he came back.

You're a genius, he texted.

Uh-huh. Now you need the new collar and leash in pink.

No.

Or you could talk Kristin into getting one that's the color of Bubbles's eyes.

Like brown.

Yes, but don't tell Kristin BROWN. Just suggest that Bubbles would love a leash that was the same color as her eyes.

> Okay. Okay. I might live through this yet. Just for the record... who knew this could possibly turn into such a traumatic issue? She was crying. Now she's not. Which is to say... It's your fault if I'm going to love you forever.

He clicked off.

Poppy fell asleep smiling to beat the band. Christmas carols played in her head. Until this year, she'd so so so loved Christmas. The presents and the tinsels, the baking and the messes, the candle smells and the sparkling tree and the ornaments and lights. This year there was Sam, and that meant so much more. It wasn't all about where they ended up, but how it was *now*, how all the time he was with her was so darned precious.

How could she not be happy?

UNTIL TWO IN the morning, when her dad called.

Poppy's phone was now on, of course. Everyone knew where she was so there was no reason to hide anymore—no *way* to hide anymore. She never hesitated to answer. At that late hour, it could be a serious problem.

"Hey, my lovely Poppy," her dad said.

She could hear the deep affection in his voice. She could also hear the slur of Irish whiskey.

"I've missed you. I understand—more than anyone—why you needed some time alone. That's always what I needed. Alone time. To work. To create."

"I know, Dad."

"But I'm glad I know where you are again. I'll be there for dinner—I was going to say tomorrow, but then it turned into Christmas Eve two hours ago. So today."

"Of course you will."

"Honey . . ."

A ball of lead dropped in her stomach. "What?"

"I haven't gotten presents for everyone. You always did that for me. You were always my wonderful, special daughter, who I could count on through thick and thin. I hope you feel appreciated. And loved. And that all the things you've always done were valued."

"Uh-huh," she said.

"But about those presents for your sisters—I'm working on a sculpture right now. For a church, if you can believe it—but I haven't had a single minute to think about Christmas shopping. I just can't do it myself, honey."

"Uh-huh," she said. He waited. She was supposed to offer to come through for him. She always had. This time—for the first time—she just said, "I'm glad you're coming for dinner, Dad," and rang off.

POPPY'S CELL PHONE buzzed again around six. Didn't matter by then. She hadn't slept.

It was Jonas—from the lab. He was just a kid. Nineteen. He loved the work, loved the apprenticeship with her, and temperamentally was an even worse workaholic than she was.

His voice was shaking. "I know we weren't supposed to call you."

"And I know you wouldn't, unless something was really wrong."

"It's our study that's really wrong. The grant about the invasive species—I think of it as the Greedy Glugger because that's how we've been calling it. You know, the invasive creep we've found in three northern lakes now—"

"I know the one." Obviously. It was her study; she'd nicknamed the sucker fish herself, but Jonas was clearly upset and she wasn't about to tease him for stating the obvious.

"Well, I was just rereading it one more time. And I found a problem. We weren't expecting anyone to see it or read it until after Christmas? But if anyone got their hands on it and discovers the goof, they'd probably wonder about the accuracy of the rest of our data. At the very least, they'd think we're careless—"

She carried the phone to the kitchen, where she could start making coffee. His voice was trembling again. "Jonas, do you know what the mistake is?"

"What I know is that it's all my fault."

"You know what? Maybe it is your fault. But however big or small the mistake is, it probably isn't going to affect world peace. We'll survive if there's a problem. You're okay. Just tell me."

She gulped down two mugs of coffee before she got it out of him. He was like her sisters when they were younger—heaven knows, they were willing to talk, but it took a deep shovel to dig out the real problem.

Poppy had dreamed of earning this grant for more than two years—when she'd first discovered the Greedy Glugger. It was a fish with a mouth almost bigger than its body—a species never seen before in Wisconsin's northern lakes—who seemed content to gulp down any fish smaller than him. They weren't reproducing as fast as rabbits, but close.

Intruders entered lake waters all the time, but identifying them could be a pistol and a half. Defending against them was always a challenging crisis. To kill all the monsters sounded easy, but it wasn't. First, they needed to know how they got in their specific lakes. How to get rid of them in a way that didn't harm the other species of fish and growth in the lakes. How to understand their breeding ground, and why they found certain freshwater lakes so enticing to breed in.

Simple solutions rarely solved complex problems. Which is why they needed a grant, with enough funds to study the darned Glugger before it did any more damage.

Wherever the species came from, perhaps it was benign. But here it was interacting with unfamiliar species. The result was unfortunately noxious. Bigger fish who tried to eat it became poisoned.

"Jonas, take it easy. We'll figure this out."

"It was my numbers that were wrong. It wasn't actually an error in calculation, Poppy. Somehow I just put in an eight instead of a six in a certain graph, and that affected the results all the way through."

"Jonas." By then she'd washed out her mug, brushed her hair, and yanked on clothes—she'd put him on speaker for part of the call. "It'll take me an hour and a half, maybe two, to get to the lab—"

"I'll be there. I'll be there before you're here."

She sighed. His voice was so earnest, his tone so relieved she was coming. "We'll fix it, Jonas. Not today. My family's coming over for a big Christmas Eve dinner. But I can spare an hour if it'll help you stop worrying about it. We'll see what's what, make a plan, figure it out. I promise, it's going to be okay."

He almost laughed, but his choked voice sounded closer to crying. She couldn't stand it. She couldn't just leave the kid that panic-stricken without answers over the holidays, and he was right that this was potentially a mighty serious problem.

Poppy sent a text to Sam—telling him she needed to be at her lab and couldn't be back until early afternoon. After that, she sent emails to family, just to let them know where she was and telling them that though dinner might be postponed by an hour, she'd be there, nothing to worry about.

Only there was. The whole drive to the lab, Poppy's heart kept drumming an ominous beat.

This was the story of her life—the story she'd been trying to change. The running nonstop. The responding to everyone's needs ahead of her own. Her reacting to whatever anyone else wanted.

Only this really wasn't the same thing. The Christmas Eve dinner might be a little late, but she wouldn't be gone *that* long. She couldn't strand one of her students with a crisis. After all, she was the boss. And she had the whole responsibility for this project and grant and everything that went with it—if it failed, it was her job, her reputation at stake.

She was making lots of progress with saying no lately. She'd said no to her dad. She'd said no to Gary. Maybe she hadn't fully confronted her sisters yet, but who could move a mountain in a day? She was hardwired to put others first.

Okay. So she'd only made inroads, so far. Not major changes. Putting herself first still loomed as strange new territory. She was still rushing. She hadn't had any breakfast yet, hadn't thought to bring even a snack for the drive. Yesterday there'd been no time for lunch at all. And now she'd be going home to a roomful of presents that still weren't wrapped, and the zillions of things related to Christmas Eve dinner that she was responsible for.

Her sisters knew how to do the dinner stuff. They'd done it a zillion times with her. They could take charge, she told herself.

Only they never had before.

Once the worry itch got under her skin, it was tough not to scratch it. Poppy pulled into the empty parking lot at the lab, feeling as if she were on a crash-and-burn course that was going to explode by dinner. The crux of the problem was Sam.

She didn't want to be someone in his life who added little more than a goofy woman who excelled at running at a frazzling pace. He needed a woman who had time in her life for him, and that's who she wanted to be. What she wanted for him.

But at the moment, all she could really do was run. She'd had almost two weeks to reboot her life—and she'd thought she was on the right path—but this sure felt like repeating old history. Grabbing her purse, running for the lab because there was a problem. Instead of sending Jonas home, she promised to rush in to fix it. Even worse, as always, she was counting on herself to fix it, too.

* * *

AN HOUR AFTER receiving Poppy's text, Sam zoomed over to her cabin. Obviously she was going to be at her lab for several hours, but that was exactly why he charged over so early.

He understood about a crazy work crisis. It happened to him all the time in the summer. He could help do the dinner prep, make sure Poppy had less to do later.

Surprising him, there were already three cars in her driveway—so her clan had shown up to help, too. That was good news—and he figured the second car had to be her father's. It was past time he met the dad, Sam thought. In fact, when it came down to it, the serious talk he'd wanted to have with Poppy was about all the unanswered questions he had about her father. Maybe it was just as well he'd have a chance to meet George before that talk.

Whistling as he vaulted out of the truck, he let Bubbles bound ahead of him, dressed appropriately with velvet antlers and jingle bells. Sunlight dazzled on fresh snow. Couldn't be a more perfect Christmas Eve.

He yanked down the tailgate, shook his head. He had a mountain to haul inside—food, cookery, general holiday stuff. Not that he was a sucker for Christmas, but he always had been, always would be. Santa fashion, he hauled a big bag of presents on his shoulder, carried the rest, and let Bubbles lead the way.

Sam opened the door with a boisterous "Ho ho ho" only to find three stressed-out people. Both sisters were wringing their hands, pacing from window to window dressed in velvets and spangles and Christmas attire—but no smiles.

Cam spotted him first, trailed by Marigold. "Sam! So glad you're here. Do you know where Poppy is?"

"Well, sure." He was confused by the question, even more confused by why the ladies both looked so freaked. "Why is anyone worried? Poppy said she'd texted everyone, so you'd know she had to go into her lab."

"We know," Cam said. "And dinner's all planned—but we don't know when to start anything. How she wants the table. We just realized we don't have a big enough pan for the ham. And she usually decides which dish to make the vegetables and potatoes in."

Sam waited a minute, but that seemed to be the gist of all the stress. Nothing that affected world peace, as far as he could see.

"Okay. Here's a plan. I brought a major-size pan for the ham just in case there wasn't one here at the cabin. For everything else, make whatever decisions you want. Fill me in if I can help. I'll take on the rest. And we'll tell Poppy anything that goes wrong is all my fault."

They went for it. His brothers should be so easy to appease. Sam started dropping parcels, carting some to the kitchen counter, some by the tree, trying to take in the rest of the situation, just in case any more problems were begging to show up.

And of course there were. The fireplace was smoking—someone didn't know much about how to light one. Bubbles was already eyeing a coffee cake on the counter. And finally he got a first look at Poppy's dad.

George was tall and lean. He had the girls' dark auburn hair, but his was liberally streaked with silver. He was a good-looking guy—hardly a surprise, considering he had three gorgeous daughters. He'd parked in the big easy chair, was sipping from a fresh steaming mug of coffee, and appeared settled in for the day.

He reminded Sam of a ship captain—his blue eyes concentrating on some far-off land, appearing pensive and thoughtful. He glanced up when Sam walked in, offered an immediate jovial smile.

Sam reached out a hand. "George? Pleased to meet you. I'm Sam Cooper. Great to share a Christmas Eve with you."

"Feel just the same. Sit down, sit down, have some coffee. I'd love to hear what you do, where you live, all that."

He would have liked to do just that, but the place really was a mess: the smoking fire had to be handled first, then the coffee cake rescued from Bubbles. They needed to get ham in the oven, and the packages dealt with, and the table set. George was oblivious.

Sam told himself he should have been prepared, but until then, he hadn't really believed their father was capable of ignoring everything around him.

"Give me a minute to handle a couple things," he said. "Then I'll be back for a talk."

"Sure, sure . . ."

The smoking fireplace, first. Somehow the flue had been partially closed, and the fire built a little too fast. A window opened helped the smoke escape.

Cam and Marigold framed him. Marigold had made the fire. "What'd I do wrong?"

"Nothing, you did fine. But in an old fireplace like this, you must always check to make sure the flue is completely open."

"Sam." Cam wasn't quite through wringing her hands. "It's after one already. Don't you think Poppy should be here by now?"

"I don't see how she could possibly get here before now. It's a couple hours there and back. We don't know what the problem was. But she had to need time to assess what was wrong. And she'd have called if something was going to affect her getting here by midafternoon."

Cam quit twisting her hands together, frowned at him. "You're right."

"I'll be darned. I'm not sure I ever heard those words from a woman before. It may take me time to recover from the shock."

There now. Not just a smile but a punch on the arm. It was his turn to grin.

"How about if we get everything started? Dinner should be around the same time, or maybe just a little later. If I understand Poppy's text, there was a mistake in some grant she was working on. One of her college students—Jonas—discovered that some figures were wrong. She said he was the numbers guru on the project, so he was really freaked at finding the goof. A lot was at stake."

"But that's *work*," Marigold said incredulously.

"Yeah." He'd assumed Poppy had sent them the same information. And maybe she had. But it was pretty obvious that nothing had gotten through. "Somehow, I can't imagine Poppy letting something important get ignored, just because of a hurricane or a tornado or a snowstorm, can you?"

Cam started laughing. "No."

"She'll be here," he said reasonably. "She'll probably be tired and crabby and hungry. She won't have forgotten it's Christmas Eve. She'll just be trying to do fifty things at once."

Now Marigold picked up a grin. "That's our sister."

"So. I figure I'll take on the ham, just because it's such a heavy sucker. I brought over a big cooker in case you needed it, but it's still in the truck. I'll pop out to get it. Nothing like that is ever a problem in my clan. We all have so many big meals together that we always have cooking gear. Anyway. You want your ham rubbed with brown sugar, sealed up, or some other way?"

"I can't believe it. You know how to cook?"

"My mom wasn't about to raise three boys who couldn't

cook—and do dishes. We're all used to chipping in for the big meals. It's no sweat. So, Cam, if you could find the tinfoil and brown sugar, I'll start on the ham. And Marigold, I see all those gifts under the tree." He scratched his chin. "I could have sworn you all said you weren't going to exchange presents this Christmas."

"Well, that's what we agreed to. But we both thought Poppy needed presents. *We* don't need anything. But we thought she did."

"Well, I can see from the bedroom doorway that her bed's heaped with packages. So apparently she ignored the rules and bought stuff, too, just never had time to wrap anything. I'm thinking—how can we make this all go a little more smoothly? Marigold, how about if you take all her presents, all the presents under the tree—and put everybody's gifts in grocery sacks and mark who they're for? That way, everyone's presents will look the same. And no one will feel bad if theirs aren't wrapped—"

"Like Poppy's. And I get to see hers and everyone else's ahead of time." Marigold offered a happy Cheshire-cat grin. "What a great idea, Sam."

Questions kept coming. They didn't want to start cooking anything, veggies or potatoes or setting a table or whatever, because they didn't know how Poppy would want something done.

"What?? She used to yell if you didn't do something her way?"

"No." Cam looked at him as if he were nuts. "You know

Poppy. She's not a yeller. But we always include her. Partly because she's so good at organizing everything."

AN HOUR LATER Sam corralled the sisters over the kitchen counter, taking a break with the rest of the coffee cake. "Can I share something private with you two?" he asked.

"Of course you can."

"Well—I suspect you know this, but Poppy loves you two more than life."

"And we love her back the same way."

Sam nodded. "A few years ago, I lost a woman I'd been positive I wanted to marry. She felt I never gave her enough attention."

Cam hesitated, but then said cautiously, "Are you saying we should be giving Poppy more attention?"

"No. I'm saying that I learned the hard way that it's too darned easy to assume what someone else needs. I had no idea what this woman wanted or needed in her life. She needed something different entirely than what we were doing. I felt bad. I thought I knew her. And hurting her really made me think about what I did wrong."

"Honest to Pete, that person sure doesn't sound like Poppy."

"She isn't," Sam agreed emphatically. "In fact, Poppy is almost the exact opposite of that lady. For instance . . . Poppy doesn't like being noticed. She doesn't like drawing attention to herself. Am I wrong?"

"You've got that dead right," Marigold affirmed.

"So, how I love your sister is obviously different from how you love her. And you've known her much longer besides. But from what I've noticed, she really has trouble finding a stop button."

Cam foraged in a holiday tin for a cookie. "You mean she can't stop working until a problem is solved, or a project is finished . . . or if someone's unhappy, she's trying to help them."

"Yeah, that's what I've been thinking, too. She doesn't need more attention—or less. Attention isn't remotely an issue for her. But what I think—if I'm going to be the right guy in her life—is that I have to find a way to shut the door. Turn out the lights. Hide her phone."

"She needs balance," Cam said. "That's exactly why she's been so worn out. She never stops. And there's no point in trying to reason with her. She just digs her heels in even harder."

Marigold frowned. "Maybe we could try harder just to talk about silly things, instead of problems. Not responsibilities. Things like where would you go on vacation if you could go anywhere? Teasing her. Not asking her for advice all the time, just being with her."

"Teasing mercilessly is a sister-acquired skill," Cam said.

"I have two brothers, so believe me, I know how that goes. I can't do what you two sisters can do. But I can make sure she gets some peace time. Some renew-the-spirit, do-something-new, lazy happy time."

"Hey, Sam?" Cam interrupted the conversation with a determined gleam in her eye. "You're more than a little serious about her."

"Are you trying to tell me something I didn't know?"

She chuckled. So did Marigold, but the youngest sister added, "You think you can rein her in, you'll have to rope her into a chair, Sam. Maybe even try a padlock."

"I know. I know. It's hard work. But someone's got to do it." He didn't add that he didn't want any other guy doing it.

He glanced at the clock. It was pushing around two thirty. Dinner couldn't be ready before four thirty, which was fine. He just hoped Poppy didn't come home *too* soon, because he had yet another one-on-one he needed to tackle.

"George . . ." He ambled over to the couch across from Poppy's dad. "Is it too early for a little nip?"

George brightened. "Not too early for me."

Chapter Thirteen

POPPY WAS BREATHING guilt, smelling guilt, tasting guilt, itchy with guilt. And that was before she finally got back to the cottage and found no places to park. The family—and Sam— were all here.

She'd left everything for them to do.

It wasn't as if she'd forgotten the time. But once she and Jonas were in the lab, poring over their study and the complete grant proposal—well, it wasn't as simple as just finding and correcting a mistake.

This *was* an actual crisis.

On the surface, the mistake was just a numerical error, no different than a typo. But because it skewed the results—in their favor—it could easily look as if Poppy had deliberately altered the results to get the grant.

Jonas would be all right, not just because she could protect him, but because the blame would fall on her—as it should. She was the boss; she was responsible. Her whole career and hard-won reputation would be on the line if she turned in suspicious data. It only took seconds for a scientist to lose her credibility, and shorter than that if the scientist was a woman. She'd have to start from scratch and prove herself all over again before anyone would ever give her a chance at another big-money grant like this one.

Uncovering the problem wasn't that challenging, because Jonas had done the work—gone over his own research and discovered the data numbers in question. It could be fixed—and hopefully before the grant was expected to be electronically delivered right after Christmas. But it couldn't be done in seconds. Much less in one day.

Poppy shooed Jonas back to his family for the holiday and then knuckled down for another hour. Now that she knew the problem, she couldn't just leave it. She needed to organize a plan of attack, set up a timetable, and establish a check and recheck system to prevent this from happening again. Finally, she felt prepared enough to lock up and leave.

The whole drive home, though, she kept thinking of everything she'd left for her family to do—the cooking, the setup, all the preparations for the holiday dinner. And Sam had to cope with her family alone—including her dad, who could be a handful.

Cripes, her presents weren't even wrapped.

Actually, Sam's present couldn't be wrapped—but that was beside the point.

At the cottage door, Poppy pasted on a hard-core joyous

smile and turned the knob, quickly letting out a wildly happy "Merry Christmas Eve, everyone!"

As if Sam had been waiting at the door, he reached her first—and had a wineglass waiting for her. He held her drink as he helped her shimmy out of her parka and snow gear, blocking her view of the family at the same time. "Poppy, you look gorgeous," he murmured.

Had he been drinking? She looked like worn-out dishwater, not that she could help it. She just said, "Sam," and then let his arms fold around her.

The hoard still made it through to her, but Sam, thankfully, could run interference in a hurricane. The sisters surged first, with kisses and Merry Christmases and you look so great, Poppy. She could smell dinner. She could see the table set, with even a couple of candles in the center. A cluster of grocery bags were nested under the tree, and Bubbles muscled in for her kiss and a petting. The fire was blazing and popping, bright and warm as sparklers.

Even her dad cornered her for a massive hug. "Hey, Poppy. I like your young man."

Good grief. How much could he have had to drink this early?

Sam ushered her to the couch and parked her next to him, with Bubbles guarding her other side. Poppy never expected to relax. She never expected to relax again in this life. But it was all so much easier than she'd expected. Anxieties and worries petered out. The chores were done, everybody happy, no one complaining, no one wringing hands.

And then, out of the blue, Marigold and Cam approached her, so close they could have been joined at the hip. They pulled up two chairs, clicked their wineglasses to hers, ignored Sam—they had *never* ignored Sam yet—and then smiled at her.

Just smiled. Suspicion sped up Poppy's heartbeat. Something was caving in. She just didn't know what it was yet.

"You two okay?"

Cam nodded. "We're both happy as clams. And dinner's about ready. But neither of us are putting food on until we have a couple minutes to talk to you."

"Go for it," Poppy said, already braced for Armageddon.

Cam clearly had been elected to take the podium. "When you texted that you had to go into the lab this morning—well, it obviously had to be a serious problem."

Poppy frowned. "It was. And honestly, it was a really serious problem."

Cam nodded. "We get that. Only we don't know what that means because you never talk about what you're doing. Like you never really explained what this grant was all about."

Poppy's eyebrows lifted. "Say what? I used to tell you bits and pieces about my work all the time—but your eyes always crossed. I got it, honest. Most of the world doesn't get orgasmic over microorganisms or percentages of deviant chemical compounds and all that."

"We forgave you a long time ago for being brainy, sis." Marigold's turn to sound downright mature. "We know you can't help it. You know we're going to blank out when you talk about algorithms and other mathematical crud like that. But when you took off this morning—Christmas Eve morning—we knew it had to be more serious than that."

"It was," Poppy admitted again. "There was a mistake in the grant we are supposed to submit in just a couple days. If it hadn't been found—and corrected—to be honest, my job would have been at risk. Pretty much my reputation altogether. I have to admit I was pretty shaken up. Even if I didn't make the error myself, I'm responsible for it. I should have checked and rechecked—"

Cam interrupted. "Wait a minute. You made a mistake?"

"*You?*" Marigold echoed.

And suddenly they both jumped up and surged toward her. "We're so proud of you, Poppy! Good for you! Good for you for screwing up. Good for you even more for telling us!"

"We want to hear more. But I'm afraid dinner's going to burn. We really have to eat." Cam's tone was apologetic.

She got one more hug and then the sisters hiked toward the kitchen. Poppy finished her last gulp of wine, glanced at Sam. "Did you put them up to that?"

"Not me. I don't think anyone did."

"It sounded . . . planned. They ambushed me."

"Yup. Sounded that way to me, too. I liked it. That they were proud of you for making a mistake."

"Yeah." Poppy still couldn't quite put her head around it. But it seemed like . . . it sounded like . . . it felt like . . . they were try-ing to help her climb off the Mom Pedestal. Tell her she didn't always have to have the answers.

Maybe they'd actually been hearing her?

"This feels like a downright miracle," she murmured to Sam. Then they both popped up to help bring dinner together.

Poppy organized serving plates and servers. Camille lit can-dles. Sam said grace. The brown-sugar-coated ham was more tender than any she'd ever baked, the potatoes tastier, the salad perfect.

All three sisters saw Christmas as an ideal time to remem-ber their mother, so dinner conversation started with their fa-vorite mom stories. George talked about the challenges and politics of his current sculpture project. Everyone found a way to chip in.

Poppy sat back, loving this. Her sisters really glommed on to Sam—no question they liked him. They took extra pleasure in telling embarrassing stories about her—but that was okay. Sam had enough siblings to know that game. Their dad had a mae-stro baritone when it came to singing carols, and he devoured dinner with as much enthusiasm as the rest of them.

Poppy could feel it building—the Christmas spirit. The lights, the love of family, the snow outside, the personal memories of their mom. Through thick and thin—and all the hardships—the sisters had cleaved together. "Like glue," Cam said. "Anyone in trouble, the other two were there. Always."

They were. Maybe Poppy knew how hard she'd tried to help

her family come together and stay together—but they all did their share.

Marigold finally stood up. "I can't eat another bite, as good as the desserts look. So why don't we rest, do a few presents now? I'll hand out."

"How come you get to hand out?" Poppy teased.

"Because I'm the most beautiful, the youngest, and the most talented," Marigold said without missing a beat. "Also because"—she glanced at Sam—"Sam said I could."

"Oh, well. If Sam spoke, I don't think anyone would dare argue."

Sam held his head in his hands.

Poppy's eyes met his a half-dozen times. Maybe a whole dozen. Every once in a while she caught a pensive expression on his face—as if he were thinking about something serious—but it wasn't as if she had the chance to ask him about it. This just wasn't the time or place. And she didn't know how he'd accomplished it, but he'd clearly waved a magic wand over her family. They were having fun, acting easy and relaxed. All their Christmases had been special, Poppy had always believed. But not like this. Each of them—including her—just seemed to be . . .

Happy.

"Okay," Marigold ordered, as if she'd been giving orders her whole life. "Everybody gets a grocery bag with their name on it. If anyone doesn't like what they got, that's okay. Just give it to me. I'll either eat it, wear it, pass it on, or sell it."

Out came the loot, which was pretty similar to most years

except there were more cries of *I love, love, love it!* And *Is this perfect or what?*

Her dad opened the fresh shirts and gave a hearty laugh. "Thank heavens. I don't think I have a shirt in the house that doesn't have paint or clay or solvent on it!" But then he glanced up. "But what's this, Poppy?"

Poppy saw the envelope her dad held up, but she'd never seen it before. From the corner of her eye, she caught Sam giving her a quick wink. She cocked her head but gave her dad the obvious answer. "It looks like a Christmas surprise to me."

Her dad slipped open the envelope and read the contents with a confused frown. "Call the Mrs.? I'm not sure what that is?"

Sam wandered close to her dad, took a glance at the letter that was confusing George, and then plunked down next to Poppy again. By accident, he moved a little closer. His arm, even more accidentally, rested behind her back. But she was pretty positive the teensy pinch *wasn't* an accident.

"Well, I'll be darned," Sam said to her dad. "I know that service. My mom gave it to my uncle a few years ago when he was stuck with a broken ankle."

"What kind of service? It says it's for six months." George showed everyone the form letter.

"So it does." Sam nodded. "What I remember is that my uncle didn't like strangers in his house, but for a few months, he just plain needed some help. So this service does all kinds of things. Like grocery shop. Or cook. Or do laundry and clean.

Or pick up prescriptions or take your car in to have it serviced. You tell them what you need done. Simple as that."

It might be "simple as that," but Poppy had never heard of it before. She wished she had. It was an ideal thing to try on her dad. She just wasn't the one who'd thought of it. She leaned closer to Sam, looked up into his big, bad eyes. "You're in big trouble with me," she whispered.

He laughed, as if she'd told him a joke. "I hope that's a promise," he murmured back.

Marigold and Cam were both entranced by the gift and gave Poppy a double thumbs-up. Marigold tried coaxing her dad into loving the idea. "This doesn't mean we'll visit you any less, Dad. But this way we'll be able to spend less time doing chores, and more time just being with you."

Clearly George wasn't as excited as his daughters. "You're making me feel guilty, Poppy. I never thought I was asking you to do too much."

Cam was close enough to mutter a whisper. "A little guilt won't hurt him. You go, girl." And in a normal voice, kicked in, "That was a brilliant idea, sis."

Poppy flashed her eyes at Sam again. "Did anyone ever tell you that you lie like a rug? I never guessed."

"I have a couple other hidden talents I haven't had a chance to mention to you yet."

He was having so much fun. And since he'd invented this idea entirely on his own, Poppy figured she needed to show him that she could keep up. She shot her most loving smile at George. "I just wish I'd thought of it before, Dad. We all want you to enjoy your art, your work—and not have to worry about distractions. I hope this will help."

And that was it. The only sticky moment. Except when Sam got up and bent behind the tree and brought out the last present—a two-foot-long skinny package, wrapped in green paper with an eaten-up red bow. He raised a hand to get the group's attention. "For the record, everyone, Poppy refuses to give me a present until tomorrow. So I'm not giving her the present from me until tomorrow, too. But tonight, I had to give her this. And on the beat-up bow . . . well, Bubbles helped me wrap it."

Bubbles lurched to her feet, clearly wanting credit for whatever was making everyone happy. Poppy unwrapped the curious package slowly, looking at Sam. "I can't imagine what this is."

"It's a very, very important present," he assured her. "It nearly broke the bank, it was so expensive. And rare. I could hardly find anyone who was selling anything like it."

She looked at him suspiciously. "I'm guessing you want a whole lot of brownie points for this?"

"I do, I do. I earned them. Trust me on this."

"Sam. I do trust you. But I've come to notice—especially recently—that you have some unexpected credentials in shenanigans."

"Me?"

And then she opened it. At first she couldn't figure out what it was. A long sterling silver handle—gorgeous—ending with something? A clamp of some kind?

He whispered, "It's a marshmallow stick. For cooking marshmallows over a fire outside."

"Sam! A sterling silver stick for marshmallows?!" She threw her arms around him, half shaking her head, half laughing. "You nut!" And then she stopped laughing long enough to kiss him. Kisses in front of families were inevitably . . . tidy. But she tried to send him secret gifts with her eyes.

"She likes it," he told the family.

"We can all see that," George commented dryly.

Everyone stayed for another couple hours, but it was late, especially with everyone driving. Poppy split up food so everyone had goodies to take home, helped gather up their gifts, their stuff. The whole crew was still chattering, still hugging, still smiling.

Then out of nowhere, the cabin was suddenly silent—there was nothing but the Christmas lights. And her. And Sam. And Bubbles, of course.

Poppy's heart started pounding. "You did something to my family. They weren't normal. Was it alcohol? Magic? A secret spell?"

"I suspect it was all of the above with some plain old happiness thrown in." Sam scratched his chin. "But I guess, right about now, you have something you want to talk to me about. And I've got something serious I need to ask you, too."

"Yikes. That sounds serious."

"Nothing so heavy it should upset our Christmas. But I do think we'll both feel better if we clear up a couple of touchy things."

"Sure. Wine?" she asked.

"How about half a glass? This won't take that long."

There was a bottle open somewhere. Malbec, she thought. Someone had opened it, but it was still almost full. She poured two glasses and carried them back to Sam by the fire. "Okay, on my dad's present, if you were afraid I was going to call you a scalawag—"

"A scalawag? Say what?"

"For buying my dad that Call the Mrs. present and making out it was from me. That was a real scalawag move. But I can't very well yell at you when I thought it was an incredibly thoughtful thing to do. And I appreciate it hugely. But, for the record—if we'd just had two seconds to ourselves, I'd hope you would have asked me first, talked it over, before you just did it."

"We haven't had those two seconds, Poppy."

"I know. The last whole week seemed like a nonstop roller coaster. And I'm just saying—really—thank you. But. You shouldn't be paying for a present like that for my dad, so just tell me what the cost was."

"It's not a big deal."

Poppy waited. She could almost see the little masculine wheels whirling in Sam's brain. He wanted to pay for it. He was considering arguing with her. But then he looked straight in her eyes, then at her mouth, and finally threw up his hands and chuckled. "Okay, okay—I'll make you a deal. What I want to talk about is a little more serious. If you promise not to be mad at me for tackling something touchy, I'll tell you what your dad's present cost."

"Deal," she agreed. "But spill it quick. I want to get to the more fun part of Christmas."

"*Me, too,*" he agreed and clinked glasses with her. Both of them took a sip of wine, and then Sam crouched down to bank the fire.

"Okay. Here it is. I've been around your sisters several times now, and because they can talk a hundred miles an hour, simultaneously, I've heard dozens of family stories and traditions. I feel like I halfway know your mom, from all the things you and your sisters have said about her. I tucked in all the stories about when one of you was sick, or sad, or upset. After a while, it really got to me, that one person was never in any of those stories. Never. Not once."

She knelt down on the warm hearth next to him. "You're talking about my dad." She didn't phrase it as a question.

"Didn't anyone do *anything*? Aunts, grandparents, neighbors, teachers, someone? If they didn't intervene themselves, didn't someone at least report him for neglect?" Sam's voice was husky, a timbre of emotion Poppy had never heard from him before. Anger. But not at her. "I'm not looking to cause a rift. But you have to know this wasn't remotely right."

She tried to swallow, almost couldn't. In all these years, no one ever asked about her dad. About how the three girls had lived, how they'd coped. "We always had food. A roof over our heads."

"Poppy."

Okay. He wasn't interested in platitudes. But she didn't like remembering those old nightmares. It couldn't be helped. It was just their reality. She had to protect her sisters from the goblins under the bed, when she was still young enough to be scared of those goblins herself. "Some things were pretty rough," she admitted.

"Rough? I'd say it was beyond rough. A pack of wolves raise their cubs with more nurturing than your father showed any of you—but especially you. Maybe if a surgeon had a reason to cut open his chest, you'd find out if he even had a heart."

The image was so awful that Poppy wanted to laugh. And maybe would have if her eyes weren't brimming. The fire spit and sparkled, warming her back. Sam's quiet, low voice warmed her more. But it still wasn't a conversation she wanted to have. "When you're a kid, you don't always know when things are wrong. You just go with the cards you're dealt."

"I understand that totally. But I hope you feel proud of yourself. Really proud."

"Maybe I am. Sometimes. But there were lots of times when I didn't have a clue what to do. And even more times when I knew things weren't like they should be."

"You were neglected. Emotionally. Physically. And every

other way a child could be neglected. As far as I can tell he was *never* there. For any of you. But especially never for you."

Poppy pulled up her knees, wrapped her arms around them. She'd never seen Sam upset before. He'd never seen her this close to tears. "There were definitely a few things that happened that weren't . . . right. Like when my sister got her first period, and I didn't have a clue how my mom would have handled it. Like when I caught Marigold putting a pack of gum in her pocket at the grocery store, which we hadn't paid for. There was nothing terrible. Or dangerous. Just life stuff. We coped. No one was hurt. But around the time I was fifteen, I admit I came close to telling someone. A school counselor. Or one teacher I really liked."

"But you didn't tell."

"I thought about it."

"But you didn't tell," he repeated.

"Sam." Poppy said his name in her calmest voice. "By then I was old enough to understand that just maybe he *was* guilty of neglect. And that possibly he could have been found incompetent, incapable of taking care of us. And the thing was—if it came down to social workers and a court ruling, the three of us could have been separated, farmed out to different foster care families. I was never dead sure if my dad would fight for us. I'm not even sure—if I couldn't keep doing the mini-mom role—that he wouldn't have given us up without a fuss. Maybe he didn't need us, but we needed and only had one another. We were *family*. I had to make it work."

He said nothing for a moment. Most people found her father a brilliant artist. Some tolerated his artistic temperament, but no one had ever asked or seemed to guess that three vulnerable girls were raising themselves. Outsiders saw a loving family. The girls were all smart, good in school, never in trouble.

Only Sam, in all these years, had cut straight to that mighty uncomfortable truth. Sometimes, Poppy was pretty positive she *should* have told someone—an adult someone—how things really were. But she'd only been a kid. A zillion crises came up all the time. She'd never known for sure what she should have done. She just kept trying. To keep them all safe. Together. Through thick and thin.

Poppy couldn't guess if Sam understood the choices she'd made. But she knew, from the heart, that he hated the position she'd been put in—especially when he growled, "I think you did terrific. Beyond terrific. It's just killing me, Red. What you felt you had to take on. What you did take on. I wish to hell I could have been there for you."

Oh, yeah. He got it. "It's okay, Sam. I'm okay. We're all okay." She closed her eyes, closed the tears away. She'd done plenty of that kind of crying a long time ago. She lifted her chin, tried to add some lightness, make a joke. "I mean, we're fairly messed up, but not more than about everyone in the universe."

"Just . . . c'mere," he said, in the same low growl and opened his arms.

He folded her up in a hug. Just rocked with her for long minutes. And then rocked her some more. His heartbeat thunked against her cheek. She felt his fingers sieve through her hair, felt the encompassing warmth of him. She wasn't sure who needed the hug more—her or him—but it was different from electricity, different from desire. This was more a fierce urge to be part of him, for him to be part of her.

Sam didn't like how she'd grown up. Hey. Neither did she.

But Poppy no longer worried that Sam was trying to slow them down. Her truth was the same as his—they'd simply had no time to be together since the first and only time they'd made love.

He lifted his head, smoothed her hair again, and abruptly looked round. "I hate to say it, but this place is really a mess."

"I know. Isn't it wonderful? I always thought this was how Christmas should be. Lots of messes, lots of good smells, lots of lights. And no brussels sprouts."

He laughed. "I'm with you on the brussels sprouts—and all the rest. So let's leave it all, make sure the food's put away—then you bring a toothbrush and let's go over to my place." He added, "So I can give you your present."

"And I can't wait to give you yours."

* * *

SAM'S PLAN WAS for her to snuggle next to him on the ride to his place. That probably would have worked out if Bubbles hadn't bullied her way into the seat between them. The dog couldn't be happier.

Poppy didn't complain, but Sam really only wanted to snuzzle against one female. Noncanine.

"Dinner was super," she said. "You all did more work than I did."

"You just got stuck doing a different kind of work. And I really enjoyed the time with your family."

She tilted her head so she could see him behind the dog. "Are you going to be okay with my dad?"

"Yup." He had a feeling they'd have to dive into that subject more than once. "Whatever I may personally think—he's your father. I'll get along with him. Promise. Don't worry about it, even for a minute." He steered toward other subjects. "Everybody gave thoughtful presents. What'd you think of your sisters coming up with a full 'day spa' for you?"

"I've heard of a 'hot rocks massage' but never thought I'd get the chance to experience it. And a whole day of being spoiled witless? Really, really thoughtful of them."

"And some mysterious someone came up with the three-foot-long chew b-o-n-e for Bubbles."

"Thank you for spelling it. The last time someone said the word, I got my entire face washed with kisses. She can have it when she's settled down somewhere. Anyway . . . personally, I thought the best gift was my sterling silver marshmallow stick."

He chuckled. She was still carrying it. No way was she willing to leave it at home. "Glad you love it . . . and that I could surprise you. And one more thing on the Call the Mrs. idea for your dad. I hope he takes advantage of it, but who knows? He could like things just the way they are. I just hoped that you three—especially you—wouldn't feel quite so obligated to jump every time he calls, if he has other options."

Poppy leaned her head back. "That gift is an unspoken permission for me to say no to him, Sam, instead of jumping every time he asks me for something. I know what you were doing. Believe it or not, I think I'm actually learning to be tough."

"Yeah, you are." Maybe Sam thought she was tough as a spring rose, but what she wanted was to be tough on her own terms. And in so many ways she was breaking new ground, doing just that.

"Are you wondering what your present is?" Poppy teased.

"I'm not sure. Is it scary?"

"Nope."

"Something to wear?"

"Nope."

"Big or small?"

"I'm afraid to answer that."

"Uh-oh." Finally he pulled into his drive. "How big?"

"I'm afraid it's going to require a forklift to bring to you."

When Poppy popped out of the truck and aimed for the door, Sam had to stop for a moment, just to look at her. She mesmerized him, silhouetted against the holiday lights, the starshine, the arc of a pearl-white moon. Impossible to beat the magical stillness of a Christmas Eve night. He raised his hand. She took it, smiling up at him.

He smiled back, until it finally registered, what she'd said about his present. "Did you say your present's going to take a *forklift*? What have you done?!"

"That's all the hints you're getting, so no more begging."

Again, there were loads of things to bring in. This time, Sam steered Poppy toward the front door, where spruce boughs dripped lights over the entryway.

"A forklift?" he repeated, but then he didn't wait to hear her answer. He just wanted the chores done and out of the way. As quickly as he could, he stashed boxes and bags in the kitchen, peeled off his parka. By the time he hustled back to the front hall, she'd hung up her parka, shed boots, and came straight for him. She wanted kisses. Now. Not later. Right now. It was one of his problems with her. She couldn't keep her hands off him.

But she couldn't quit talking to him either. "Sam?"

"Hmm?"

"Now I'm worried that you're not going to like it. Or that you'll think I'm a nutcase for giving you something like this."

"I already think you're a nutcase," he assured her.

"Whew. That's a relief. Where are we going? Up? Down?"

"For a couple minutes, I have to wait for Bubbles to come in. She's still out, taking care of business."

"Okay, then I'll wait here with you. What's up for you to-morrow?"

"Going to Conan's. We rotate. But Kristin being six, this may be her last year to believe in Santa, so we're going to his house this year. And I'm counting on you to come."

"I'd intrude."

Darn woman forced him to kiss her again. "You're incapable of intruding. Besides which, this way you'll meet the whole family at the same time. They're scary for sure, noisy and rowdy and mess makers extraordinaire. On the other hand, everybody brings something, so there's lots of great food. Only there's no sterling, no fancy dishes. BYO or whatever beverage you want. It's easy. But—"

"But?"

"But you think your sisters are bad? We'll barely get there before my brothers—and the females in the family—pounce on you like meat at a carnivore convention."

"That's such a pretty image," she said wryly, but he just grinned.

"It's pretty much like meeting your sisters. Most strangers would be terrified, but it won't be remotely scary for you. You already know about people talking at the same time, and asking questions that are none of their business, evaluating our relationship without knowing a darn thing."

"That just sounds normal."

"See? I told you you'd be fine. You'll love it. And they'll love you. Aha, here's the baby." When he opened the door, Bubbles galloped into the house, shook off the snow, and galloped down the hall.

"Where's she going?"

"It's time for bed."

"Um . . . is she sleeping with us?"

"I had in mind—no. But I can't swear who'll be in bed with

us at four in the morning. She can open doors. And if a door is locked, she howls until you can't sleep and have to open it anyway."

"Sam?"

"Hmm?" He'd taken her hand, was leading her up the stairway.

"*Why* is it so easy to be with you?"

"Because. It's so easy to be with you. Which I never found with anyone else, ever. Just in case you were wondering."

When they reached his room, Sam ignored the overhead, just turned on the light in the bathroom, so Poppy wouldn't have to worry about stumbling around an unfamiliar room in the night. Still, especially for tonight, he switched on the logs in the lapis fireplace. Immediately the flames shot up, glittering gold, scattering light and shadow all through the room. The darkness blurred everything but what he wanted to see—her. Just her.

* * *

FOR POPPY, HIS sudden silence unnerved her. She had no idea why her heart picked up an uneasy drumbeat. She wasn't remotely afraid of Sam. She had no doubts about wanting to be with him. And it wasn't their first time.

But, she realized, *this* time was in his bed, his house. His world. Sam wasn't a player any more than she was. The first time had been as natural as sunshine. This time, in every way, he'd invited her into his life.

Those were much higher stakes.

Poppy hadn't changed her mind. Looking at him, she couldn't imagine changing her mind. The way he looked at her was mesmerizing, as intimate as any touch. The fireplace kept shooting ribbons of gold fire, providing soft light and smoky shadows. Enough shadows to block out everything else—but him. Just him.

He'd been talking nonstop. She was the one who usually talked nonstop, not him.

Slowly she approached Sam, lifting her hands to his shoulders. Looking straight in his eyes, she slid her hands down to the bottom of his sweater. Lifted. Carefully. All the way over his head.

The sweater flopped on the floor. His eyes, in the firelight, suddenly changed from dark to ebony dark.

"Are we through talking for a while, Sam?"

There seemed to be a frog in his throat, because his voice came out husky. "I hope so."

"Me, too." Under his sweater was a long-sleeved tee. She pulled that over his head, too. "I can't imagine why you've been worried about this."

"I'm not worried. Even remotely." Sam tried clearing the frog from his throat again. "I just need this to be right. To be perfect. And I'm not sure I know how to make this perfect for you."

"I have an idea." Her fingers found his belt buckle. The buckle was a thick heavy metal that wasn't going to give in easily—but then she'd never been one to give in easily either. "Let's both hope this goes terribly."

"You think that's a good idea?"

"I do. Then we can practice it over and over and over, until we get it right."

There. His breathing eased. That black shine in his eye was still mighty sexy, mighty serious . . . but Sam's sense of humor kicked in. "I love how you think, Poppy."

Suddenly his hands got busy. He was a lot faster than she was. Her sweater sailed through the air. Then his hands slid down to her leggings, sneaked inside to her bare skin, and then slowly, slowly skimmed them all the way down to her ankles. She kicked them away. Rather violently, for her.

"I'm not worried anymore," he assured her.

"I can see that."

"But I *was* worried. That this was too soon for you. That you weren't ready to put me on your serious list, much less on your forever list. That I was pushing you—"

She pressed a single finger on his lips. That problem needed to be nipped in the bud right now. "After I was grown and on my own, Sam, I could never pin down what was wrong with my life—for years. I knew what I didn't want. I knew what made me unhappy. But not what was right for me."

Poppy unsnapped her bra. "Then I met you. And in less than two weeks, I totally knew. You think that's fast? I think I wasted all these years *not* knowing you. Not loving you. Not going after what I really wanted in my life."

"And now you're in a hurry."

She wasn't. Until she got the darned belt buckle loose and managed the zipper. Then . . . well, she lifted both palms to his chest and pushed—just lightly, but the big man fell on the mattress as if jet-propelled.

Accidentally, Sam pulled her with him. Poppy was almost laughing when he kissed her. Then . . . not.

It only took a few more seconds to make the rest of their clothes disappear. The shock of intimacy, no-secrets intimacy, total vulnerable intimacy, seemed to inflame them both.

Closing her eyes seemed to ignite other senses. Taste—his mouth, his neck, his fingertips. Salt and sugar, cream and cool and tangy. Sounds—groans and moans, whispers and hissed-in breath. And touch—ah, touch. Every texture of him invited her, exited her. The slope of his shoulders, the sleek muscles of his upper arms, the flat of his abdomen. And then the power, the right, to touch *him*. He was long, throbbing soft, then in a fury of hot and hard.

He lifted her above him, on him, so she was straddling his thighs. Then he shimmied in, slow and deep and careful, until she was all full, all filled, filled up to her navel—or so she felt. When she opened her eyes, his gaze was on hers, intense and possessive. He started slow, silky strokes, his palms cradling her behind, giving her all the control over this pony.

Suddenly restless, she bucked to speed his pace, but Sam seemed far too greedy to go fast. He aimed for torturously slow.

Neither wanted this to be over, no matter how fierce the

yearning, how desperate the need. She'd never been lonely in her life, never had the time. But she felt lonely now, lonely to belong to him, to be enriched by him, taken by him. Loved by him.

From somewhere, he whispered, "All for me, Poppy?"

And she whispered back, "All for you. Only for you."

He turned her again, this time so she was beneath him, covered by him. She had the power to stroke, to clench, to tease . . . to shower love on him—until both of them had ridden too close to the cliff and soared off, in a gush of release and a sweet scream of satisfaction.

She was pretty sure he swore her name. She was positive she swore his. Eventually both of them started breathing again. Both of them sank into the pillows, still wrapped around each other.

She remembered touching his cheek, his neck. She remembered his slipping a sheet over them both, then a warm blanket. Then nothing, beyond the shelter of his arms.

Chapter Fourteen

SOMEWHERE AROUND DAWN, Poppy heard an odd sound—an almost imperceptible pattern of tapping.

Sam climbed out of bed before she could. He walked to the door, let Bubbles in, snapped his fingers, and the dog promptly leaped on a long couch against the wall.

"Her bed," Sam murmured and climbed back under the blankets with Poppy. He rearranged everything. Her arm across his chest. Her head snuggled just right against his shoulder. The down comforter pressed just so, so there were no air leaks, no nasty drafts getting anywhere near her. "Keep sleeping," he said. "It's crazy early."

She closed her eyes. So did he. But then he murmured, "Did I tell you I loved you last night?"

"About forty times. Did I tell you I loved you?"

"You did. But you were pretty happy, so I didn't know if you really meant it."

Her eyes popped open. "Seriously?"

"Well, if you *really* meant it, I'd think you'd want to tell me about the present that requires a forklift."

She laughed. And punished him with a tickle, which seemed to call for more kissing and murmuring sweet nothings rather than talking. Eventually, though, between Bubbles's snoring and daylight and Sam's big smile—well, it was pretty obvious that neither of them were going to be able to sleep in.

"Merry Christmas, Poppy."

"Merry Christmas, Sam. And I do think it's about time I gave you your present."

"*Finally.* Although wait a second." He stormed out of bed again, took something from the pocket of his jeans, and came back under the covers. "You first."

It was her turn to leap out of bed, scrounge around for the sweater she'd worn yesterday, unzip it, and bring out her cell phone. She opened it—once she was snuggled next to him again.

"This wasn't a present I could carry or wrap up. For now, all I can show you is a picture." Poppy took a breath. "I found this place where a guy carves pictures or script onto stones. And then I found this beautiful, huge white rock." She spread her arms out, indicating the rock's size. "About that wide and half as tall as me, which is why it's so heavy. It came from a quarry in North Carolina, so it's a mix of marble and white granite. It'll be ready in another couple weeks. I'm having it engraved to say SAM'S SLICE OF HEAVEN."

She thumbed through the pics, showing him the rock, the carver, the plan, what the finished rock would look like.

Poppy held her breath, unsure whether Sam would like it or think her idea was nuts. "I thought it could be a marker at the start of the driveway? You know, kind of helping people trying to identify your place." She hesitated. "Or anywhere you wanted it."

The longer he looked at the pics, totally silent, the more she worried it was a terrible present. But then, his eyes met hers and simply held that gaze.

"Poppy."

"Tell me."

"I haven't cried since I was eleven years old and broke my arm. And I'm not about to cry now. But I have to say that's the most thoughtful, personal gift anyone ever gave me. You *know* me."

She let out a huge, happy sigh. "I'm hoping to know you a whole lot more. Were you afraid I was going to give you a tie? Socks? Who— What's that?"

He'd unearthed a small green velvet box from his jeans' pocket, but that's all she could see; he was clutching it pretty tightly. "Now, you may not like this. And that's okay. We can exchange it for something you do like. I'm no good at things like—"

"Sam. Quit being mean. Fork over the box."

He started to. But then his cell phone bleeped a loud drum roll . . . and that call changed everything.

* * *

SAM KNEW THE instant he heard his mother's voice that there was trouble. When she said, "Now don't worry, there's no crisis," he knew immediately there was a crisis.

His dad had fallen, doing something stupid. Getting on a stepladder to get some big old bowl out of the top cupboard. "He says he's fine," his mom said. "But he fell on a hip and his shoulder. I want him to go to the ER. He won't. Your father is a stubborn goat, Sam—"

He missed some of this, because he'd heard some of those phrases before—probably most of his life.

"He says he's coming to Christmas at Conan and Karla's and I can't stop him. I don't think you can talk any sense into him. I don't think anyone can. But—"

"But," Sam said calmly. "You'd like me to come over and see what's what. So if we have to strong-arm him, there'll be two of us on the same side."

The relief in his mom's voice said it all. "He'll be mad if you come."

"I've survived his being mad at me before."

"Honey, I want to meet your Poppy. One way or another, there'll still be Christmas at Conan's. Everything could still work out just fine. I just—"

"I know. You're worried. So. Take me less than a half hour to get there. We won't make any plans or changes in plans either way. Let's just see what the situation is, decide together. He's sitting down?"

"Yes. In his chair in the living room. He's pretty much swearing nonstop because of my making such a fuss."

"You get an A+ from me, Mom. You're always the one who knows when it's time to make a fuss. I'm proud of you. And I'll be there in two shakes."

He turned around, saw Poppy pulling on clothes, looking at him with sympathetic eyes. "Your dad is hurt?"

"A pretty good fall, I gather. If he's feeling good enough to swear, he's probably okay. But my mom's shaken up."

Poppy said, before Sam could, "You have to go. Of course. I'll just head home, Sam. I can walk easily enough—"

"No. Poppy. I have to go over there, see what's what. But there'll be a Christmas at Conan's no matter what. I really want you to come. They all really want you to come—"

She shook her head. "I don't think we should plan anything or worry about it. You're going to your dad's; you may have to take him to an ER or a doctor. I'd just totally be in the way—"

"Wait. Yeah, I have to do that. But whatever happens with my dad, I'll know within a couple of hours. If he's in trouble, that's that, I'll be canceling out of Christmas at Conan's. But if Dad's okay, he'll be adamant about coming to Christmas. That's a guarantee. So I may drop you at your place right now, but I'll call you as soon as I know what's going on and what the next plan is." He loped over, tilted her chin, popped a kiss on her mouth. Then softened that first kiss into another, slower one. "I want Christmas with you, Red."

Poppy got that look on her face. The reasonable one. She was going to raise sensible, practical problems with her getting in the middle of the family's commotion.

"Please?" He added an extra punch. "It's not just for me, Poppy. Kristin will be upset if her grandpa is hurt, but she'll talk to you. Bubbles has to come because I can't leave the dog for the whole day, and you *know* she won't behave well. And my dad can be ornery if he doesn't feel well. You know how to handle ornery. You're perfect with ornery. And sooner or later the chaos'll be over and we can still have part of the day together."

She threw up her hands. "I'm on board. But only if it all works out with your dad and the doctor. You have a heap of other things to think about besides me today."

Actually, he didn't. He had a sudden sharp premonition that something wrong could happen if he let her out of his sight today.

But that was ridiculous. He never had premonitions, never claimed to have any superstitions. He just naturally wanted her with him, especially on a day that could cleave them even closer together.

Still, there was no help for starting the morning rambunctiously. He drove Poppy to the cottage—where she unwillingly admitted this part of the plan was pretty good. She could get a chance to shower and choose fresh clothes. And Bubbles, being the traitor she was, was happy to stay with Poppy.

It was a half-hour drive to his parents' place, where Sam found pretty much what he expected. His mom, Elys, answered the door and just motioned him in. "*You* try dealing with him," she said.

Taran—an old Cornish name that meant *thunder*—suited his dad perfectly. He was bear-size, like his sons, trapped in his easy chair where his mom had packed his hip and shoulder with ice bags. "She keeps yelling at me," Taran immediately complained to Sam. "I'm going to Christmas. I don't care what your mother says."

"I'm not the one yelling!" Elys yelled back. "And you're not going anywhere but to the ER. Unless Sam says it's okay for you to go to Conan's. And that's that."

"And since when do you tell me what to do?" Taran demanded.

"Since the day we met and you realized how much smarter I am than you."

"*Hah*," Taran grumbled.

Sam long knew that they could both be a handful. Especially when they were both worried about each other, for unknown irrational reasons, they took to arguing. Sam let them both rant on, pulled up a chair next to his dad, gently touched the shoulder, then gently rotated it.

"I'd know if it were broken, son. It's not. I'm going to have a couple big bruises by tomorrow. No big deal. I can sit at Conan's house no different than I can sit here. I'm not dying. I don't need x-rays."

Sam wasn't quick to believe him. "Can you stand up? Walk a bit? Show me what's happening with the hip."

"It's just a hip. I'm getting older. Naturally everything hurts now and then."

"You listen to Sam, Taran!" His mom spoke from the kitchen, where she'd sped off to start packing things up for the family Christmas. "If we're going to the ER, Sam'll take the food and presents over to Conan's."

Again, Sam ignored them both. "Dad, I want you to slowly stand up. Show me where it hurts. High hip, low hip? Is it sharp when you put your weight on it?"

"No," his dad said, sounding both surprised and relieved. "Yes, it hurts. I know it's going to be purple and blue by tomorrow. But there's nothing broken. I broke enough bones as a kid to know what a broken bone feels like. And it's not like this."

Slowly, eventually Sam capitulated, brought in his mom. "Here's what I think. I'll pack the car. Mom, you drive the two of you to Conan's—"

"Sam—"

"Hear me out, Mom. I'm going back to pick up Poppy and Bubbles and our Christmas stuff. I'll call Conan to give him a heads-up. Dad's going to behave himself, settle in a chair with some ice. We'll do a little Christmas, see how he is. If there's any sign he's in any real pain, he goes straight to the ER. But I'm pretty sure it's a reasonable decision to just wait and see for a few hours."

"I told you, Elys!"

His mom started to speak again, but Sam interrupted. "I need you to drive him, Mom, because I don't think he could comfortably get in and out of my truck. But if you two are going to squabble the whole way—"

Both claimed they never argued, and of course they could ride together peaceably.

Personally, Sam didn't see how it could possibly be harder raising kids than it was raising parents—an opinion he wanted to share with Poppy, and did, around a half hour later.

* * *

POPPY WAS READY. More than ready. She'd spiffed up, obvious in hope that Christmas at his family's was still on. Her hair was all soft and glossy; she'd added some makeup, a white velvet tunic, and Christmas-red lipstick—which quickly transferred to his lips. The kiss was too short, though. It was obvious she'd been nonstop thinking. "Sam, we should plan, in case you need to take your dad to the hospital later, and how I'd get home—do you want me to drive separately?"

He should have known. Give her a family crisis and she ran to take responsibility. "I'll handle all that. But what is all this?" He saw the mound of stuff on the counter.

"It's not my fault. I can't go to someone's house on Christmas without bringing gifts, Sam. They're not what I would have picked if I'd had time to shop. But there's a hairband for Kristin with sparkly lights. One of my handmade Christmas bulbs for your mom, another for Conan's wife. A bottle of wine. Another container of spaghetti ice cream—because I didn't have anything else homemade around. But there's also a container of cookies . . ."

SAM COULDN'T BELIEVE it. The whole Christmas to-do came together like clockwork. They'd barely arrived at Conan and Karla's before his two brothers leaped on Poppy on sight. "Our hockey buddy, and are we looking for a rematch! We're think-ing the three of us against Sam—"

Conan's wife had decorated the house within an inch of its life, some trimmings gorgeous, some clearly made by Kristin, all equally displayed. Bubbles took one look at Karla and slunk over to Kristin, where she was safe. Elys took one look at Poppy and let out a sound of delight. "Why, you're gorgeous. And here he said you were just a plain-looking woman . . ."

Poppy laughed. It was obvious she'd hold up to the teas-ing. Even better, she sank next to his dad—ostensibly to meet Taran—but mostly to have a quiet conversation with him. His dad calmed down as if someone had sprinkled him with fairy dust.

Sam parked next to Poppy at least a half-dozen times, but someone always pulled her away. Kristin, to show the presents Santa had brought her, and then to discuss them at length. The women, who started carting things to the dining table. Karla asked her for help "for a second" because she was right in the middle of mashing potatoes when their young toddler woke up and started crying. Poppy changed the baby and put her down—which started the crying again—so she hauled the little one to her shoulder and carried her around, led by Kristin, who hadn't finished her conversation yet. Eventually Sam's mom pulled Poppy aside for a secret tête-à-tête—just behind the Christmas tree—and he could guess she was being grilled.

Since Poppy was laughing with his mom, he wasn't worried that she needed saving. She was doing fine. More than fine. She fit in his family like the perfect cherry in a cherry pie.

She touched base with him. He touched base with her. But somehow the two of them kept getting separated. Maybe it was Christmas. His mom and Karla were ecstatic about their handmade ornaments. Kristin dragged her into a game involving "jewels" chasing around a board, only the toddler was with them. Sam crouched down to play with them, but then the toddler took off, trying to climb a bookcase, and by the time Sam had rescued the squirt, someone else had taken off with Poppy.

It was his mother, that time. Who'd unearthed some baby pictures to show Poppy. Like the one of him in a diaper, splashing in a mud puddle. And worse.

Finally, it was time for dinner, and before anyone could grab Poppy again, he claimed her and the seat next to her. Bowls and plates started sledding around the table, the clan all crowded into the small dining room, everyone happy—including him. Including her.

Or she seemed happy, through the salad, through the main course, until desserts were brought in. Groans of *Mercy!* echoed around the table, but no one actually turned down dessert. Poppy became more quiet, though, her attention clearly distracted.

Finally, she said, "Sam," soft as a whisper.

He leaned closer to hear.

"Just take a quick look at your dad," she whispered.

His head whipped toward Taran, but initially he didn't see anything. His dad had been having a good time, seemed to walk into the dining room okay, and certainly had piled mountains of food on his plate.

Now, though, Sam noticed his dad's plate had barely been touched. And Taran's complexion had changed from a natural ruddiness to pale. He was still talking. Still pretending to eat. But his smile was set on automatic rather than natural.

Sam almost vaulted out of his seat, but Poppy's hand on his arm steadied him. "Think for a second," she murmured. "I know what you want to do. But let's make it less chaotic so everyone isn't freaked? It'll be easier to get him out of here if everyone stays calm."

He *was* calm. Sort of. He was mad at himself for not watching over his dad more carefully—and mad at his dad for hiding that he'd been going downhill. But Poppy was right. The darn woman was downright wonderful to have around in rough times—which he could have guessed long, long before this.

"Hey, Brer?"

His brother heard him, lifted an eyebrow. Sam motioned him into the living room. Conan saw his brothers and immediately joined them. The powwow didn't take three minutes.

Sam came back to the table, calm and easy. "After a fabulous dinner like that, I suspect we'd all like to put our feet up. What a great Christmas. The guys and I are going to take off for a bit, though."

"What? Where?" His mom asked the start of the questions.

"Right now, everybody relax. But later . . . Mom, I'd like you to stay with Conan and Karla. Maybe for the night. Maybe just for a bit. When you want to go home, Conan will take you. Brer's going to drive my truck and take Poppy home. And that's so I can drive Dad in the folks' car, more comfortable for him. We're just going to have him checked out."

"Sam, I told you, I'm fine." Taran started to stand up, but then he sank back in his chair again. "I'm fine," he repeated, but a bead of sweat had shown up on his forehead. Even that slight movement turned his complexion from pale to ash.

"I think you're fine, too, Dad, but we're all going to worry unless you get checked out, have an x-ray or two. Won't take long. Promise. I'll be with you. And I'll get you home. Conan will take Mom home whenever she wants—or to the hospital if it turns out that's a better idea. Right now there's nothing for everyone to do but put your feet up, enjoy the rest of this great day. And I'll call home, just as soon as Dad sees a doc. No discussion. Let's just get this done."

The women came through, brought jackets, coats—even his mom calmed down. Taran didn't try arguing again—which scared Sam, because if Taran wasn't strong enough to argue, there could well be something seriously wrong with him. Possibly, though, seeing his three strapping sons standing together like an impenetrable wall was just too exhausting to try fighting with.

Sam finally grabbed two seconds with Poppy, starting with a kiss. "Thanks. You were right. Needed to think, put it all together before raising the fire alarm."

"You knew that without my saying anything. It's just that when it's someone you love, like your dad, you want to jump in, not slow down."

"Don't contradict me. You're wonderful and that's that. I'll call you as soon as I know anything."

"Who is Bubbles going with?"

"Brer. Whoever has the truck. But once we figure out what's happening with Dad, we'll get all the transportation organized. And you'll already be at the cottage, so you'll have your car in case anything goes on too long."

"I hope nothing goes too long. And that your dad's totally okay." She gave him a hug from her heart. "Just call me when you hear something, okay?"

"You know I will."

Brer stole her away. Sam couldn't stand there long; he wanted and needed to get his dad into the car and off. But he didn't want to take his eyes off Poppy. To him, as worrisome as part of this Christmas had turned into, it was just another measure of how perfectly they suited each other. How they communicated above and beyond. How she got him. How—he hoped—he got her.

But that was a squiggle of worry in there. Everything always seemed perfect when they were together. But when they were apart, he sensed it was harder for Poppy to believe.

Chapter Fifteen

POPPY DIDN'T REALIZE, until she got back to the cottage, that she still didn't have her Christmas present from Sam, though compared to his father's health, that didn't remotely matter now. Her sterling silver marshmallow stick was a treasure beyond treasure, but she had hoped to see what he had in mind with the small green box. The obvious was never obvious with Sam.

Still, it was foolish to think about that now. And the instant she walked into the dark, silent cottage, there was plenty to occupy her time.

Somehow, no elves had shown up to clean up the mighty mess from the Christmas Eve gathering. The food had been all taken care of, no sweat there. But another round of dishes needed to be fed to the dishwasher, and some of the fancier plates and serving dishes still needed to be hand-washed and boxed up. Ribbons and bows and wrapping paper were strewn around.

Poppy tugged off her Christmas velvets and holiday jewelry, donned sweats and a sweatshirt—then just pushed up her sleeves and dug in. She washed, cleaned, straightened, took out trash. By ten o'clock, Sam still hadn't called, which she told herself wasn't worrisome. No one ever visited the ER and escaped there fast. Even if all the news was good, there was still paperwork, nurses taking history, someone getting the insurance stuff on the dotted line, basic procedures done. And after all that, the doctor still had to come in, and order the stuff he cooked up—x-rays and/or blood work and/or whatever else he thought was a good idea.

Poppy doubted that Sam would call before midnight. And although she was tired, she wanted to be there for him, so there was no way she was going to sleep until she heard.

The chores had zapped her last zip of energy, but once Poppy walked into the bedroom, she saw her Christmas clothes, presents, other things she'd worn—and abruptly realized the painful obvious. She wouldn't be needing any of those things again. Not here.

Technically she had two more days to get packed up and moved back to Madison. Work started on the third day, Monday, and she couldn't hold off returning to the lab any longer than that. The grant crisis needed to be imminently handled.

Her real life was waiting for her. She had no way to postpone returning to it. She'd known this was coming and so had Sam. It was time for her to leave.

That didn't mean she had to stay in Madison forever, or that she always had to live in her house, or that she would never see him again. Of course she would. But trying to be "a couple" with a few hours' distance separating them would naturally change things.

Poppy tried, hard, to push all that out of her mind. She poured a glass of soda. Grabbed a cookie. Then surveyed the debris she'd accumulated over two solid weeks of living in this wonderful, magical place. Finding a wonderful, magical man.

She wanted to curl up and just think about Sam, his wonderful family, how much she liked them—how easily they'd been to talk to, be with. She'd adored his dad. Yeah, Taran was on the gruff side—but sitting at Conan's, he had been scared. A big, vulnerable strong man who just wasn't used to feeling helpless. Of course he was swearing . . . but he hadn't been swearing at her.

Sam's mom was no-nonsense, the kind of serious strong woman you'd have to be to mother three boys, all close to the same age. She'd survived it. She ruled her roost. Poppy felt as if she'd been checked out by a brain surgeon—not in a mean way—but Elys wanted to examine who Her Boy was cavorting with. Elys had clearly wanted to be certain that she wasn't like That First Woman who was as shallow as a candy dish, pretty but superficial, a girl who wanted the romance a whole lot more than she wanted a marriage. She'd hurt Sam. Elys didn't go so far as to threaten Poppy with poison or bodily harm, but she made it darned clear there'd be Big Trouble if another woman failed to appreciate a damn good man.

How could she not love Elys? Poppy would have felt exactly the same. And once they got that personal stuff out of the way, she was just drawn into being family, doing family stuff, serving food, picking up the cranky baby, taking away dirty glasses, cuddling up with Kristin, stopping to joke, to laugh, to bump hips in the kitchen.

The more Poppy thought about the day—the last two days of Christmas—the more she worked like a fiend. Thinking was making her sad. She wanted to just *do*. Outrun what was coming.

And there was plenty of "fiend" work still to do. The tree had to come down, the bulbs packed, and those boxes packed in the back of her Subaru. The clothes she wasn't likely to wear again might as well be packed and stashed in the car, same way. The Christmas dishes had to be carefully packed, so did all the extra silverware and so on.

The cabin started to look worn out and dated and a little on the shabby side. Not the home she'd savored for two weeks, but turning back into the stranger's place she'd rented. She didn't want to keep on packing. She was starting to feel so darned sad she could hardly stand it.

But if Sam had any free time over the next couple days, Poppy wanted to spend it with him—not on chores and carrying and packing. So she kept going . . . until the phone finally rang, just after midnight.

"I was afraid I'd wake you." Sam sounded beyond tired.

"You didn't. And there's no way I was going to sleep. How's your dad?"

"Not great, but not terrible. No broken bones." He took a breath. "It's so good to hear your voice."

"It's so good to hear yours. So." That pause told her there was trouble. "You're worried."

"Yeah." Poppy heard Sam pull in a long breath. "He has to stay overnight. Maybe two nights, depending. I offered to go get Mom, but he said, no, absolutely not. Mom would just fret and fuss—which is true. So I'm staying with him."

"I'd do exactly the same," she said.

"I wanted to be with you tonight."

"Me, too, Sam. But obviously family comes first. You still haven't said what's wrong."

"It's his heart. The darned fall was probably a blessing. They think he has a blockage or two. It'll take a few more tests before they set out a plan of action. Nothing's a crisis. They'll do another EKG tomorrow and then get the cardiac guy in to review the CT scan. Probably there'll be some kind of procedure involved. Stents or like that."

She tucked the phone against her ear. "But he didn't have a heart attack."

"No. And hopefully he won't. No one's saying he was about to keel over, just that there were too many signs that say it could happen—chest pain he never owned up to. Dizziness— probably what made him fall—a sign of not getting the oxygen he needed, and that means there are probably blockages. Apparently a doctor gave him pills over a year ago and he 'forgot' to take them."

"Forgot? I think I'd call that a king-size fib. He really sounds more stubborn than a mule. I'd beat him up for you, Sam, but to tell the truth, I kind of fell in love with him. Flaws and all."

There was a moment's silence from him, but then came his bark of a laugh. She could almost picture him leaning back, closing his eyes, letting loose some of that tension. "That's the first time I've laughed since I saw you a hundred hours ago. And I *should* beat him up. All he had to do was take the damn pills and get his checkups."

"I hear you. And if your mom discovers he had medication and neglected to take it, she might just blow the roof off. You really need to keep wearing your Calm Hat."

Another chuckle. "That's exactly why I'm staying with him at the hospital—so he won't be alone and she won't feel obligated to come. Although, if and when push comes to shove, she's as strong as a lion. They were both just scared today. Neither one can stand the idea of being fragile. Or of losing each other. But my mom, when she gets her strength on, can be a powerhouse of calm."

"Good family. I loved them all, Sam."

"That was sure mutual."

Poppy didn't want to end the call. Neither did Sam. But she knew he had his hands full, and likely a long day ahead of him besides. "Listen, you. Get some rest. If I can do anything, give a shout. Tell me tomorrow if I can visit him. Or if there's anything I can do for you."

"Well, I know what I *want* you to do for me, but it's not possible if we're in two different places."

He meant her to laugh, so she did. But smooth as silk, she murmured, "That's another that-goes-for-me-too—but just let me know what's what tomorrow, okay? I decided—since I only have two days to pack up here before heading back to Madison—that I'm going to get all that nuisance work done. So. Your dad and family come first. But if we can catch any time, I'll be here. Can you picture me giving you a huge seductive wicked kiss?"

For a moment Sam didn't answer. Poppy wondered if her bringing up having to return to Madison had startled him. Even though they'd both known it was coming. They'd just both blocked thinking about her having that whole different life apart from him. But maybe not. He answered in a particularly wicked whisper.

"I can picture that kiss perfectly. In fact, I'm counting on your giving me more trouble than I can handle."

"Well, that's not even a challenge."

When she severed the call, he was laughing. So was she. But alone in the cabin, as she started switching off lights, locking the door, preparing for bed, she couldn't seem to stop feeling . . . lost. Sad. Anxious. It was such a change. A total letdown from two days of constant activity, constant togetherness, constant seeing how their families related to each other. Without Sam here, there seemed nothing but this lonely silence.

* * *

SAM CALLED AT seven the next morning.

"Did you get some rest?" she asked, her own voice still groggy.

"Not really. But they took Dad for all the tests, finally got him settled down. The hotshot team came in a few minutes ago. They're going to put in a couple of stents. They say there's a risk, but not a bad one. He'll hopefully feel stronger and better almost right away. But they want him to wait one more day, to ensure he's solidly stable before the procedure, so he'll be here a few more days."

"I'll bet talking him into that was as easy as cuddling a tiger."

He chuckled. "You said it. I'm going to get my mom here, but just for a short visit, to see how she does. She'll want to be here for the procedure. And we'll need to hear what kind of preparation needs doing before he comes home. Unfortunately, I have no idea when . . ."

Sam didn't need to finish the sentence. She knew what was coming. "I understand, totally. You're stuck there. You can't guess what either of them are going to need right now."

"Conan's got his hands full. Brer will happily come, but—"

"Brer's terrific, but not with stuff like this. You're the one who keeps the clan calm and on track."

"How come you understand everything so easily?"

"Because I'm brilliant and cute and have you buffaloed about how wonderful I am?"

"Poppy. I swear you're the only one in the universe who could make me laugh this morning."

"You worried?"

"Not exactly. I think we're lucky we got here before his condition got any worse. I also think this is the time of life when parents develop medical problems like this. We weren't prepared, but now we need to be. For right now, though, I'm the one who has the most flex time, workwise, so I really feel I should be here."

"I'd feel the same. And I can come and sit with you, if you want, but I suspect you need to grab some rest when you can get it. You'll have family coming and going pretty much non-stop. And if I can get the grunt work done here—the packing and closing up of the place—then I can be free whenever you are."

"I wish I could help you with the closing up."

"I wish you could, too. It's a total pain. But it's not hard, Sam. I can get it done." Poppy took a breath. "Okay, saying goodbye with a major smooch and an even bigger hug."

"Back atcha."

* * *

THE NEXT TWENTY-FOUR hours, Poppy practically stayed glued to her cell phone. Sam called. His mom called. Sam called. Her sisters called. Sam called. Shocking her, her father called to say he'd tried the Call the Mrs. and he was amazed to discover "it was kind of nice."

Once the packing was done—except for the food—Poppy pulled on gloves and seriously cleaned the place. It was spotless when she got here. She wanted it spotless when she left.

When Sam didn't call for several hours on Sunday, she tried his cell. Conan answered. "We're all here, Poppy. Dad did great. Think we can spring him tomorrow if he behaves himself."

"And Sam? You're answering his phone?"

"I think he was up for forty-eight hours straight. When he crashed in the cot in Dad's room, we just let him sleep. But if you want, I'll wake him."

"Heavens, no. Let him rest. He knows I have to vacate the cabin by tomorrow, and it's not like I'm disappearing. I just have to get back to my job. Tell everyone I love them all? And give your dad a hug from me."

"You bet."

To cheer herself up, Poppy took her skates, one more time, to the rink by the church. She couldn't imagine the next chance she'd have to skate again. The sky was gloom gray, the rink deserted, no kids, no adults, no anyone. Still, she laced up her skates and took off, hoping to regain the feeling skating gave her. The inner peace. The power inside herself to just let go. Be who she was. Value who she was. All the wonderful things her mom had not only taught her, but showed her.

When she got back to the cabin, there was a text from Sam. She called him, but his phone went to voice mail. The next call came from her lab rats—they'd texted her that they were ready to work on the grant study as soon as she got home. Even if it was in the morning. Even if they were still on Xmas vacay.

Poppy had to smile. She was so lucky with her team. Even the youngest of the grad students loved the work, loved what they were doing. They all felt seriously great about doing something that actually mattered.

So did she.

She just really didn't want to go back, quite this fast.

She called Sam again. And again, got his voice mail. This time, she was almost glad she had to text him, because the lump in her throat was so big she doubted she could talk.

Sam. I can't believe I have to leave without seeing you first, but I really need to be at the lab early tomorrow. It's killing me not to say goodbye—but then I realized how silly that was. I'm not saying goodbye. You know where I am. I know—and you know—how crazy family responsibilities can be. It's okay. Hope to hear more about your dad when you have the chance. She added a heap of heart emojis.

* * *

THREE HOURS LATER, Poppy was back in Madison, turning on lights, looking forward—NOT—to unpacking the car. Her cell phone buzzed, giving her an excuse to sit down and put her feet up before tackling chores.

Her sisters were sharing the line, both all abuzz. How good

Christmas Eve was. How good the presents were. How was Sam's dad? Could they come over and help her unpack, make her some dinner, help her with anything? They could be at her place in minutes.

"Hold on for a minute." Poppy squeezed her eyes closed, feeling the sharp stab of stress she'd almost forgotten. The last two weeks had changed her. Sam had changed her. She'd worked at recognizing and changing herself.

Everything was better . . . but she saw how easily it would be to slip back into old habits. For her. And for her sisters. Their bubbling exuberance was wonderful to hear. Only not exactly. She'd tried to gently coax change, but sometimes you just had to aim straight for the bull's-eye to reach the goal.

"Poppy? Do you want us to—"

"No, you two. But could you both stay on the line for a few minutes?"

"Sure," Cam and Marigold both said at the same time.

"I'd rather talk in person, but somehow I keep failing to get that done. So let's just do it. I want to clear the air. About why I took these two weeks off. What was troubling me. What I wanted to fix."

"*Good.*" Cam's no-nonsense voice, strong and clear. "Let it out, Poppy."

"The reason I wanted that time off was to think through our relationship. Us. Who we are together. Who we could be."

Cam spoke first. "I don't know what you mean."

"I mean . . . when Mom died, the three of us cleaved together like glue. Maybe we had some tough times, but we took care of each other, protected each other, nurtured each other. Honestly, I don't think we could have made it without each other. I hope you feel as proud of us as I do."

"There's a 'but' in there, Poppy." Marigold rarely sounded serious, but she did now.

"But . . . I think we got into a habit of depending on each other. The three of us are family. Always will be. I can't imagine ever losing that special bond. But we really don't *need* each other the way we did when we were little."

"You think we depend on you. Too much." Cam's voice was calm, but already sounding hurt.

"Yes. I do. We're all adults now. But I think you do overdepend on me. Not because you need to. Just because it's our habit. How we made our lives work for so long."

"You didn't want us to find you? Is that what you're saying? You didn't want us to have Christmas together?" Marigold's voice turned wobbly.

Damn it. That's exactly why this issue had been so impossible to talk about. Poppy had spent a whole darn childhood trying to make her sisters feel safe and happy, so they wouldn't have to cry. And now she could hear unfallen tears in Mari's voice. And her own eyes were welling up and stinging.

"I wanted you to know that you could have had a great Christmas without me. That you don't need my approval or support or protection. You don't need me. Not anymore. Not like when we were kids."

For a few moments, there was total silence from both sisters. Poppy gulped, then tried again. "Let me say it a different way. I was only the substitute mom because you two were too little to take on the job. But I don't want that mom role in our lives anymore. I don't want to be the boss, or the organizer, or the rulemaker. I just want to be your sister."

"Well," Marigold said. "I can kind of get that."

"I never got a chance to just be a sister."

"You're whining now." Cam's teacher voice.

"It's not *our* fault you always took on those jobs, Poppy." Marigold.

"None of it's your fault. None of it's my fault. It's just the way the cookie rolled out after Mom died. We just never stopped to think about changing the rules."

"Maybe because you were the only one who wasn't happy?" Cam, again, not willing to let go. Not willing to cry. Just upset.

"Here's part of the problem. My problem. I do want to be a mom. But to my own kids. If I ever get married. If I ever have any."

"*Of course* you're going to get married."

Cam still had more to say. "I never thought I acted over-dependent on you. Needy. Glued at the hip. I just always wanted you to be the first person I told when something important happened. If you don't want that—"

"Quit sounding hurt, Cam. You were never anything like a needy Nelly. But we all trust one another so *tight*. Neither of you need a mini-mom anymore. You don't need my advice or approval, not like you did. *Don't* misunderstand me. I wanted to be the best almost-mom you could have. But I need something different now—and I think you two do, too."

"I'm listening, Poppy." Marigold sounded thoughtful.

"I don't want to be less close. I want to be close in a different way. I just want to be another sister. I want us all on the same level. And I need your help to do that. I pushed you out of the nest when you were old enough. Now I want you to push me out."

"Poppy, you're older than we are. And you've achieved so much on your own—"

"Work stuff, yes. Academics, yes. But I haven't achieved anything personal, Cam. I really never risked leaving the nest I had with you two. But now, I need to create my own life. It's so past time. I need to take risks. To own my own life. Don't you both feel the same way?"

"Sheesh, Poppy. You don't have to go on and on. I got it. But I need to think about it all, before I have anything else to say." Marigold was obviously ready to ring off.

Cam, not quite so fast. "I'm upset."

"I know. I can hear it in your voice. It's killing me."

"I don't want to talk to you. For at *least* a day."

Well, in spite of herself, that brought on a smile. At least a small one. "A day? A day is all you expect to be upset?"

"I just don't have time to hold grudges. And someone's at the door. Talk to you in a day or two."

Poppy heard the click, knew Cam had hung up as well. She let out a huge sigh, as if not realizing how long she'd been holding her breath.

Maybe this cake wasn't fully baked yet, but finally, all the ingredients were in and the oven on. Change just couldn't happen overnight. The big things, the serious things, all took time to really change. But for the first time since she was eleven, Poppy felt lighter, easier. More certain that she could identify what she needed and wanted in her life.

And now more than ever, she couldn't wait to see Sam again.

* * *

ON WEDNESDAY, SAM parked on the street by Poppy's house around three. He'd had it. Five days was enough of all this flimflamming around with texts and missed calls and voice mails. Obviously midafternoon wasn't a good time—unlikely she would be home from the lab this early, but he wanted to see her place. Do a few things. And since both her sisters had offered him a spare key to Poppy's house, he'd graciously agreed.

He liked the neighborhood—all grown-in trees, lots of stone and brick. And her house was small, but one of a kind. The architecture included the gables, a massive window in the arched roof, pretty brickwork, casement windows.

When he turned the key, his eyes took a moment to adjust to the dim light, but it didn't take a brain surgeon to find light switches. Sam plopped a grocery sack in the kitchen, then rambled around the first floor for a few minutes, just doing a basic discovery tour.

The house was likely built in the 1940s, no youngster, but it had seriously good bones. Poppy hadn't quite moved in yet—but he'd half expected that. He didn't know how many years she'd owned the place, but she'd been insanely busy from the time she was a kid.

There was no reason to put up paintings and personal stuff if you were only crashing here. He suspected Poppy wouldn't say it quite that way, but she'd the same as told him. She had no time for herself. Never had.

Now, hopefully, she would.

He poked, opened doors, kitchen cupboards, headed upstairs, and found Poppy's one sanctuary—a mighty inviting office. The ceiling was slanted too low for him to stand up except in one spot, but it was clearly her place, not meant for anyone else. Here were the pictures, the ancient curl-up-in chair, the purple throw to ward off drafts.

Sam smiled as he clomped back downstairs, set his overnight bag in Poppy's bedroom—hey, there was only one bedroom. And he wasn't leaving until he'd finally caught up with her.

Back in the kitchen, he turned on her oven, opened cupboards until he found the right-size pan, opened the fridge for other stuff. Not much. He'd brought what he needed to make Bengal tigers—a chicken recipe his mom had given him years back, because it was male-proof. That was meant as an insult, he understood at the time. But she was right. You could forget it for an hour or two and it'd still come out tasting good. He didn't know how or why. He just knew it took fifteen minutes to throw together, add potatoes to bake, and still have time to chill some white wine and dark beer.

SAM NEVER HEARD a car drive up, but he picked up some kind of sound—a thump on her front porch? Either from bootsteps or possibly she'd dropped something. Either way he sprang to his feet and surged to meet her, throwing open the door.

Only it wasn't Poppy.

It was a guy. Sam sized him up in a millisecond. The guy was good-looking, if you liked a sharp Gallic nose and a boxy frame with no neck. Sam could smell his too-fresh aftershave. He was wearing a wool coat instead of a parka. Shoes instead of boots. His hair had that fresh-barbered cut, his face shaved within an inch of his life.

Sam could smell a predator at fifty paces. He really didn't need to analyze the rest of the details.

"Hey," he said cordially. Since he happened to be carrying a kitchen towel, he feigned wiping his hands dry, as if he were familiar with her house, her towels, and everything else inside the place. "I'm Sam Cooper. And you're . . ."

"Gary. Gary—"

Sam missed the last name, mostly because he wasn't listening, didn't really care. He snapped his fingers. "I know about you. Feel as if I almost know you. You went to school with Poppy—"

Gary's mouth dropped. "You knew about that?"

Of course Sam didn't. But the guy looked the same general age as Poppy. And he was here. And wearing a winsome smile when he put up a hand to knock on the door—although the winsome had worn off fast when he saw Sam.

"Sure," Sam said. "She loves telling stories about growing up here, her school days—I'm sorry, she's not home from work yet. Was she expecting you?"

"No," the guy admitted.

Thankfully that was the right answer. Sam wasn't expecting a difficult situation, but it was so much easier to be kind. Gracious. The Bigger Man. "Well . . . would you like to leave a message? I'd ask you in—but we planned quite a special evening once she gets home."

"No, no. I didn't want to interrupt. You don't even have to tell her I was here. I was just going to say hi."

Yeah. And cows danced. "Well, I'm glad to meet you. I'll tell Poppy you came by." Sam waved, en route to slowly, graciously closing the door.

He'd bet the moon and back that Poppy had quite a few of those hard-to-get-rid-of guys from her school years. Some men just had to be squished down before they got the message. It was hard to deal with a predator when you were five foot four. Much easier when you were taller than he was and had the muscle to go with it.

Getting rid of the guy almost started Sam whistling. But not quite. Nothing was going to shake off his nerves until he could see Poppy again.

They were so good together, but being separated was a whole different ball of wax. Poppy was just defining her own brand of strength, learning to give herself permission to . . . well, to be the woman she wanted to be, on her own terms. Sam had been afraid, because of falling in love with her so fast and hard, that he'd screw up. He'd screwed up once—badly. *Now* he knew easily that was never the woman for him, but that was the difference.

Poppy was. The one and only woman. For him.

But with their crazy lives—and crazy families—it was going to be challenging to make it all work. If not impossible. Unless she felt the same.

* * *

POPPY NOTED AN unusual number of vehicles were parked on her street, from trucks to cars. Since it was Wednesday night, she figured someone was likely having a party or maybe a family gathering. It wasn't a problem, easy enough to wiggle around them and pull into her own drive.

Her house had lights on—which was weird, since she always turned off the lights when she left in the morning. But this workweek had been a frazzler. Finally, the grant project was done, perfect, sent out, legally protected, the whole shebang. The staff were as exhilarated as she was—and probably just as worn out.

She hoped she wasn't out of peanut butter, because she was too darned whipped to cook dinner.

Poppy opened the door before she realized that she was still holding the key in her hand and hadn't needed it. So she'd left the house unlocked all day? Open all day? Maybe it finally happened. She'd lost her mind.

She dumped her work bag, her purse, her gloves on the table by the door, had one sleeve out of her coat when she saw him. Sam.

Now she was *really* worried she'd lost her mind. Obviously she was dreaming him. Scarier yet, the dream came with wildly realistic details. His unbrushed hair. His black-and-white flannel shirt. His eyes homed in on her face like lasers locking on a target, a smile on his lips that wasn't quite steady. He was holding a spatula.

Imagine having a dream that included Sam holding a spatula. It was more than she could handle. She galloped toward him, dropping her jacket midstep, and pretty much jumped in his arms. "It *is* you. I thought I was dreaming you. If I *am* dreaming you, for Pete's sake, don't wake me up. I've been so worried."

"About my dad? He's fine."

"Not about your dad. You texted me all the stuff about your dad. About us. How we were ever going to do this. How we could possibly make it happen. Whether I was dreaming to think we could find some way to pull it all together. Whether I was losing you."

"You couldn't lose me." Obviously she had to kiss him. Seriously kiss him. She watched his eyes close, then closed her own. There it was. The haunting taste of him. The sinking in. The texture of his mouth, his tongue. The way his tough, strong body molded perfectly against hers.

And yeah, the way fire sprung between them, those kisses expressing urgent words, hot needs, the wildness they found together. But her face suddenly reared back, looked at him. "I smell something burning."

"It's not burning but it's really close. Figured you'd be hungry."

"I am. Starved. Missed lunch. But I'm not *that* hungry for food, Sam. It'll wait."

"But I need to feed you. And me. Before it burns. And because we have stuff we need to talk about before we get to 'us' time."

"Okay. I'll eat fast." Poppy smiled at him, a private smile, and then was about to stampede into the kitchen before she noticed the living room. "Whoa. What's going on here? Some kind of game?"

In the center of the carpet, Sam had apparently been playing with money. He'd used rope to make four lines within a circle. One line held silver dollars; the next held two-dollar bills, then the quarters, and the last was a pile of bright copper pennies.

"Let's get plates, and I'll tell you. How about if you sit and I just serve us?" Sam brought in the beer and wineglasses, so she could pour. Next, silverware, since he forgot it. Then finally he came back with plates covered with Bengal tigers, hot buttered potatoes, beans that he claimed had been cooked with dried cranberries and a little maple syrup.

"Wow. Are you kidding? I'm never cooking, Sam, if you can come up with chef-style dishes like this. That really does look a little like a tiger." She tasted. "Mmm. You really slayed it. Totally delicious." But her gaze was focused on the rope lines dividing the strange variety of currency. And on the small green velvet box that had suddenly appeared right next to her wineglass.

Her gaze kept bouncing around. From the circle. To the box. Back to the circle. Back to the box. To the circle. Then back to the box.

Then to his face. Just his face.

"This looks pretty confusing, Sam," she said gently.

"I know." He scratched his chin. "I was afraid if I just started talking, I'd bumble it. And I wanted to cover some extremely serious things. Before kissing you. If I didn't create some kind of convoluted nonsense to get us through this, I'd kiss you before I got the big stuff said. Poppy."

"I'm here."

"I have some huge stuff to say."

"It's okay. We'll get past the convoluted. Survive any bumbling. It's going to work out. I'm about a hundred percent positive."

He pointed a finger at her. "Don't let me start kissing you until I get this done."

"We'll see. I'm not promising." Night had come on strong. The windows reflected nothing but black sky with a wink of starlight. Only shadowed lamplight illuminated where they were. Sam's face was always strong, his eyes always gentle. But Poppy rarely saw stark vulnerability in Sam. Now she saw it, soft as a heartbeat, in the way he looked at her.

He was the real thing, she mused. Her pulse simmered like a promise waiting to bubble up and happen. Like a moment she never wanted to forget.

But he was obviously trying to stay seriously serious a few minutes longer. "I drew some lines. I know that sounds silly. But we've both had trouble drawing lines in our lives. So this was just a way of making a plan. A way of looking at how we could manage our lives. But also—know we could change the plan at any time." He added firmly, "This has nothing to do with loving you."

She was 110 percent certain it did. But she said, "Heavens. Don't worry. That never crossed my mind."

"Okay. So here's the idea. The line with all the silver dollars— that's about you and me. The two of us are in that lane. No one else. We take care of each other, put the two of us first. We protect each other, from all the bad people. But also from all the good, wonderful people who love us, but sometimes demand too much of our time. Okay so far?"

"Totally okay," Poppy agreed. And since he set down his plate and sat on the carpet, so did she. Not too close. Just hip-bumping, knee-grazing close. Not kissing close, but just in case that possibility came up, neither was going to need a five-mile hike to get there.

"We can move any of the lines, Red. This isn't about my making the rules. It's about both of us considering how to establish our priorities."

"Got it."

"So the line with the two-dollar bills—two-dollar bills are rare. Because we both know that sometimes, we have to change the rules and do what we have to do. You can't plan for everything. There'll always be crises that come up, because that's how life is—but that doesn't have to mean it's a crisis for *us*. It just means we have to think up unusual solutions, color outside the lines, to find solutions for those. A crisis doesn't have to be bad. Doesn't have to be scary. Actually, I think it's part of the fun of being together. Two heads are always better than one. Especially your brain and my brain. We're already both problem solvers."

"I like how you think, Sam."

He frowned at her. "Not yet."

She hadn't tried to kiss him. But possibly he guessed she was thinking about it. "Go on," she urged him.

"So the quarters—they're basic currency. Family and loved ones go specifically in that line. They matter to us. They're basic and important to our lives. And we want them to have a slot of our time and attention. But they can't own every second of us."

"Got it."

"Okay. Now the last line is copper pennies. I'm using them

to represent work. You and I have completely different jobs. Always will. In the summer I work like a maniac. Can't help it. It seems like when you're in the middle of a project, you're working maniacal hours as well. That's okay, for us to have different priorities there. To respect what each of us needs to do. But I made a separate line for work with pennies—because we both love our work, need our work. It matters. But we can't let it steal all our time, all our energy."

"Got it."

"Poppy." His voice turned dead serious. "We're alike. I didn't first see it, but I do now. When there's a trauma in either of our families, we show up. That's who we are. Besides which, I hope we have half a dozen kids and all their families come over to feast with all their families. I believe in families."

"So do I."

"My family isn't perfect."

"Mine isn't either."

"But that just doesn't matter. It's like when you're on a plane with a baby and the jet engines fail. You put on your mask first. Not because you don't love the baby, but because you do. Only you can't save anyone if you don't save yourself."

Poppy didn't answer that time, because she really did understand what Sam was saying. This was exactly what she'd failed to do before. Establish lines. Not because she didn't want to be there for her family, but because she was getting swallowed up without lines. And what he said wasn't about her. Or him. It was about them. Putting on their own masks first.

"You can't help anyone else if you don't survive," Sam finished. "Now. This has nothing to do with loving you. Or marrying you. Or having babies with you."

"Oh, I think it does, Sam. I think that's exactly what you've been talking about."

He took a long breath, scratched his neck. All that talking seemed to betray how worried he was. Anxiety just didn't suit him. She had a solution for that.

She half turned, curled closer, kissed off that anxiety. She couldn't do that for anyone else, but she knew what worked for Sam. Cut off his thinking button by nestling against his lap, stroking his nape, into his hair, with combing fingers. Her lips hovered over his, close, breathing close, heartbeat close. And then showed him what a kiss could be if—and when—she pulled out all the stops.

She closed her eyes, locked everything from her mind but Sam. No sound, no light, intruded. Just the whoosh of his sigh, the silky easiness of his mouth. The rustle of his shirt coming off. The ache of his heart, beating on hers, heating on hers.

Years ago, Poppy had learned that you couldn't fly without taking a risk. You couldn't find joy unless you opened your heart to it. And you couldn't find grace within yourself if you weren't willing to dare being all you could be.

It all came back to her now. When she most wanted to soar. For herself, for her guy. Swift fingers tugged at his shirt, at his belt. Her mouth came back to stroke his, take a different angle, then sweet-nibble his lips again. Her hands slid up, into his hair, so she could hold him still for another kiss. A slippery kiss this time. The taste of her tongue, his tongue. The taste of intimate promises and flagrant, wicked intentions.

They both surged apart for about two seconds. They both just needed to come up for air. Sam seemed oddly out of breath. His voice sounded oddly hoarse. "Wow," he whispered. "What happened to you?"

"Love, Sam. Just loving you."

He reached out. She leaned in. He smiled a kiss. She smiled one back. But once his arms came around her, she couldn't think of a single reason to talk for a very long time.

Epilogue

LIGHTS WINKED AND blazed from every window in Sam's house. Both of Poppy's sisters had brought guy friends for New Year's Eve. Sam's dad was full of the devil, as if he'd never had a heart issue—and as if he wasn't wasting a second more of his life. Laughter rang from all three floors. Poppy was checking on everyone, making sure they were having a good time.

There seemed to be an extra dog around somewhere. Sam's cousins and spare kin had all showed up for the New Year's gig. So far Poppy hadn't met anyone who was remotely shy. Kristin was playing under the tree with the manger, talking to Joseph and Mary so they'd know how to behave in the Christmas story next year. Bubbles was everywhere, but primarily, once Karla's toddler baby had crashed on the couch by the fire, the dog took up residence as a baby protector/backstop.

Poppy and Sam had fed the whole crew a couple hours before. The feast was impossibly easy. All the women brought salads or deserts. Sam grilled the steaks. Everybody brought dishes and silverware to the huge old table in the dining room. Sam's brothers could fill dishwashers like nobody's business.

Someone was playing a game of hearts at a side table in the living room. Heaven knew how the baby could sleep through their noisy laughter. Cam and Marigold explored the house, enchanted by the architecture and aura of the place, in love with Sam's famous stone wall. Sam's dad kept finding Poppy to sneak a hug now and then. His mom kept doing the same.

They all seemed to be having fun, even the little ones who'd fallen asleep. No one was honoring regular bedtimes on New Year's Eve—but they didn't have to. Everyone ate until they were stuffed, then either crashed or played or settled into talking somewhere or another.

Poppy just felt . . . happy. Both families together seemed to meld as if they'd been born friends. She took one last check around, but nothing seemed to need doing. She was about to track down Sam when he showed up in the doorway, motioning her with a come-on gesture. She chuckled and surged toward him.

"We throw good parties, did you know that?" She tucked under his arm, glad to share a quick hug.

"I never doubted it. I have a little fear we'll never get rid of everybody. But for a couple minutes, I was hoping you'd come outside with me."

"Sure." She cocked her head, thinking some fresh air sounded really good—even if it was cheek-freezing cold outside.

"I have a tiny surprise for you."

She looked up, thinking, *Finally*. They'd been so busy. Actually they'd only been *really* busy being happy, but somehow Sam had forgotten all about that little green velvet box. In Madison, he and Poppy had gotten caught up in each other and the discussion about their lives, then getting ready for this party, and opening the box was overlooked. Her Christmas present. Not that he hadn't given her all kinds of gifts. She certainly didn't need more. It was just she was starting to suspect he'd either lost the box or forgotten about it altogether.

Sam led her downstairs, where another family group was playing pool and sampling some homemade brew. Clearly he'd put their jackets and gloves and hats by the fireplace earlier, because they were toasty warm. By the time they'd collected their outdoor gear, he herded her past the exuberant pool players toward the back door. Right off, she saw two pairs of skates. "I'll be darned," she said, "those white ones sure don't look like they'd fit you."

He grinned. "It could be that I lifted your skates when we were in Madison yesterday. By then, I was already thinking about setting up a rink in the backyard. Don't expect anything fancy—but the ice is smooth, and with all the Christmas lights on, there's ample light to skate by."

They both pulled on winter trappings and headed outside. The air was almost too fresh to breathe, the night as silent as a song. And then she saw his rink—not regulation size but better. "This is wonderful, Sam!" The glaze of silver ice filled out a low spot in his yard and was shaped like a kidney pool. She glanced up. "You think it's okay if we just enjoy this ourselves? Don't you think the others will want to join us?"

"They don't want to. I'm positive."

She blinked. "How can you be positive?"

"'Cause I told them all to stay inside or risk my wrath." He murmured, "I think they might have gotten the idea I wanted a few minutes alone with you."

"Oh? Any special reason?"

"No worries. Just wanted to play a little hypothetical game with you." First, though, once they took off their skate guards, Sam lifted his hand to invite Poppy on the ice. For a hockey guy, he had some surprisingly graceful moves. He tucked a hand around her waist, lifted her hand to match with his, and led her into a slow, lazy dance.

"Where'd you learn to do that, Sam?" she asked suspiciously.

"Love. Loving you. It taught me pretty much everything I know."

The darn man made her heart ache. He had that winsome expression—that halfway grin that lit up her world, always made her smile back. "About this game you wanted to play . . . ?"

"Yup. This won't take long. I was just thinking. Hypothetically, what do you think about Christmas weddings?"

When she suddenly skidded sideways, he was right there to help her reclaim her balance. "You haven't asked me yet, Sam," she reminded him. "So I kind of have to imagine my theoretical answer."

"So shoot. In theory, what do you think?" He spun her around once, twice, then hooked her close to him again. Skating backward. Letting her take the lead. Only she was looking at his face, and she no longer cared who had the lead.

"Well . . . it seems like a long time to wait. But I love the idea of a Christmas wedding. And if the hypothetical couple have a lot to figure out, where to live and all that, that would give them plenty of time to plan and play with how they want to do it all."

"I confess it's been growing on me. Kind of thought the same thing. And then I couldn't get my mind off the whole theoretical idea. I keep imagining you in a white dress, carrying a bunch of mistletoe and holly and red roses."

"Hmm." She lifted an eyebrow. "I could really—theoretically—picture you in a tux. It's almost enough to make me swoon."

"Yeah? I'd love to see you swoon."

The devil made her swoon right there, lowering her into his arms, skating at soaring speeds down his magical rink. But then . . . he lifted her again, close, face-to-face. "I was thinking . . . you have enough sisters to have bridesmaids. And I have enough brothers to have groomsmen."

"And we have Kristin, in case we needed a theoretical flower girl. And Bubbles, if we could trust her to carry the ring."

"Um . . . I'm afraid that theory won't fly. We can't trust her."

"We're just talking theoretically, though, aren't we?"

"Uh-huh. Poppy, could you put your hands around my waist, just hold us both steady for a sec?"

"Sure." She was still searching his eyes, when he started talking again.

"I'm not real fond of destination weddings. It's okay if I'm outvoted. But I just think, there's this big house with a great staircase for a bride to walk down. I can picture the snow outside, the fireplaces all lit up on the inside. Family and loved ones being there for us. But . . ." She wasn't sure what he was doing, but he seemed to be digging something out of his front jeans' pocket, which was impossible to do with gloves. So he ripped off one glove, dove a hand back in his pocket. Suddenly she seemed to be the only one keeping them steady on the ice.

"But I like the idea of a destination honeymoon. As in, a place just for us. Mountains. Ocean. Islands. Any secret spot."

"All of those sound great to me." But she could see he was still struggling. "What's wrong?"

"Nothing's wrong. Everything's perfect. It's just—"

"What?" If he tilted any farther, they were both going to tumble on the ice.

"Something's stuck in my pocket. I can't get it out. I think my fingers are just too cold. I may need help."

"Is this a wicked trick, Sam?"

"No. I love the idea of pulling that kind of wicked trick with you. But not this time. Now I really want to get this out of my pocket and I haven't a clue why it's so stuck."

"All right, all right. I'll help. But I'm warning you—"

He was right. Something was stuck in there. Of course, when she took off her glove and put her hand in his front pocket, he convulsed in near laughter and then she did. But not before she felt the soft furry texture of the item. It was velvet. And the shape of it was a box, even if she couldn't totally get her fingers around it. "Don't panic. I'll get it."

"Are we going to risk our future children in the process?"

"Don't make me laugh any harder, Sam. The problem is, we both have cold fingers—"

"Temporarily my *only* problem is that *you* have cold fingers."

"Sam!!!! I want my ring!"

Now he got serious. "Who said it was a ring in my pocket?"

"Possibly I just knew because I have supernatural powers?"

"I don't doubt that, Red. But I did worry that you wondered what was taking me so darned long."

Something stilled in his face. Something stilled in hers. "What I *didn't* worry about was your loving me, Sam."

"That's what I was waiting for. We *do* have a lot to figure out. From my perspective, that isn't daunting but the opposite. Intriguing. Interesting things to figure out together. What other people call problems, I figure we are going to have a blast dealing with together. Every minute we've had together, we've had stuff to cope with, haven't we? And every minute I've known you, I hope you were feeling as happy as I am. How right we are together. Poppy, I totally believe we can work out anything as long as we're together."

"I totally believe it— Oh! Sam! I got it!"

He grabbed the box the instant she released it—but they'd

both definitely waited long enough. He just wanted to open the box himself for her.

The ring sparkled like a star. She yanked off her left glove and slipped it on her finger, and it sparkled even more. Definitely like a star. Her star. Their star. But it took her a moment before she could say anything because her heart was too full. Love brimmed out of her eyes, her throat, filled up her heart.

"It's beyond beautiful. I love it. Not just because it's a beautiful ring—which it is—but because it means something to me that nothing else could have." She lifted her hand to show him. "Every time I look at this, I'll be thinking that it's not just a star but a Christmas star. Because I found my way to you, Sam."

"I found my way to you," he insisted. "Say yes, Red."

"Yes. Yes! *Yes, yes, yes.*"

They did circles on the ice for a few more moments. Just to hold each other. Just to feel the joy. Their joy.

In the distance, she could see Kristin's face in the window. Bubbles's face was next to hers. His brothers were trying to peer out from another window. Clearly they all expected what was happening and couldn't wait for them to come in and celebrate.

Well, she loved them all. But they could wait.

She wanted to soar on the ice with Sam a little longer. Soar in his arms a lot longer. Love with him for a lifetime.

About the author

About the book

Insights,
Interviews
& More . . .

Meet Jennifer Greene

JENNIFER GREENE is a bestselling author of over eighty-five books, the winner of multiple awards, and an ardent reader herself. She's written romances, romantic suspense, single titles, anthologies, and numerous nonfiction articles as well. She's known for her unforgettable characters, sneaky humor, and the vital women's issues she loves to explore with her readers.

She lives in orchard country, near Lake Michigan, in an old historic house—with an 1830 log cabin in her backyard. Jennifer has a weakness for stray animals, and so do her two kids—they were forced to raise Newfoundlands, Basset hounds, German shepherds, and Australian shepherds, as well as assorted riffraff breeds. (That's not counting the raccoons, homing pigeons, cats, and whatever hungry wildlife needed a home.) While the kids were growing up, the clan took an aging motor home through the United States, where she picked up most of the settings for her books.

She modeled all her heroes after her husband—or that's what he continues to claim! ❧

Courtesy of the author

Recipe for Spaghetti Ice Cream

About the book

I had this at a friend's house one time and fell in love with it. But when I looked up the recipe, there were a lot of different versions. This is the one I found to be the easiest.

I think the background for this is German—they call it *Spaghettieis*—and it's available on many menus in Germany. (I only wish I had a chance to try it there!)

Prep time: 10 minutes
Freeze time: About 15 minutes

INGREDIENTS:

1 cup strawberries, mashed (you could use some other fruit, but the red in the strawberries makes it look like spaghetti sauce)
1 tablespoon orange or lemon or lime juice
1 tablespoon granulated sugar
½ cup heavy cream
1 tablespoon vanilla sugar
2–3 cups vanilla ice cream
2 tablespoons shaved white chocolate ▶

Recipe for Spaghetti Ice Cream *(continued)*

DIRECTIONS:

1. Start by putting an ice cream scoop, serving plates, and a potato ricer in the freezer for 15 minutes.

2. Put the strawberries, juice, and granulated sugar in a blender or food processor. Pour the mixture into a bowl and store it in the fridge.

3. Whip the heavy cream and vanilla sugar into stiff peaks. Put a spoonful of heavy cream on each chilled plate. Add a couple scoops of vanilla ice cream into the potato ricer. Press the ice cream through, swirling the ice cream spaghetti over the whipped cream.

4. To make it look like spaghetti with spaghetti sauce, use your strawberry sauce and a sprinkle of white chocolate on top.

5. Serve immediately . . . although I've frozen this for a few hours before a dinner and it didn't seem to do it any harm. ∽

Reading Group Guide

1. Could you relate to Poppy's dilemma—of doing so much for others that you're burned out?

2. Have you ever felt that you had no time for yourself—no life— and you didn't see a way to fix this?

3. Did you feel it should have been easy for Poppy to confront her sisters and demand they change? Just have a big fight and get it over with?

4. Have you ever had the urge to run away or escape just to have time for yourself for a while?

5. Did you feel that George—the father in the family—was actually neglectful? Or that the girls, when they were growing up, were in a dangerous situation with no direct parenting going on? Do you know of a family where things look good to outsiders, but inside the house, children are exposed to risk and hardships?

6. Did you like Poppy? Did you like Sam? Do you believe they are going to be happy together long past the story ending?

7. In a sense, Poppy has always been a hero—whether she wanted to be one or not. After her mom died, she took care of her sisters, their lives, everything they needed; she's responsible for a big job; she's been ▶

hardworking and capable and successful every step of the way. Does she actually need a hero in her life? What kind of man could make her life better or richer?

8. Whether in a marriage or a personal partnership, what "ingredients" are needed to believe the couple have a chance to survive and thrive together? Are those ingredients the same for everyone?

9. Poppy's mom has been gone for a long time, yet she still has a presence in the story. Are there people long gone from your life—for whatever reason—who have had a lasting impression on you? Words they said, wisdom they passed, or life lessons they shared that you've never forgotten? ᴄᴡ

Discover great authors, exclusive offers, and more at hc.com.